MAFIA KINGDOM

paige press

MAFIA KINGDOM

New York Times Bestselling Author
CD REISS

ALSO BY CD REISS

THE DILUSTRO ARRANGEMENT

Some girls dream of marrying a prince. I was sold to a king.

Mafia Bride | Mafia King | Mafia Queen

MANHATTAN MAFIA

I was stolen on my wedding day and forced to marry a man who wants to get vengeance on my father. Now I'm falling for him and we're going to run away together... if my family doesn't kill us first.

Take Me Capo | Make Me Cry | Break Me Down

THE SUBMISSION SERIES

One Night With Him | One Year With Him | One Life With Him

THE GAMES DUET

Adam Steinbeck will give his wife a divorce on one condition. She join him in a remote cabin for 30 days, submitting to his sexual dominance.

Marriage Games | Separation Games

Copyright © 2023 by CD Reiss

All rights reserved.

No part of this book may be reproduced in any form or by any electronic or mechanical means, including information storage and retrieval systems, without written permission from the author, except for the use of brief quotations in a book review.

All persons and events in this book are fictional.

PROLOGUE

MASSIMO

I KNEW my father ran an empire outside the laws of New York City. I was aware that I would inherit his rule, but it wasn't until the appearance of my first wisps of beard that I learned the breadth of my birthright.

Deep underground, below even the church we had dug before permits and pipes, when horses pulled carriages along Fourteenth Street, my father, who ruled the Colonia with a tight fist on a cobra-head cane, showed me the Lines.

In a room with a seven-foot ceiling and metal filing cabinets pushed against walls chiseled so roughly they looked like a battered birthday cake, he pulled out file after file. Book after book. Some were so old they crumbled in his fingers.

The Colonia history. Almost one hundred Italians who kept the old ways, arrived in New York on a single boat when Naples was part of the Kingdom of Sicily. Catholic, but pagan. Pagan, but Catholic.

They were fleeing something, but of everything that was remembered, the name of that exact something was forgotten.

For years, after my regular studies, I pored over the oldest of those books. Memorized them. Our scribe, Ivy, showed me the newer Lines, the ones that went backward to our home in Naples and forward again to the present day. She said I had to know it because I would be the king of any Line that had ever touched New York.

That information, in all its detail and consequence, has proven completely fucking useless.

Without a king recognized by all the people, the Colonia go into a kind of hibernation. We coexist with Outsiders in a crowded city, so there are rules to prevent infiltration.

Without a leader, the ceremonies and rituals stop. The law firm that we hired padlocks the places we gather. Our children go to Outsider schools and though our legal business continues, it does so for the good of individuals, not the collective.

To us as a people, this is a disaster. It's a scattering that will only compound with every second it continues.

To me, as a son and brother, it is a tragedy. My father was murdered. My sister shot me in the leg rather than come home. I was beaten, broken, and dragged back to Naples like a sack of rice. Ruler of Nothing. The King of Shit.

I have been stuck here for half a year, in a miserable corner of Naples, forced to work as muscle for the Orolios.

All I can do is sit on this hard bench with my father's cane between my legs and stare at her.

And stare. And stare.

I'm no scholar, but day after day, I visit a painting that's on loan from another, bigger museum, and I stare as if trying to find its soul.

Parmigianino's Lucretia. Blond braids twisted around her head. Cheeks ruddied from her efforts at justice. Her pale neck elongated against the flat black background, looking up, lips parted, Greek nose profiled in all its perfection, breast exposed as she plunges a dagger into her chest. The wound is so bloodless, her blade looks broken, but history knows the dagger killed her, and a republic was born from a rape.

Nice story. Fuck the republic. I would have saved her. If I had been king, servant, or pariah, I would have ripped apart any man who hurt her. Before she even had the chance to stab herself, her rapist would have been torn limb from limb.

I keep coming back to her, telling myself, in a way I'll never be able to articulate, that she is mine.

And then—like everything else I've ever claimed—the loan period ends, and she is gone.

CHAPTER 1

SEVEN DAYS TO ARMISTICE NIGHT

DELFINA

A bomb has gone off in my family. The women hustling around the kitchen don't know why it went off or who dropped it, but we all have to get this wedding off in two days instead of four months. Thank God it's not mine. I'm already twenty-one and Papa hasn't arranged anyone, which means I may get to pick whoever I want. I throw up a quick horn gesture to ward off any bad results my gratitude attracts.

"It's not fair!" Liliana sobs, pushing a balled-up tissue against her nose. "Why do I not get to decide anything?"

She's never complained about being told to marry Paolo Alessi. That choice was taken away very early. As the oldest, she was always going to have to marry whoever Papa said, so the rest of the decisions down the line have taken on greater significance.

"Better sooner than later, no?" Her future mother-in-law, Assunta, hands her a fresh tissue. We're in Assunta's kitchen with a cross-section of aunts, cousins, mothers, and friends.

Liliana nods and balls up the new tissue. We'd been

carefully planning her wedding—up until tonight, when we were all called across the Spanish Quarter to make it happen in forty-eight hours. The women weren't told why. Something about letters and summons. Follow-up questions were waved away.

"I just want it to be nice." Liliana sniffles. "Now here we are, making sure we have enough sugar to make our own pastries."

"It'll be nice," I assure her. "We've done this a million times. Now we just have to do it faster."

"On a Tuesday?!" Her face crumbles again. "No one gets married on Tuesdays. It's bad luck."

Assunta *tsks*, but I'm not sure if it's because she thinks Liliana's being unreasonable, or because she agrees on the hierarchy of the days of the week.

"God made Tuesdays the same as any other day." Aunt Lina leans over the counter to continue a list in her spiral notebook. Normally, the bride's mother would be making the lists, but ours didn't survive giving birth to me, so we were raised by her five sisters. Lina is the most practical, and right now, I appreciate that. "Let's not waste time with superstitious nonsense. Your uncle Fosco can get us the big room in the club for the reception."

"Oh, God," Liliana says. "That club is a dump! We were going to have it at the Stigliano!"

"Enough!" Aunt Greca barks. She was always the disciplinarian, and had to be with seven children of her own. "You're being a child."

Liliana bolts out of the kitchen in tears. Aunt Greca shakes her head and goes back to counting sacks of flour. They're all too busy with the wedding to care for the bride's heart, so I grab the box of tissues and follow her outside.

Our city was built in the sixteenth century and is as dense as lard bread, with unexpected pockets of open air between buildings and mansions, like ours, tucked behind iron doors.

Paolo's family owns a shipping route Papa says is important, but it isn't much. The Alessis are not as rich as us, nor as poor as most, so their house does not have its own courtyard, but a shared outdoor space paved in stone. I find Liliana there, crouched on one of two metal chairs under the single tree growing from a patch of soil. I put the box of tissues in her lap.

"Aunt Greca is such a bitch," she says, cradling the box and bowing her head so her light brown hair covers her face.

"She's overwhelmed too." I sit in the other chair. "And she was married when she was fifteen, so, yeah." I can't imagine how awful it would feel to be trapped so young, before seeing any of the world.

"Ugh." She snaps out a fresh tissue. "I'm not ready and I'm twenty-three. Did they tell you, Delfie? About the sex? What it is? What actually *happens?*"

"I get the idea." I shrug. It was always described as one of the many things a wife has to cope with in exchange for... well, I don't really know what.

"I'm so scared. How can it not hurt?"

"Orelia says it's nice."

"Well, she's a *puttana*." She blows her nose. "And I mean that in the nicest way. Good for her."

Sitting back in the chair, I let the Quarter wash over me. The smells of food and garbage. The multiple arguments and discussions. The human and canned television laughter. Mopeds crisscrossing the city. Traffic on *Via Medina*, a kilometer away. A car stereo. If I listen closely enough—crickets, and the breeze flicking the leaves of this one, lonely tree. Humanity crushes the senses while the stars are silent.

"Is he still taking you on his boat for the honeymoon?" I ask.

"Not until after Armistice Night."

Armistice Night is an annual event celebrating peace between the colonies. It's a big deal. I've always wanted to go, but it's for the families of the System, and Papa's been clear that though he pays into the System and remains friendly with Cosimo Orolio, he and his children are outside of it.

"Imagine how quiet it is on the ocean."

She blows her nose, while I look through the archway of old stone to the dots of stars, trying to imagine a world with only the sound of water splashing thickly on a boat's hull.

"Delfina!" Aunt Silvia calls from above.

"Yes?"

"I need you to go home and put Enzo and Emilia to bed."

Sighing, I straighten. "Okay."

I love my little cousins, but they're the exact opposite of the roaring silence of the sea.

"Your father will get Aris to walk you over." She disappears without waiting for a response.

"It's going to be all right, Lili." I throw my arms around my sister. "It's going to be amazing."

"For you." She holds me tightly, then separates. "Because you're amazing."

"No. You are."

"No, you. And go, before Emilia gets her second wind."

I run upstairs to meet Aris so he can rush me home.

As the Capo of the System in all of Naples, Cosimo Orolio sits at the head of the dining room table with wide-set brown eyes and a slab of hair combed over his bald head. He is the oldest of the older men. The fathers and uncles, some in the System and some, like Papa, who are outside of it, sit around the table, while the brothers and sons stand at the edges, against the walls. There is background murmuring, but most of the room is focused on Cosimo, who speaks plainly to Papa.

"—under your house, starting in the morning."

"My daughter is getting married. The disruption—"

"That's our deal, Gentile."

They fall into silence when I enter. There's a dead weight in the room, and I'm not the cause. Papa seems distracted when I ask for an escort. Not just distracted, but troubled.

"Aris," Papa says to my brother, "take your sister home."

"This is too important," he protests, as he always does. "I know it's not fair, but the kids can wait."

When he escorts me, he walks too fast and I get home breathless and blistered.

"I got it," a man says. I've never seen him before, and I've seen everyone in the Quarter. He's the only one my age sitting at the table. "There's nothing else I got to tell you now anyway." He stands and bows to Cosimo, who offers his ring to kiss. Gross.

"You know the way?" Cosimo asks, taking the decision out of my father's hands. Even Papa has to choose his battles with the capo. "I don't want her to end up at your house in Velletri."

"I grew up near the galleria. I got it." The pretentions of his Northern accent are clear when he mentions the old neighborhood.

"Go, Rafi. Come back quickly. And Delfina?"

"Yes?"

"I have a niece coming from America. Her name is Luna. You will welcome her."

"Yes, sir."

He waves me away. Rafi is already out the door. I hope he doesn't walk as fast as my brother.

CHAPTER 2

DELFINA

Rafi has much shorter legs than Aris, but he still starts out too fast. From behind, his shoulders are hunched and the overgrowth at the back edge of his hairline doesn't get any thinner closer to his jacket collar. He turns his wedge of a head halfway toward me. In profile, his nose is bridgeless, like mine, but with a Roman bump. It's very nice.

The hard soles of my shoes slip where the cobblestones are worn. I pick up my skirt a few inches to keep it from getting caught between my knees, passing the narrow storefronts with their night gates drawn over the pastry displays, the colorful peppers, the dim mysteries of the barber shop. Somewhere above, televisions entertain the hard-of-hearing with loud laughter or louder anger.

"I'm going too fast for you?" Rafi asks, walking backward a few steps. I'm not that far behind, so I almost run into him. When his eyebrows go up in surprise, his widow's peak doesn't move.

"I can keep up." I drop my skirt for a moment, taking a deep breath. "You'll be back in no time."

"Doesn't matter. Done is done."

He matches my pace instead of me having to match his. I speed up a little out of consideration.

"So, you're from Velletri?" I glance at him to see if he's listening. He is. He's even looking at me. "When did you move?"

"I was a kid. My mom and dad got married to make a peace. We stayed here, with my mother's family, then my dad took us up to Velletri."

"Is the System different up there?"

My question is perfectly innocent, but he seems a little surprised I dare ask about the organizations run by capos and soldiers parallel to the system run by politicians and police.

"You know a lot about your father's business?"

"It's not his..." I shake out the defensiveness. "Nonno was in the System, but he made sure Papa wasn't." I point at the closed butcher as we pass. "But Papa still has the connections, you know? When Piero cuts me a quarter pound extra and says it's for the Colony, he's talking about Nonno, but when someone spraypainted over Maradona"—I point at a restored painting of the *calcio* player on the rough wall—"it was Papa who paid for the restoration. The kid who did it... the System took care of. Papa had nothing to do with that."

I shake my head. Just a kid. They beat him up pretty good. You do not mess with Maradona in the Quarter.

Rafi looks back to confirm the condition of the painting. "The System, yeah... different in Velletri. We don't light candles over shit like that. The business is more like business. It's quiet, you know. No waves. And nobody's half-in, half-out like your dad."

"He's not half-in." I say it as if I mean it, but I'm not really sure I'm right.

"How old are you?" he asks.

"Twenty-one."

"Really?"

"Yeah, really."

"What's he waiting for? The guy you're promised to?"

"No." I find his question too insulting to entertain with another syllable.

"Boyfriend, whatever. He didn't even buy you a ring yet?"

"You presume a lot." I'm trying to be polite and correct this ridiculous person at the same time. It's not easy.

"You get married young down here, no?"

Liliana is twenty-three, so I don't know where he got the impression we're all teen brides. He really is insolent.

"No, actually. Not any more."

Now I'm walking fast because I'm not enjoying this person's company.

"Come on." He catches up. "Don't be mad."

"I'm not mad."

"Fine. Hey. Let's go through the *vicoletto*." He stops by a narrow passage between two apartment buildings. "It's a shortcut."

I know the Quarter like I know my own hand, so this particular alley isn't a mystery to me. It does shorten the way, but Aris usually stays on the wider streets and makes up the time up by practically running half a kilometer.

Rafi's company is grating on me. The sooner I leave him at my front door, the better.

I follow him into the *vicoletto*.

CHAPTER 3

MASSIMO

I lay the pool cue on the carom table and remove a thin wad of cash from my pocket. Six months, and I still can't get used to this rainbow of money that's worth either ten percent more or ten percent less than real money, which is all the same size and the same shade of green.

"We can play again," Corrado says, twisting chalk on the end of his cue. With his short sleeves, I can see the scar on the inside of his elbow, marking him as a member of the System and not to be crossed. "You can take the *carambola* at ten, I stay at four."

I've sinned too often and too well to ever be a hero, but I won't let him handicap me to cheat himself. After eating shit for six months in this hellhole, I can take a loss at the carom table.

I flick four orange fifties on the worn green felt instead of making him fish it out of a corner pocket. Not my choice. Italian billiards is all bumpers and no pockets.

I still lose this game fair and square half the time. Tonight

I'm down. Next time I'll be up. The water stays calm enough to tread, and my limbs keep moving.

"No risk." Corrado scoops up the money and pinches it into a fold. "No reward. That's why you're not king of New York."

False. I didn't lose my father's territory because I played it safe. I took too many risks. Now Corrado is my keeper in here in the Spanish Quarter of Naples. He makes sure I stay in line. He's only known the Massimo Colonia who waits, who does what he's told, goes where he's allowed, and does the jobs he's given.

Until Armistice Night, when weapons are laid down and grudges are held in check. Then I'll petition the heads of the families to be freed, and I'll return to New York to take back what generations of Colonia built.

"Tell you what." I pick up my cane. "I get to my room without your eyes on me"—I wave my hand at the orange fold of cash—"you give it all back, plus fifty."

Corrado is bored of watching me, and I can't blame him. He's trapped here, away from a woman in Abruzzo who he wants to marry. To amuse ourselves, we play a stupid game where I try to get back to my apartment without him seeing me. Sometimes I win. Sometimes I lose. Same as every miserable thing here.

"You're on."

Sixty seconds later, the new brass tip on my father's cane is tapping on the pavement, the bullet wound in my thigh is aching, and I'm looking at the curved sliver of night sky between rooflines, wishing there was a way to just fly the fuck out of here.

Naples is a new city where it's new, and where it's not, it's a thousand years old. A scab on my middle knuckle cracks, sending a line of blood around my finger and onto the brass cobra head at the top of the cane. The gift of flight won't be granted, no matter how tightly I ball my fist. All it does is open scabs.

Sometimes, I travel between the rooftops. Maybe I'll do that tonight and beat Corrado back. I need a win right now.

My purgatory in Naples started by making Corrado follow me all over the city. I tested every road and boundary, running every tunnel and walkway, grinding my teeth and gripping the head of the cane. Whenever I lost him and tried to leave the Quarter, someone else on the System's payroll always caught me at the exits.

The street between two stone buildings is so narrow an open door blocks the way. I close it to pass. With creaky hinges, it bounces back open. I take out my handkerchief, wiping the cane before my hand. The abrasions are from a contract I did yesterday for Cosimo Orolio. Simple job extracting tribute from a plant nursery. It wasn't the father holding up the payments, but the son, with his white Nikes and Manchester United cap. He said he'd pay us in Bitcoin. I came to extract a rainbow of euros.

I get hired because I get in easily. They don't know who I'm working for, so they don't really see me coming. I'm not part of their System. I am Colonia. No one owns or owes me. We don't play.

Or we didn't, back when we were who we were. After a few hundred years running our own corner of New York, we aren't anything anymore. Our buildings are locked and empty. Our artifacts and records gather dust, and our rituals only exist in a few living minds.

We are a hollowed kingdom ruled by a broken, exiled monarch.

That's me. Massimo Colonia. King of my father's imagination. Plucked out of a two-runway airport like a nameless criminal, relieved of my passport and sent to Naples by the DiLustros and the Orolios—two families who hate the Colonia more than they hate each other.

Under the hum and buzz of the tightly-packed city—the mopeds and conversations, the music and cars—I hear a grunt that's more of a *huh*, and what catches my attention is that it's coming from the dark side of the alleyway. That side curves around and out of sight, making it look like a dead end. It's not. It's actually a way to the rooftops I've used to beat Corrado home.

The stairwell door is open. A sign that this was the right way to come.

Another grunt of expended energy, like a tennis player serving. This one is a woman's. It's followed by glass breaking. A moped guns in the opposite direction. The noise swallows everything.

Instead of going up the stairs to the roofs, I go into the slim walkway and around the turn, convinced that, of all the decisions available to me on a daily basis, none have the power to change the drift of my life.

From a TV above, a comedy laugh track explodes into guffaws and applause, almost hiding a woman's shout.

Limping into the narrow passage without the support of my cane, so that the tap of the tip on the stone won't give me away, and my scraping, uneven footfall cloaked by the blast of TV comedy and tragedy, I don't know what I want or what I will see. I do know that I am no hero. I am at the periphery, nose pressed up against the glass, looking in, convinced there is no role for me. In the dramas of men, I'm barely the villain.

The struggle is taking place in a widening alcove between two alleys, and the source of it is... Lucretia. The woman rendered in paint, now real, moving, feeling. *Here.*

She's bent over a dry stone fountain, looking up with an elongated neck, blond curl dropping over her shoulder, lips parted, cheeks ruddied with the effort of getting a troll off her back. Her shirt's been torn, exposing a breast that—in its soft vulnerability—doesn't elicit arousal but rage.

For a moment, I have to stop and ask myself if I'm interrupting something consensual.

What would I have done if I'd seen the son of the emperor raping Lucretia? Torn him limb from limb or stood there and wondered if her body was saying yes?

From an apartment above, a studio audience laughs at the idea that I'd be of any use.

The troll doesn't see me yet. He pushes her down with one hand while the other pulls up her skirt.

She almost falls, catches herself, and looks at me. Finally, Lucretia tells me who she is, what she wants, teasing a complexity that paint will never reveal. Without a single sound, she tells me that she needs me.

I hoist my cane, but before bringing it down, I put two fingers against my tongue and blow one sharp, attention-getting whistle.

He looks at me, the source of the interruption, as if I'm lower than dirt. Maybe I am. Maybe I am in no social position to inconvenience this shitbag.

A joke floats down from a television as I swing my cane, and the canned laughter starts when he realizes the tip of the brass cobra is about to meet the side of his head, and it's too late to move.

CHAPTER 4

DELFINA

Rafi's hand grips the bottom half of my face, covering my mouth so hard my cheek presses painfully against my teeth. His fingers smell like tobacco and sweat.

"Take it easy, and I'll save you from what's coming." He's stronger than he looks, but all men are.

"Mmph."

"Scream, and you'll be in the line."

I don't know what he's talking about, but I know what he wants. I can feel it against my hip. Part of me can't believe this is happening. Another part expected that, at some point, a man would try to do the most difficult thing the easy way—claim Gentile Gargiulo's daughter with violence—and bind me to an ambitious, vicious husband.

But what's the line? What does he think he's saving me from?

And why was I sent home with a man from Velletri in the first place?

I can't think and I can't get away from his clawing hand,

pulling my neckline open, my bra away. Tightening my exposed nipple in the cold air.

"You got it? It's me or the line."

I shake my head against the press of his hand.

"Just take it. Let's get this done."

When he moves his hand off my mouth, I can scream all I want, but I know he'll do it anyway, then I'm supposed to be afraid that he won't marry me because of something I don't understand. I look up at him with his soft chin and low forehead. I don't want him. He's doing this as if it's a job, and I'm so scared my body's gone numb.

"What's the line?" I ask.

"Stay still."

He stops holding me up, and I go boneless from the waist up. I can't feel myself, but I can see, and my eyes meet those of a man at the entrance to the alcove. He is tall, broad, straight as the cane he's tapping on the cobblestones.

Am I afraid or relieved?

He's a wraith with a face of shadows, waiting for what, I don't know. He could stop this or walk away. I've heard of men joining in, making the woman barely marriageable by any party. He's a question asked of a stone, and he'll do nothing I expect, because he's a phantom.

Am I afraid or relieved? I am neither. I am impatient with him, because though he only showed up a split second ago, I have the sense I've been waiting for him a long time.

Before Rafi can get his fingers between my legs, the wraith moves toward us. He is crooked, yet frighteningly fast, as if his brokenness is part of his power.

He swings a stick. I flinch. The dull crack from behind me doesn't result in any pain. He didn't hit me. Rafi makes a sound that's objection, anger, and surrender, just before another crunching sound.

My skirt falls below my knees. I turn. The wraith's back is

to me. Rafi is on the ground with his arms up to shield his face.

Papa always said if you see something, say nothing. Do not be a witness. Run. Close your mouth, turn away, and run. Knowledge can only hurt you. Run. Run. Run.

I didn't know why he was so strong on this point, until now. I remember what he told me, but I cannot obey the command. The cane comes down on Rafi again. Where they connect is at the end of a sharply pointed cone widening into my full attention. The head of the cane is metal. It is bloody now. The wraith is a man with one foot on either side of Rafi, kicking him flat when he tries to roll over.

"What—?"

I stop myself when the wraith looks over his shoulder at me. The light cuts through the short, dark blond beard to reveal the hard line of his cheekbone and jaw, and when he glances quickly at my exposed breast, the light glints off the edge of his iris. Green. Brown. Gold. Rainbow windows into the soul of a ghost. Absently, I cover myself. So many statements and demands try to break through the noise in my head, but only a question gets through.

"What is the line?"

"Run." His voice is husky and deep, and the one word has the tinge of a brutal foreign accent that only gets stronger when he repeats it. "Run."

The wisdom of the command is lost on me. My legs won't move.

CHAPTER 5

MASSIMO

A king rules without ruling. He speaks and the word is law. The threat of violence maintains the peace, and the peace can only be enforced with displays of ferocity.

It's a tightrope. On one side—collapse. On the other—chaos.

It wasn't until I was cast out and trapped that I stepped onto that rope between scion and king, beating a man with the head of my cane. When he tries to roll over, I lean on my good leg to push him to his back with my bad leg. The pain in my thigh is another thing to conquer. Bring me an army of enflamed old wounds and I will bear them to break this man.

The cane is an extension of my arm and my arm is controlled by a mind hijacked by righteousness. I am King of The Alley, and my word is law here. I am the only voice of justice.

The man puts up his arms and my cane finds a way between them. When I'm hitting him, I am clear water. A riptide flowing in one direction. Unmuddied. Complete. I want nothing I don't already have.

And then it's over. The currents close over me, and I am just sandy foam and the never-ending repetition of waves curling and crashing into chaos.

The man is silent. A sob breaks through the rush in my ears.

It's Lucretia. Looking at the spot below us where my cane landed over and over, I know what she sees—the frightening aftermath of violence. But when I look at her, she doesn't know what I see—a virtuous woman glimpsing a reality she was sheltered from.

"I told you to run." I want to sound sterner, but her frailty is sharp enough to cut my command to pieces.

Her eyes go from accusatory to glossed-over, as if she's turned her gaze inward.

"But I didn't." She seems surprised by what's in her own mind.

"You should."

Her eyes meet mine. Brown. Hazel where the light catches the iris. "He's alive."

"Because I chose not to kill him." Knowing that I am no greater than the King of the Vicoletta Right Now doesn't keep the confidence out of my throat.

"You're the American. The betrayer."

"Is that what they say about me?"

She looks away, brow tightened, hands balled together in the center of her chest.

"They'll punish you for this. It's going to be bad. Really bad for you." She takes a step back.

"I'll be fine."

Above us, leaning out a window, a man murmurs on the phone. The tightrope slips from under me. My little kingdom is collapsing.

"What's your name?" I ask.

Lucretia.

"You need to run."

"Tell me where to find you. To check on you."

"Goodbye. And thank you."

"Just a name."

But then she's running down the dark alley with clicking heels. I chase her, leaving the bloody face behind, to a world where I am no ruler. The cobra head is slippery and the cobblestones are uneven. I kick sideways and slam my shoulder against a cracked wall. Push away from it and look one way down the street, then the other.

No sign of her.

This is her city, not mine.

If she's gone, she wants to be.

CHAPTER 6

DELFINA

Walking the streets of Naples at night has always been presented as a walk past a lion's den, but it's too late to go back to the wraith and demand he take me to the Gargiulo Gate. He told me to run, and I ran—eventually. He won't stay long enough to ask Rafi if he's feeling all right any more than he'll take a nice walk across town with me.

Crossing to my side of the *Via Cedronio*, I can't breathe, even though all I'm doing is breathing.

"You're alone?" Nunzio asks, lifting the muzzle of his gun a fraction of an inch while looking over my shoulder to make sure I am what he said I am. He can carry a gun even though he doesn't have the scar inside his elbow. Papa pays for that too.

Does he see the wraith? Was I followed here by my protector?

"Let me in." I can barely get words out between gulps of air.

Nunzio moves his eyes into the crevices of the street,

where he must see nothing, because his attention has landed back on me. "You okay?"

He's known me since I was a toddler and he was already older than his years, and I like him, but I am so tired of being everyone else's problem.

"Let me in!"

I've never yelled so loud to enter my own house. Maybe that's why he gets out of the way without another objection.

The huge metal door in the middle of the street opens into a leafy courtyard surrounded by the halls and balconies of my childhood. A different world where I am as safe as a chick in an egg.

Papa runs his business empire out of this compound, the same as his father and his father's father did. It's populated with offices and polished floors to the right. The left hasn't been touched in forever, and that's where our extended family lives. We have seven kitchens and I pass three of them to run to my rooms, where I can be alone.

Nunzio will tell Papa I came back alone. I don't know what that will mean for me, or Rafi, or the wraith of a man with the American accent.

Splashing cold water on my face, I watch it drip down my cheeks.

What just happened?

My reflection is smudged. I wipe loose drops off the mirror. Behind me, there's movement in the open window. Shadow-on-black. More a feeling than a sight. On edge, I turn with a gasp, fearing it's the wraith from the alley only slightly less than I'm hoping it is, but it's just a raven, staring at me with one side-eye.

"Shoo!" I wave it away and close the window, leaning on the sill with a sigh.

Bad things almost happened. Then a different bad thing

happened. Something specific and unnameable and massive and minuscule.

His accent was American, but he was no tourist.

Massimo Colonia.

Men like him are the reason I need an escort home from the Orolios. The filthy American. The descendent of traitors so untrustworthy that their deceit is passed from generation to generation, like thick lips or high cheekbones. They say God gave them clubfeet and lame legs so they can never run away from what they did, though the specifics of their misconduct have been all but forgotten.

Did the devil make him that handsome to aid him in more crimes? Because that face is burned into my memory by fires hotter than hell. Jaw tight, a loop of hair swaying across his forehead as he brought the cane down into Rafi's face.

With the mirror cleared, I can see the drop of red on my collar. It's not a gentle little dot. It's a line from thick to thin. A brushstroke. Movement. A velocity. How far did it have to travel to land there? Five feet? Ten?

It's a message across an infinite space. Something bad almost happened. Something worse took its place. And someone is going to pay for it.

CHAPTER 7
SIX MONTHS EARLIER

MASSIMO

My last moments of freedom were spent chasing my sister. If I had known that would be my last day of wanting something besides being home, I would have appreciated what a privilege that choice was and left Sarah alone to make her own life.

But I was going to save her from the man who took her. A man she said she loved.

I knew better. I knew the difference between captivity and love.

I *thought* I knew.

My father's body wasn't even cold. I was wounded, broken, pushed into an unanticipated succession fight for the Colonia First Chair.

Maybe I was chasing my sister to the Caribbean because she was all I had left. I wanted desperately to be a hero to someone.

In a tiny airport on a speck of an island known for nothing more than bank fraud and three resorts, they caught me.

Santino DiLustro. Cosimo Orolio. The Old Country we left a hundred years before their great-grandfathers were born, calling me home.

It was about a knife, apparently.

I never gave a thought to the wedding knife we used to cut couples together in marriage, but I'm stuck in Naples because of it.

The Colonia came to New York when Manhattan was half-wilderness. Before indoor plumbing. Catholicism may have been the official religion of the Roman Empire, but when we left Naples, we built our own rituals. Our own walls. As the world grew around us, we protected ourselves and our culture from any kind of dilution. We were perfect.

"Where's the knife?" A man in his forties held the gun, speaking English with a heavy Italian accent. His fingers were so thick, one barely fit in the trigger guard.

"Who are you?" I was on the floor at that point, thinking if I knew who they were, I'd know what they were talking about.

"The black knife!"

There was only one of those that I knew of, and Father Grimson had told me it was only black in the sunlight. Underground, in the Dome, it was plain polished silver. I never saw the difference for myself.

"Who are you?" I repeated and got smacked for it. I couldn't retaliate. There were too many hands holding me down.

"We get the knife and you go home."

The wedding knife had sat in the center of its table with its blade pointing toward heaven for as long as I could remember. It's cut men and women into marriage for hundreds of years. Why would this guy chase me into the desolate terminal of a barely-secured private airport for it?

"Who. Are. You?"

A younger guy with slicked-back hair and dead-pale skin—who I'd later know as Corrado—translated back to the old man wearing two suit vests under his jacket, high-neck under low-neck, as if he needed to show both.

Two-Vest mumbled a long answer. Corrado nodded. Listened. Didn't interrupt. My Italian is serviceable in New York, but he was talking fast and I couldn't discern names from words. I would only learn later it was not Italian, but a Neapolitan dialect.

When the old man finished, he jerked his head to Corrado, who turned to me and translated flatly, "I am Cosimo Orolio, son of Gaetano Orolio, first of Alfunzu Orolio of Abruzzo, whose father and whose father before him led the Carbonari to war against Bourbon occupiers. I am of the last Carbonari, the fighters who stayed in the Kingdom of the Two Sicilies to live or die. You, Massimo Colonia, are of the first Carbonari, the secret society who ran from the Holy Mother Church to preserve their rituals. You are a traitor. I want my fucking knife."

He wasn't going to have it.

I was Massimo Colonia, First of Peter Colonia who put his wing over the Dome my entire life, and who gave it all to me to protect as he did. That knife bound men to women. It is stored deep, past a dozen locked doors. I wasn't giving strangers the keys to my kingdom so they could retrieve a bauble.

"It's ours," I growled. "If we have it, there's a reason."

Cosimo nodded to Thick Fingers, who reached into my jacket, pulled out my passport, and handed it to his boss, who opened it, nodded, slid it into his pocket, and said, "Then we take you instead."

Corrado did not need to translate.

CHAPTER 8

SIX DAYS TO ARMISTICE NIGHT

MASSIMO

"Get up." Corrado whips the covers off me. He has a key to my little room over the butcher, but his presence is still surprising.

Six more days until I can plead my case and get permission to go home.

The count of days to Armistice Night is usually the last thing I think of before I sleep and the first thought in my head when I wake. But not today. I was dreaming of Lucretia in profile, lips parted, shirt torn open to reveal what is hers alone, and the blood-caked face of the man who tried to rip more from her.

"What the fuck do you want?" I'm told my Italian is grammatically terrible, or too heavily accented, or lacking in musical finesse. All I know is I'm misunderstood less and less frequently.

He sits in the chair next to the bed and puts my cane over his knees. "You sound like a tourist who took a class."

"Fuck you."

He lights a cigarette and blows the smoke toward the window. It's the least he can do, and I'm not getting any more consideration. "Leave out the *cosa*."

"*Che vuoi?*" Up on my elbows, I ask what he wants again, with fewer words.

"What did you get up to last night?" He picks up the cane and taps my bare chest with the bloody brass cobra head.

I fall back, looking at the water-stained ceiling without answering.

"Don Orolio wants to know."

"He doesn't already?"

Corrado stands and leans the cane on the chair. "He wants to hear it in an American accent." He's usually a fucking asshole, but he sounds a little sad to deliver this news.

"Let me shower and—"

"*Subito*, Massimo. You fucked up. Bad."

Fine. It's out of my hands. I'll go with a man's blood in the cracks of my skin.

On the second floor of the building where Cosimo Orolio put me, there's a bald man who, every morning, sits on his balcony drinking espresso. Whenever I leave, he stands, holds his cup over the edge of the railing, and with the concentration of an adolescent boy at an arcade game, dumps it on me.

His aim is always flawless, but his timing took a few weeks to perfect. It landed behind me with a little splat and I thought he was just a slob, until the day he got it right. When I looked up at him, he shouted, "Bull's-eye!"

Entrapment is so much more than a locked door. It's walking the streets in circles, unable to go farther than the outer walls. I cannot leave. I've tried. There are only a handful of ways out of the Quarter. It was built to shelter the Spanish army, so the exits are easy to man with people willing to stop me—sometimes gently, sometimes not. The tunnels under the city are the same. I have no passport, no money, no privacy. I'm trapped in less than a million square meters, living in a room over a butcher.

For a knife, of all things.

And yet, my Lucretia is here, somewhere in this crowded pocket of an already dense city.

Who is she? Does she live behind one of the anonymous windows? Has she ever hung her laundry on the lines strung from balcony to balcony? She can't live too far away. How did I not notice her before?

When the street is too narrow to walk abreast, I walk behind Corrado. The grocer sweeping the sidewalk spits in my path and sneers. As a bike-riding teen passes, he kicks me. I move quickly enough to avoid the worst of it. I am hated here. I am a worthless betrayer. A back-stabber. A sixth-generation coward and a traitor to a country that no longer exists.

I jump ahead to walk next to Corrado, just in time to miss a moldy orange thrown from a balcony.

"Just around the corner," my companion says. "We'll be there before someone ruins your jacket."

"I'm used to it."

"Unfortunate." That's the second thing he's said to me today that has the slightest hint of compassion. "You must think we're animals."

"Never saw cats or dogs hold a grudge for six generations."

He smiles at me, then looks up and shakes his head at whoever's about to pelt me with something.

"You gonna tell me how I fucked up last night?" I ask. "I shoulda just let it happen?"

"You did what I would have done. What any of us *should*

have done. It's a shame you had to be the one to do it, and shame does not sit peacefully on a man's heart." He turns into a dark doorway as I feel a pebble hitting my sleeve. "Up here."

As I follow him up the stairwell lit by only a skylight, I wonder if Lucretia has thrown things at me. Does she hate me the way everyone else does? She didn't seem to, at all.

No. She doesn't hate me like the rest of them, though she may resent the rescue. She could hate me for exposing her to the violence of it. I'd do it again. And again.

At the top of the stairs, I hang on to that knowledge like a prize. Let them all despise me. That beautiful creature is whole because of me.

This comforts me as I walk into the room where I'll take the weight of men's shame.

Three slim glass doors cut into eight rectangles lead to a wrought-iron balcony with flowers spilling over the edge. That's my only escape.

The room faces west, so it's dark in the morning, and the men sitting around the table are in shadow, but I know Cosimo Orolio at the head before he even stands.

"Massimo Colonia." My name is a sorrowful responsibility in this room.

"Don Orolio," I say with my chin up. I am not the one here who needs to hang my head in shame.

"Sit." He indicates the chair at the foot of the table, facing into the light.

I sit and lean my cane against the table. Cosimo introduces the other four men. His son, Aris, a real fucking prick; Galante Gargiulo, a rich guy who lives just outside the Quarter; and Fedele Scanga, a barrel of a man in his fifties with a widow's peak much like the one I aimed at last night. I've never seen him before. He doesn't even nod at me when introduced.

He must be that animal's father.

Good job, asshole.

"Massimo," Cosimo starts, "a man with a cane was seen last night on *Vicoletto Tofa*."

"That was me. And I'm going to save you the trouble of—"

"Hush now, boy." Cosimo isn't unkind, but he's dead serious. "The man had a cane and used it to beat another man. Was this you?"

"*Sì.*"

"You beat him?"

"I did."

"Why?"

Scanga slaps his hand on the table. "What is the difference? My Rafi is in the hospital, almost dead. The left side of his head was crushed. His mother has not stopped crying. She won't eat. His sisters already wear black. What could he have done to deserve this animal attacking him while he's unarmed?"

"He was assaulting a young woman," I say.

"Do not." Scanga growls an unspoken threat. "My son was doing no such thing."

"Do you know the woman?" Cosimo asks me.

"I do not."

"Can you describe her?"

"Can I?" I ask myself more than anyone present. "She was blond where the sun touches her head. Light brown where the hair is hidden. Her eyes were dark in the moonlight, but may be hazel in the sun. A perfect Greek nose. Like a marble statue of a goddess. Straight as geometry itself."

"Did she call for help?" Scanga demands.

Cosimo waves to one of the younger men standing in the corners. The subordinate leaves quietly.

"She was defiant, but out of her depth," I answer as the door clicks shut.

"Did she *call*?" Scanga asks.

"What are you implying?" In a rage he's built up while I was busy answering dumb questions, Gargiulo leans into a sliver of light, and I see her mouth and forehead. He's my Lucretia's father. "Say it loud."

"I am implying"—Scanga leans forward—"that I sent my son down here to do business, to warn you there was a summons, and now he's dying for some *mezza sega* you're keeping as a trinket."

He calls me an insignificant half-man and no one bats an eyelash.

This is when I realize that no one's leaving here without blaming someone for what happened, and that someone is me. I am the sacrifice, offered to save Rafi's father from shame. If I defend her and say she called out, Scanga will resist it. The witnesses might say otherwise. I will be a liar, and in the eyes of these men and her community, she will have consented. I won't do that to her honor or my own.

"This was my father's cane," I say with my hand on it. "He had a clubfoot. Spent most of his life hobbled. Leaning on that foot was incredibly painful for him. But every day, he walked up the stairs and down them. He walked to see his people, perform our ceremonies, and mark the boundaries of our territory. He was feared. He ruled by tradition and blood. He was a king with this cane, and he never had to use it to discipline one of his subjects, because he held them in line with just the threat of it. If we were in my kingdom, that boy never would have touched a woman without her father's permission."

I have pissed off both Rafi's and Lucretia's fathers. Scanga, I understand. I accused his son, again. Gentile's tight jaw, red face, and narrow eyes are inexplicable... unless he was asked for permission. But to do what? Take what his daughter wasn't willing to give? That makes no sense.

I'm trying to sort this out when the door opens. The young

guard comes through, and behind him, quiet as a thunderstorm, she steps in.

There are only fourteen thousand people in the Quarter. A mere three million in Napoli. With just fifty-nine million in all of Italy, how had I not seen her before last night?

"Delfina," Cosimo says. "Come. Stand near your father."

She obeys, but even in obedience, she is not diminished in scale. She is not small or weak. She captures my full attention like a touch of bright color in a black and white photograph. She is the one point of light in a pitch-dark room.

She doesn't look at me as she takes her place behind her father's chair, and I'm grateful. If she did, the building would explode.

"Delfina," Cosimo says, "is this the man you saw last night?"

She glances at her father, not me, before turning back to Cosimo. "I didn't see his face."

She's lying, and I can't figure out why.

"He's already admitted to it."

She looks at me then, and her expression turns the explosion I expected into an eruption. She thinks I'm crazy. She is awed by me and I don't know why.

"It was me," I say. "And the question is whether I intervened or interrupted."

A knot forms between her brows, as if she doesn't understand.

"That is not the question!" Her father's hand curls into a fist on the table.

"It is," Rafi's father says, fist rising from his lap and turning into a tight point in her direction. "No one heard a cry for help. You tempted my son and drew him into the dark to avoid the line."

The dynamics here are getting clearer, and this is going

to get ugly. I'm not in the business of taking sides, but unless I step in, she's going to bear the brunt of the outcome.

"His hand was over her mouth," I say. "She was struggling. Look at her. She's innocent. Is that a woman looking to seduce a man in a dark alley?"

"What is the line?!" Her demand for an answer cuts through all the bullshit. Whether or not she screamed is irrelevant in the face of her ignorance. "Rafi said, last night, it was him or the line."

My brain does not have time to process what I see. My Lucretia, but more alive than even the first time I saw her. Not passive. Not begging for her life or for justice. She is not a victim. Not in the full light of day. Her cheeks are red from exertion, glowing with sweat that catches her wheaten hair, darkening it and sticking the curls to her face, hazel eyes narrowed and focused on her father like lasers.

Cosimo and Galante exchange a conversation with a glance.

"Don't worry about it," Cosimo says. "It's not our problem."

"We try to warn you and this is how we're repaid." Fedele huffs a derisive laugh. "You think it's just our women. You think you're immune. Time is not on your side, Orolio." He turns to Delfina. "You should prefer a dark alley to what's coming. You're no better than the rest of us. You're going to present yourselves and one of you's going to be sold to a monster."

Delfina freezes. She didn't expect this response. Neither did I, but I make a decision then and there. Delfina Gargiulo will not be sold to any monster, any man, anyone.

"She asked a question," I say. "That answer doesn't cut it."

Delfina moves her attention my way as if seeing me for the first time. I feel much the same, because this look completes her transition from a work of art to a fully present woman who breathes electricity into the air. My skin tingles with it. Was I even alive before this moment?

"You impudent—" Fedele's face turns purple with rage.

I meet his gaze, because I want a fight right now. Foolishly, thoughtlessly, I'm charged with energy to defend her right to ask a question. Fedele must see this when he turns to Delfina.

"My Rafi was trying to do you a favor, *signorina*." Fedele stands. "You'll wish this cabbage hadn't come for you." He turns to me. "You think they'll protect you? These men? They hate you because your women don't get in the line. Instead of facing what needed to be done, the Colonia ran away and hid. They thought they could move across the sea and keep their women away from it. He will come for you. You are a dead man, Massimo Colonia."

"He is worse than dead," Cosimo says with the authority of a man who's been don as long as anyone can remember. "He's barred from Armistice Night."

"What?" I stand quickly.

"For assaulting Raffaello Scanga, your punishment is exclusion."

"Armistice Night is open to the Colonia." I state the law as if I have power to enforce it. "I am the rightful successor."

"Your birthright is defunct. Your family is scattered. Trash. You no longer exist."

His words would be unbearable under any circumstance, but in front of Delfina, they're humiliating.

"You will never have our knife." I grab for the last straw of dignity.

"Then you should make yourself at home." Cosimo smirks.

I glance at Delfina, because I'm sure she finds me repellent and worthless. I am sure the disgust in her eyes will be easy to read, and I'll know where I stand with her. But her head is down, and I am shut out from even her revulsion.

Every man has his limits. I've been discovering what I'm

able to tolerate for months now. Being cut off from my only hope of freedom is almost too much. My first impulse is to leap across the table and wrap my hands around Cosimo's neck. That would surely get me killed or worse, pulled off him and beat up.

That will not happen in front of her.

My Lucretia won't know the depths of my shame. Not today.

So, I take a deep breath and point my chin in my captor's direction. "I will die here if I have to."

He nods, assuring me that I will.

CHAPTER 9

DELFINA

Massimo promises Don Orolio he'll be happy to die rather than give him his people's knife. His misery soaks through every word. He hates it here, and yet he won't give up. I hate one of those things and I like the other.

More than anything, I want to see faraway places. I want to be free to go where I want, when I want. I want to be above all the constant noise. Still, I don't understand how anyone can hate this city. It's not perfect, but it's real, with a visible history of strong people. It has roots deep in the earth and branches touching the heavens.

Can't he see that? With those intense hazel eyes, can he see my heart's desire?

The men speak and I hear them, but my attention is on the American. Out of the corner of my eye, I watch as his desolation becomes darker and thicker.

Scanga seems satisfied with the outcome and walks out with his man. We're left in silence.

I can't look at Massimo. The wraith of last night is

completely real today, with all the frailty and presence of a human man. Without defenses and accusations flying around the room, I don't know what to make of him. Something else weighs on those of us left here.

"She asked a question," Massimo repeats. I believe he'd never dismiss me or shoo me away. He'd never tell me that my dreams are silly or selfish.

"Papa?" I put my hand on his shoulder. "What does it mean?"

"Nothing yet." He pats my hand.

"What does it mean?" Massimo's repetition is defensive—as if he's asking not for himself, but for me.

Mr. Orolio and Papa exchange glances.

Papa stands and leans both hands on the table as if he's going to crawl over it and choke Massimo. "You will stay away from my daughter, betrayer." With a huff, he draws himself back. "Come, Delfina. I will take you home."

"One thing," Don Orolio says, freezing the room. "My niece, Luna Beneforte, is here from America. We don't have women in the house, so she'll be staying with you."

Papa seems unperturbed, and normally I'd welcome a visitor without question, but I'm annoyed by the lies. How many can there be all in one day?

"What about Serafina?" The tone of my question about Don Orlio's most-beloved daughter is laced with venom. She's catty and awful and always managed to get out of unpleasant obligations at school.

Papa looks at me as if I just flung shit across the room. But Massimo smirks, staring at me as if seeing me for the first time, again. Somehow, I've pleased him, and I like that. A lot.

I'm shocked out of our stare when Don Orolio answers.

"Serafina is on the *Dragon Bones* with her sister." He says the name of his yacht as if I'm supposed to know what he's talking about, which I guess I do. "She cannot be returned in time to entertain her long-lost American cousin."

"We'll take her in as one of our own, of course," I say.

"*Bene. Grazie.* You may go."

I comply, leaving with one last glance at the beautiful man who may have destroyed himself saving me.

Massimo Colonia has opened the door to my mind, turned on the light in a room I didn't know existed, and made himself comfortable. He's sitting on the sofa of my attention, with his feet up on my curiosity, breathing in the stale air of my unspoken cravings.

He's not saying anything. His presence in my consciousness demands nothing. I don't feel pulled toward the thoughts or feel the need to block him out. But he's changing the gravity of my awareness, putting it squarely between my legs.

In the back of Papa's limo, alone behind tinted glass, I slide down to the edge of the seat and put my feet far apart, inching my knees closer together until the stiff seam of my jeans presses against the hard nub of my clitoris. I discovered this one day on the way to St. Magdalena School, when I was so tired I tried to get horizontal for a few minutes. Every bump in the old streets was a revelation, and my arrival at the school gate was more of a disappointment than usual.

Rocking my hips slightly, I imagine Massimo Colonia on top of me. His eyes are half closed with desire. His lips are parted, whispering my name. He is in ecstasy. A helpless breath escapes him because he is with me. Only I can make him feel this way.

The door opens. I close my legs quickly, even though

there's nothing to see here really, but I feel overripe and flushed.

Papa stands there but doesn't get in. His hand goes out for a girl about my age to slide in across from me. She has freckles and wavy brown hair that curls into coils around her face. Her eyes are hazel like Massimo's, but with darker lashes.

"Hi!" She smiles, delighted to be shunted from her uncle's house to ours, and holds out her arm for a handshake, like a man. Then she makes nonsense sounds I don't understand.

"Ah, um, I speak not Italian. Speak I English?" She looks at me hopefully.

"No English." I shrug.

Papa gets in the car and clears his throat. Our driver closes the door.

Luna holds up a phone with a screen and draws her hand across her throat. "No *bene*."

I look at the screen. No Service sits at the top. I show her my flip phone. Shrug again. Smile. It'll be fine.

"She can help with Liliana's wedding," Papa says.

"Yeah. She'll go back to America knowing how to cook, at least."

On the way home, Papa sits next to me in silence, while Luna and I try to communicate in hand signals. It doesn't work, and when the traffic snarls us at an intersection, we all fall into silence, and I fall into Massimo.

He's tilted my world a little sideways. Everything is slowly sliding in his direction. I look for him everywhere. Where does he live? What does he do? Where would I go to run into him again?

"Papa." I look at him. "What will happen to Massimo?"

"Eh." He waves away any concern. "He won't make it another six months."

I suck in a breath so sharp my ears ring. "He didn't do anything wrong."

"Count the eggs in your own nest."

When the car is inside the walls of our family home, my day slides back into reality. The dressmaker's Fiat. The grocer's truck. The batting and bunting being loaded into an SUV for a rushed wedding.

"I don't want to cause him trouble."

That's at least half the truth. What I want to cause is an ecstasy so intense that his lips part and his eyes flutter closed.

Luna looks at me, pink-cheeked.

"Delfina," Papa practically barks, "you are to stay away from him. Do not even think of him again. Do you understand?"

I do, but I don't. I nod anyway. "Yes, Papa."

The car stops. Both back doors open. Papa pats my hand as if this is done, but it's not. If I can't think about Massimo, I can ask a question about something else.

"You moved Liliana's wedding because of the message Rafi brought."

"*Capretta.*" He's half in, half out of the car when he calls me by my little girl name.

I roll my eyes, because no matter how many times my little self got caught in the proverbial fence wires trying to get out of wherever I felt trapped, I'm not a baby goat.

"I'm not a child anymore," I say, but he's already walking away. I rush out to follow and catch him in the short walkway to the back door. "Papa!"

He turns, and Luna comes to a short stop beside me. "You want to know, and you should know." His expression is soft. Pitying. His compassion is terrifying. "The Montefiores are back, and they're demanding their tribute."

"Those are just stories."

If you're a bad girl, the Montefiores will come in the night and ruin you. They will come as a cat or a wolf while you sleep and you'll be paralyzed as they take your virginity. They will rip you apart and break your will.

The tales are all different. They were born from Vesuvius. They sleep under the ruins of Pompeii. They are all dead. They all live forever. No one over the age of twelve believes any of it, but when we get old enough to take care of the children, we tell the same stories to get them to behave.

Luna clears her throat. Her brows are knotted with concern and I wonder if she reads minds or understands Italian.

"Yes." Papa sighs deeply and rubs his hands on his brown pants, leaving out which parts of the stories aren't *just* stories. "Those are stories. Some are true. I can make Liliana unavailable by setting the wedding earlier, but I couldn't spare you so... we will play the odds, and the odds are you'll go to Armistice Night and come home no worse for it."

Armistice Night? One night a year, the heads of all the families in the System and their wives meet in peace to arrange marriages, make treaties, and gossip. We aren't in the System, yet I'm going?

"How? I thought—"

"The Montefiores have been gone fifty-some years, and fifty-some years ago..." He shrugs as if to say he can't do anything about the passage of time. "This family was inside. We may get called. It is what it is."

"You said the odds are I'll come home."

"Good odds. If we get a letter."

"What if the odds don't work out?"

"I don't want you to worry about that."

"Papa! Tell me!"

"You go with them. That's all. They take you as a wife and you go with them. I'm sorry. The odds are good."

He's talking as if this is all real. My questions can't seem to line up properly for the fire drill, and in that sliver of shocked silence, Papa walks into the house.

"Come on," I say to Luna, then make a gesture that says the same thing. She looks at me, stricken, as if she heard the whole thing. *"Parla Italiano?"*

She says something back in nonsense.

"Neapolitan?" I think, maybe she didn't want to tell us she knows our dialect, but she just blinks. Is she hiding what she understands? I can't bear a sneak. "There's a tarantula on you!"

No reaction. She really understands nothing. She was probably making that face in reaction to her own apple pie thoughts.

We'll have to make do with hand signs.

CHAPTER 10

DELFINA

Preparations for Liliana's wedding have turned our kitchen into the center of the universe. Even little Emilia, who's six years old, has a job halving maraschino cherries for the cookies. Thank God the caterer could do the food on short notice. The bakery, however, could only guarantee bread. The pastries are on us now.

I introduce Luna, who smiles wanly. Finding out none of us speak English has shaved the edge off her cheerfulness.

"Come on!" Aunt Etta takes Luna by the shoulders and pushes her toward the sink. "You have dirty pots in America, right?"

"She doesn't understand you, Ma," my cousin Rizzo says, stirring cake batter with a wooden spoon. Her hair is up in a scarf like the rest of us, but she cuts her curly dark hair short because she hates the attention of men.

Like all my cousins, Rizzo lives with us in what we call the Gargiulo Palace, which isn't a palace at all, but a big house built around a courtyard and connected to neighboring buildings. It takes up half a city block and is hidden behind big iron doors leading onto the street.

"Everyone understands cleanliness." Aunt Etta hands Luna gloves, which she puts on.

"How did it go, Delfie?" Liliana asks, stirring custard to bring to Aunt Lina's side of the courtyard, where we'll stuff it into pastries. Her eyes are red and puffy with tears. Yesterday, she was ticking off reasons her marriage is going to fail. It looks as if she's been crying about it ever since. "You're still okay to be in the wedding?"

"*Santo!*" Rizzo seems deeply offended.

"What?"

"After what she went through? You're worried she'll be ineligible to be your bridesmaid?"

"I'm just asking."

"I'm fine," I say, slicing hard sausage.

"It's just another bad sign." Liliana swipes a circle of salami. "Nothing's ready, and it's going to be a mess. You're fine, right, Delfie? Look at you, chopping away."

"It's fine, Liliana." I slap her hand away from another disc.

"More please." Little Emilia pushes an empty maraschino cherry jar toward me. Her cutting board has a small pile of halved cherries and her mouth is bright red.

I get a fresh jar from the cabinet for her and slap the bottom.

"Are you upset that I'm getting married?" Liliana asks quietly, once everyone else has moved on to other topics.

"What?" The jar pops open.

"I'm leaving you, but I'm not. We're living in the house, just on the other side. I'll always be your sister, and you'll be married soon. I promise."

"You think I want to be married, like, right now?"

"You were always the beautiful one."

"Shut up." I slap the jar down in front of Emilia and look around.

Everyone's working away, talking about their tasks, collaborating on getting it done. Even Luna's scrubbing a huge pot as if it's her job. I guess everyone does understand cleanliness.

"You'll have a big wedding and all the attention someday." Liliana's big sister voice is soft and reassuring.

She's not trying to offend me. She's trying to comfort me. But the only thing I'm offended about is that, after a lifetime together, she's decided not to know me at all.

"Liliana. I love you, and I'm happy for you."

"I'm not saying you aren't."

"You want to live the same life our mother lived, and our grandmother lived, and every other woman in this city lived. You want to follow the same rules and stay here forever. I get it."

"Oh, Delfie." She presses her lips together and blinks slowly before looking me in the eye. "Travel for a bit and you'll see. There's nothing out there. Not really." She speaks from the thin experience of a summer in Paris. "Everything we need is right here."

"Yeah, well, I might get taken away by the Montefiores, so let's see if they have everything I need too. Why don't you ask them since you know so much about what I need? Give them a list!"

Emilia's eyes get wet. I'm yelling. I don't mean to yell.

"*Basta!*" Nonna barks. She's actually our great-grandmother, but we call her Nonna.

"You're going?" Rizzo's eyebrows are raised in surprise. Her dad is in the System under Don Orolio, as well as her brother Corrado, so she was bound to go to the line at some point.

"I guess I'll have to if I have to?"

"Oh, God, I don't want to go alone if we do." Rizzo comes to me and we hold each other's forearms in a nervous embrace. "But you guys aren't even—"

"We were," Nonna says. "When I was a girl." She slaps the flour off her hands with a sigh. "We will get summoned soon. And when we do, the unmarried girls they ask for will be candidates. They will line you up so you can be chosen or not. You will do it. All of you." She makes it a point to make eye contact with Rizzo and me. "Same as I did. Twice."

We all freeze as Nonna nudges me away from the sink to wash her hands.

"The first time," she continues, running a brush over her nails, "I was sixteen. The second time, I was engaged to my husband, but my father didn't spoil me and move my wedding." She gives Liliana a passing glance then drops the brush into the dish. "We knew better than to break the Vow."

"What is the Vow, Nonna?" I try to be casual, wiping down the side of the big pot.

"When the Montefiores call, we answer." She shuts the water and shakes out her hands. "The letters come in the North first, then to us, then to the Second Sicily. They request certain daughters appear at Armistice Night. Some are favored, some just named. They stand in a line, and the ones who are chosen as wives are taken away."

"How many?" I ask.

"Depends. I've seen one and I've seen two. Most I ever heard of was four, but that was before my time."

"Where do they go?" Rizzo asks.

Nonna dries her hands in silence.

"*Where?*" Rizzo demands.

Nonna shakes her head and sighs again. "Some say the Montefiores live under Vesuvius, in caves, eating nothing but the darkness, but I've been close to them, and they are men. Human men. Beautiful men."

"This is stupid," I mumble, stripping the skin off another sausage. "We don't even have letters."

"So you don't know what happens to the wives?" Liliana pops a maraschino cherry in her mouth. This is just a scary story for her.

"We don't see them again."

Rizzo's face has gone so white she's blue. Aunt Etta has been putting the same chocolate chip at the center of the same cookie the whole time. Little Emilia looks about to cry.

"Nonna." I never snap at my grandmother, so she raises an eyebrow but doesn't reprimand me. "You're scaring everyone with this superstitious nonsense."

"Delfina!" Aunt Greca scolds me for accusing our revered nonna of spouting nonsense.

"One time." Nonna holds up one finger. "I went to Firenze for an appointment with a special doctor and I saw Elisabella LoVullo. I saw her chosen, years before, with my own eyes. But there I was, with my legs spread and my feet in stirrups when she walks in. White coat. Hair up in a bun. Holding my chart." She throws open the oven with her free hand and, with a towel to protect her from the heat, slides out the rack. "She sits down, takes one look at my name, then sees my face and walks right out." She slaps the hot tray onto the counter.

"So..." Rizzo hesitates, as if the idea is too weird to leave her lips without another few seconds of consideration. "She became a Montefiore wife and then a doctor? In Florence?"

"I had five children without her help."

"You almost died every time, Nonna," Liliana says softly.

"But I didn't. No doctor has the power to make easy what God wants hard. My mother prayed for me every time and here I am." Nonna points at me. "And I'm the one who prayed to Saint Gerard to get you out of your mother alive. I left my own wedding ring at his altar, and look at you. Came into the world feet first." She slides a cookie tray into the oven. "But you're here."

"Mother isn't," I whisper.

"I only had one ring." She slaps the oven shut. "I regret that. I saved you at birth. I cannot save you from this. The Montefiores wreak hell on any family that does not present their daughter. May the Holy Mother avert his eyes to another bird they might pluck, because after Elisabella, no other of the chosen has ever been seen again."

"Do you believe any of what Nonna said?" Rizzo asks me, smoking a cigarette at the wall.

It's dark, the night before my sister's wedding. All the cookies and breads are baked. The birds and crickets sing the way they always do. It's hard to imagine anything will ever change.

"I believe she believes it."

"I like the doctor story though." Rizzo pulls on her cigarette and offers me a drag. I decline. "You feeling okay? After last night, I mean?"

"Sometimes when I close my eyes, it's happening all over again and I can feel his hands on me."

"Ugh."

"And it's scary like it's real. But sometimes, when I close my eyes, I see the American with the cane, beating Rafi's face in, and I'm not scared anymore." I hold out two fingers so Rizzo can put the cigarette at the center of my fingers' V. "He was there today, when they went over what happened to Rafi."

"Yeah?" Rizzo seems intrigued. "What's he like?"

"He's..." I blow out the smoke, holding back a cough. I decide to answer a different question. I don't know what he's like, just that he's not like us in ways that have no name. "They were all acting like he interrupted something."

"Men are gross sometimes."

"And I saw him, really clear for the first time."

"I heard he's handsome."

"Well, yeah. Definitely. But he seemed so sad too. Like he has no one. Everyone hates him. I felt… not bad. More, I guess I wondered how he holds his head up the way he does. Like he's wearing a crown, and he has to because it's heavy and he'd rather carry it than fold under the weight. And I just kept thinking, 'What do I need to do to save him again?'"

"Save him?"

"See him. I meant see him. What should I do to see him again?"

"I don't know."

"Come on, Rizzo, you've snuck out to see a man before."

"Yeah, and it almost ruined me." She scoffs and takes a last drag of her cigarette and offers it to me. I refuse. "If you figure out how to see him…" She throws it to the ground and stamps it dead. "Make it before Armistice Night. After that, who knows where we'll be."

CHAPTER 11

FIVE DAYS TO ARMISTICE NIGHT

MASSIMO

On Tuesdays, Corrado and I move bags of money. Campagna Florist to the Bella Frisco Café, to the Taverna Verdi, then under the tunnels, to the barber, which buzzes with activity. The dressmaker doesn't even come out to chat with Corrado.

Nino Catering is also busier than usual.

"What's going on?" I ask when Benny tosses me Nino's bag of Cosimo's tribute money.

"The Gargiulo wedding," he says, getting back to his kneading while my heart turns to stone. "Supposed to be in October, but everything's fucked now."

I'd know if she was getting married, wouldn't I?

Why would I? It's not as if I'd be invited to eat and drink with her family, or stand in the corner while she dances with her new husband. My blood goes into a rolling boil, cooking any thought I had in my brain that wasn't of her.

"If you're staying," Benny says, slapping the dough, "grab an apron."

His voice snaps me away from the head-pictures of another man's hands on her.

It can't be Delfina's wedding. There would have been a fiancé to protect her from Rafi. My God, I'm not thinking straight at all.

"Bigger load next time then." I hold up the bag and peer over the counter at the slips of paper tacked to the edge of a shelf. Nothing. Then I see the stacked steam trays with the delivery tag scrawled with the where and whens.

"Potato peeler's in that drawer to your left," Benny says.

"I'm not much of a cook. See you next week."

Corrado waits outside, on the phone to the faraway girlfriend I'm keeping him from. He turns his back to me. I stuff the sack of money in the bag he has slung on one shoulder. When I'm done buckling, he hangs up and we walk.

"The whole place is upside down over one wedding." An empty sunflower seed shell falls onto my shoulder. I brush it away.

Corrado never gets hit. These fucking people can aim like nobody else. They should never lose a war.

"It'll all get done." He lights a cigarette without slowing down. Real skill.

"You going to this wedding tonight?"

"She's my cousin."

"And they moved it from October?" I dodge a pebble I see hanging in the air, mid-flight. The person who threw it is already gone.

"You trying to say something?"

"Yeah. It's been how long since these Montefiores were around? They said fifty years?"

"That's when their villa burned down. And *poof*. Never seen again. There's been peace ever since, or nonstop war, depending who you talk to." He makes a quick, unexpected left turn. "Cosimo's moving some stuff through the tunnels and we have to set it up."

I'm not sure what he means, but I follow him anyway.

Cosimo Orolio has a lot of shit.

Corrado and I are in a basement under Cosimo's house that connects to the tunnels crisscrossing under the Quarter. The room is stacked with pine crates stenciled with numbers. He's sitting on one of them, checking stuff off on a ledger.

I call out the number on a crate. "Eleven, twelve, fifty-two. Nineteen forty-four. That a date?"

"Yes." He marks it in the ledger. "Next."

The job is so mindless I can worry with ninety-nine percent of my unused attention.

Assuming the letters come, and assuming Delfina's requested on this line—which isn't a given since her father's not in the System—I'd have to assume again that she's chosen to be a wife. Who would they choose but the most beautiful woman in the city?

A lot has to happen. But that doesn't stop me from imagining another man touching her, or building every detail of that contact so that I can piss myself off even more.

"Seventeen, zero six. Nineteen forty-six. Long time."

"Yeah."

"That when he got it?" I ask.

"You think Cosimo's putting neat little stencils on boxes? Look at this place. It's a mess. Next."

I give him a date in the nineteen seventies, let him write it, then ask, "Fifty years since the last line. That's a long time to go without a wife. Gotta be a different guy now, right?"

"We're not taking any chances. You done with that row?"

"Yes." I walk down the aisle to the beginning of the next

row. "There hasn't been a letter or a line in your entire lifetime? Cosimo was how old then?" I brush the crate to remove a layer of dust. "This is stupid. He knows it's stupid. That's why Serafina's on his boat. I bet you every euro I have that she's not coming back for Armistice."

He looks up from the ledger. "You know what happened the last time a family didn't bring a girl to the line? My father was there. The house on *Via Mattia* smelled like a slaughterhouse. There was blood everywhere. No one was spared. Not even the children."

"Fifty years ago?"

"Go to the library. Read the papers from that day. The women were ripped apart. All of them, except the one who was taken. They left her hands behind. Just her hands gripping the stairwell banister like she'd been torn away from them. So, you know what? I don't blame your ancestors for running to America. This is a fucking curse. Next."

"Fix it. Stop whining and fix it."

"Stop whining and give me a number so we can get out of here."

I give him the number, but he's agitated. Maybe I'm a little agitated too.

"Next," I say before he does.

He puts down his pencil. "You want to know the best part of falling in love with a girl from Abruzzo?"

I don't, but he's going to tell me all about Angela. "You want the number or not?"

"I have an excuse to live there. Get away from this." With a flat hand, he indicates the entirety of everything. "Call us ignorant if you want. You're having shit thrown at you by people you never met for something you didn't do. I get it. But us? We're inside the System, and we're fucking cursed by it."

Delfina proves his point. She should be worshipped, not lined up like a cow at auction. She's cursed too.

If you believe in curses, which I do not. I believe in doing things.

"You know a Dario Lucari?" I ask before giving him the number. February, 1966, and a stamp from the Italian Ministry for Cultural Assets.

"We have some Lucaris around. They're trash."

"I had one. Fucking asshole too. Spent his whole life thinking of ways to destroy us, then did it."

"You got fucked by a Lucari? Man, sorry for your loss."

"Stole my sister like a bag of rice, then fell for her. And I keep thinking, he swam through shit to get what he wanted. No one told him what to do." I kick a stencil of an eagle holding a bundle of sticks. The crate doesn't budge.

"No one told you to beat a guy to death."

"He's not dead. Stabilizing even."

"Better light a candle of thanks or you'd be on the payback end of a blood debt."

"I'm tired of keeping my head down."

Corrado looks at me as if I'm suddenly not a dog to walk, but a puzzle to figure out. "What are you saying?"

"Nothing. I'm saying nothing."

"You should say less than nothing then."

I give him numbers and he writes them down, but there's something heavy in the air. It's the decision I'm processing. The one I know I'm going to make when I'm done. Then all the heaviness will break and the consequences of making Delfina Gargiulo mine will rain down on me.

CHAPTER 12

DELFINA

The wedding ceremony goes off without a hitch. Liliana and Paolo's union is a business deal, but they seem to really like each other. She looks beautiful. The families on either side of the center aisle look pleased. The priest does his priestly duties without acknowledging that the ceremony is on a Tuesday in June instead of the planned Saturday in October.

It's fine.

I stand there in my pastel dress, hands clasped in front of me, expressionless so as not to take the focus from the bride.

"Wake up." Rizzo jabs me with her elbow.

They are pronounced husband and wife. Permission to kiss.

It is done. My older sister is locked in a new box. At Armistice Night or after, I will be next.

When we get to Uncle Fosco's club, I smile for the pictures and sit up on the dais feeling a little dead inside—like a puppet who thought she was a real girl and is only starting to notice the strings pulling her mouth into a grin.

That's when I see him.

In the back of the hall, with his cane and his dark gray suit, Massimo is as much a wraith as he was in the *vicoletto*. I notice the not-him. The nowhereness. He is a shadow sucking up the light, drawing me to him from the line of bridesmaids. The music is persistent and the couple dances clumsily, creating bursts of laughter from both families, but my attention is pulled back to his form. He's not supposed to be here, standing stone-still in the center of a forbidden vortex of risk and reward.

Papa told me Massimo isn't for me. I'm not even to think of him… but he didn't say I couldn't *look*. I don't have a choice. The world blurs around him.

When I look away from Massimo, the gravitational pull of the shadow is gone, and so is its source. I am adrift.

There's a process to the reception. The introductions. The bride and groom dance. Later, we'll do the garter and the bouquet. It's all been disrupted by the schedule change, and it's Tuesday. Can't get away from that. Nothing is going to go right.

"It's fine," I whisper into Liliana's ear and refill her wineglass. I've slid three empty seats over on the dais to sit next to her. She looks like a confused puppy and her new husband is across the room, talking to a couple of the Orolio guys as if they're having some kind of business convention.

"We're doomed." She picks up the wineglass and pauses before draining half of it. "Honor the line. My wedding is cursed to honor the fucking line."

"This is all to keep you off it."

Liliana considers the rest of her wine and decides to put

down the glass, scanning the dance floor. Her eyes land on Paolo at the bar, nodding as one of the Orolios explains something in his ear, counting off fingers with his thumb.

"It's probably nothing." Liliana adjusts her gown and turns to me. The curls at her forehead are losing some of their spring. "Paolo says it's rigged anyway. On the lines before, they knew who he was going to pick, the rest is just proving you'll show up."

"Who are they going to pick?" I didn't realize how terrified I was until this moment and the possibility that I can let go of the fear. "Tell me!"

"He didn't say. I think they don't know yet."

"But they might."

Behind the bar, in an arched walkway, a dark form flits from pillar to pillar. It's not the staff carrying a tray or pushing a cart, because the sight of it sends an electrical current from the base of my spine to my brain, which lights up like the Bell Tower on the Night of the Tammorra.

"My God, tonight is my wedding night," my sister continues, turning the subject back to herself as I watch the shadow in the shadows—the void pulling my attention toward it—calling out to the part of me I've silenced and ignored. My own shadow. The impatient, demanding scream of lustful hunger.

"What if you like it?" I barely know what I'm saying. The crooked shadow has stopped, and I stare, waiting for it to fold up into itself and disappear.

"Ha. You'll be the first to know."

She takes my hand as the shadow moves into a shaft of light, and I gasp, grabbing her hand back. It's Massimo, out of the shadows for a moment.

"No." Now that I see his face, I'm worried for him. He can't be here. He's not allowed.

"I will tell you, I swear." Liliana thinks my refusal was made in her direction, but it wasn't. Sure, I'm afraid of the unknowns of the line, but I'm more afraid of what I'm about to do.

"Stop being a fucking baby." Letting go of my sister's hand, I stand, eyes on Massimo as if he's about to disappear, which he does. I anchor my concentration on the spot where he was. "We all busted our asses to save you from a shitty deal."

"What?"

His face appears in another shaft of light, one arch over.

"Delfina!"

She says that louder, so I can hear as I slide sideways along the length of the dais, past my cousins Gracia and Emilia, who wanted to sit up here to feel important and loved. Holding the rail, I walk down the steps carefully because I can't look at my feet. I can only look at him as he disappears again.

Will he show up at the next arch over?

I feel the press of a hand on the back of my neck.

"*Ciao*, Delfina." It's Aris's friend, Franco. I know the voice, so I don't have to look at the face when I dodge around the tux. "How about a dance?"

"Not now."

"When you come back."

"Sure." I push through the crowd and onto the dance floor to get knocked by my cousin Maria as she spins away from Enzo.

"Sorry!"

He does appear at the next light, but in profile, moving. I dodge a dancing couple and muscle past a line of women, into the center of a circle.

"Delfina!" Rizzo cries. "Do that dance you did—"

I'm on the other side of the circle before she can finish.

At the other side of the dance floor, I see his silhouette by one of the pillars behind the bar, where the staff take empty trays. He sees me and shifts behind the column.

I stand in front of it.

"Massimo?" I say as low as I can, but I'm fighting against a live band.

Palming the painted plaster, I shift around the column to get a little closer to him. The edge of my hand touches something warm and alive. Him.

"Delfina." His pinkie flicks to mine.

The unconscious patterns of my body stop. I don't breathe, or blink, or swallow. The music is muffled by the silence. My heart goes quiet until he moves a hair closer, and I know this touch isn't an accident. Time moves forward again. I exhale, blink, shift my hand to meet his.

"You shouldn't be here," I say, leaning my back against the pillar, gazing into the dancing crowd without seeing a single person in it.

"But this is where you are."

"What if my father sees me here?"

"Tell him you're deep in prayer." He hooks his pinkie over mine. I could get away if I wanted to, but knowing he wants me to stay keeps me in place.

"Whose hand do I say I'm touching then?"

I want to go around the pillar to him, but I can't. My whole family is here. If someone sees me, they'll know.

"The subject of your prayers." His pinkie stretches across my knuckles, running along each one.

"Who would believe that?"

"Me." His whole hand grabs all of mine, and I gasp at the boldness of his desire. "Because I'm holding the object of mine."

"Delfina." This time, the speaker is coming from the direction of the dance floor.

Massimo's hand turns to vapor, and I pull mine back from around the pillar.

"Papa?" I find him coming toward me from the bar. Even in the light, I can't tell if he saw Massimo or wonders why I was reaching behind the column.

"I want to speak with you."

"Can it wait?" Catching Massimo's shadow down the service hall, I get between it and my father. "I have to use the bathroom."

"We can talk on the way."

Papa puts my hand on his forearm and leads me past the arches, toward the hallway Massimo just escaped down. My life and his are separated by an ocean of generational hatred, but I don't want him to get caught here.

"I think the ladies' is on this side, actually." I pull back toward the dance floor, counting on him not knowing it's the other way.

"Just one moment." Papa continues in the same direction.

I stop under an arch and turn so that my father's back is to the last place I saw the shadow. That entire small section of hallway is in full view, fully lit when a busboy exits the back room.

Massimo is not there. I take a breath and relax.

"You're nervous," my father says, his breath heavy with cigars and Sambuca. His cheeks are already rough with stubble.

"I just—" Wait. What am I nervous about? And is it the same thing he thinks I'm nervous about? "I guess I... am?"

Right now, I'm a little agitated from not knowing where Massimo disappeared to.

"Understandable. It's been fifty-some years since we had to honor the line. You're not used to it. You've never seen it. But you need to know... hey." He takes my chin and points my face toward his. "We didn't get letters. We may never get summoned. It may be he knows who he wants."

Why does Papa always look at the bright side of things, even when it's not reasonable?

"And what if they come?"

"The odds are very good you'll still come home. Very, very good."

"Papa, you told us not to gamble, and this sounds like gambling."

He drops his hand. "I can't tell if you're not taking this seriously."

"There are no letters, so what's to take seriously?"

He sighs and scratches a spot on the back of his head. "It's…" He ends on a *tsk*. "Difficult to make plans. Your mother would know what to tell you."

Papa gets the sorrowful cast in his brown eyes that he always gets when he needs Mama. He had it when I got my period and when I asked why Aunt Greca bled when God took her baby. He got it bad when I came home crying because Carina DeSoto told me that, on your wedding night, the groom stabs the bride with his penis. Aunt Sylvia came that night to explain what really happens. It sounded awful, so I cried all over again and Daddy didn't look me in the eye for days.

The best way to deal with the fact that he can't do Mama's job is to let him off the hook. It's also the best way to get to Massimo.

"Can I go to the bathroom now?"

"Go," he says with both irritation and relief.

Now I'm in a predicament. The ladies' room really is in the other direction, across the minefield of the dance floor, and I have no idea where Massimo's gone, but he certainly isn't that way, so I'll cross for nothing.

Actually, Papa won't ask why I'm going in the wrong

direction for fear the answer would make him wish Mama was around.

"Thank you." I get on my tiptoes and kiss his cheek. "For trying."

I rush past him and into the crowd, turn and wait just long enough to see if my father is still there.

He's not. For the moment, I'm free.

I go back to the column where Massimo's pinkie touched mine.

Now what? Which way? I don't see the shadow anywhere. I do not feel his electricity or warmth. I'm going to have to decide which way to go before someone stops me to dance, or reassure me, or throw a bouquet in my direction.

The STAFF ONLY swinging doors open for a waitress, revealing a short, dark hallway with a water station and bus cart, and another set of swinging doors behind that—each with a square window to the brightly-lit kitchen. I don't need to see his shadow to know that's the way. I feel it. I can't hesitate, or worry, or convince myself I can't do what I shouldn't, so I don't.

Rushing like a woman too busy to interrupt, I crash through the first set of doors, then the second, squinting in the bright, white light. Dishes clack together and pots and pans make metallic *thucks*. Somewhere to my right, water runs. Men shout everywhere. Maybe about the dessert or about a guest wandering where she doesn't belong.

Keep going.

I can't stop now.

Gathering up my skirts, I rush around the first stainless steel barrier, into the proper kitchen with the blackened burners and hanging pots, finding a way through until I'm stopped by a tall man in a white double-breasted jacket and houndstooth pants. I hold my stomach and look down.

"I need air. Outside," I say, pointing at his thick gray clogs as if they have targets on them. "I'm going to puke."

"That way." He points through a pantry with an ajar door on the other side.

Massimo went through that door. I know without knowing. I feel it.

I rush through, a woman on a mission, to the bottom of a three-meter-by-three-meter shaft. A couple of chairs are strewn around and a garden of cigarette butts grows in one corner. The buildings bordering it are five stories high.

"Why isn't the intermezzo out?" Paolo's voice comes from the kitchen.

If he finds me, he's going to report back to his new father-in-law that I was hiding, or worse, chasing a forbidden shadow. I press my back against the far wall, next to a closed door. I look up. Time has pushed the sky into a crooked square.

There's nowhere to go. Nowhere to hide.

Did I choose poorly?

To my right, the door opens with a squeak. I gasp as I'm grabbed by the arm and yanked into darkness. A hand over my mouth, and in my ear the sound of a man shushing me.

The last time a man put his hand over my mouth...

This is different. His cologne is pepper and wood, not the rank offense of Rafi's scent, and his grip on me is gentler. A suggestion more than a demand.

The door closes, leaving a slit of dim light under it, illuminating the brass nub at the bottom of the cane leaning on the far wall.

"It's okay," he whispers with his thick American accent. "I won't hurt you."

Believing him is one thing. Letting him silence me is another. I move his hand away from my face. He does not resist and I do not scream.

Voices.

"Intermezzo!" The kitchen staff is mocking Paolo. "After I smoke, *storpio*."

My back against Massimo, I feel his breath, his heartbeat, the tension flowing off him with every lift and fall of his chest. I turn to face the man in the darkness, hitting the cane. It slides down in an arc slowly enough for me to see what's happening, but too quickly for me to stop it. It's going to make a sound and the kitchen guys will see us.

With a move smoother than I can fully process, Massimo leans past me and snaps it up before it hits the ground. He faces me as we listen to incoherent mumbling from the other side of the ajar door.

"... Tuesday?"

There are three kitchen workers and one man standing close enough to be my entire world. Sight of his darkness. Scent of his sweat. Feel of his body. Sound of his breath.

"... nobody safe inside the System..."

To taste him would fill my entire body.

"They'll get their lemon ice when..."

"I'm sorry," Massimo whispers. "I need more than your little finger."

"You took my whole hand."

"Your beauty provokes me." His murmur becomes more urgent. "If your lips say the word no, your refusal will be the last word my heart ever hears."

The kitchen workers say things to make each other laugh, but I stop trying to make sense of them. In a tiny stairwell landing, there's only me and a man I shouldn't be safe anywhere near. A man too toxic to know. His breath is heavy enough to fall on my collarbone, warming me to his proximity.

The sound in the courtyard dims to silence.

Still, we wait. When the quiet electricity we generate

between us crackles darkness into sparking light, he speaks with the command of a man who knows what he wants and will take it.

"Refuse me."

"I don't want your heart to live in silence."

"Come with me." His authority is a whisper. I have no answer for it.

I will follow him anywhere.

CHAPTER 13

DELFINA

The Quarter was built before elevators existed, so I'm no stranger to walking up five flights of stairs. By the time I get to the landing halfway up the third story, my skirts are gathered in one arm, above my knees.

He's behind me, following in silence. The cane taps every other step, but whatever's wrong with his leg isn't slowing him down.

"One more," he says when we get to the last landing.

There's nothing but a door at the top of the next flight. The roof. He could throw me off it. But he won't. I am sure of it, so I open the door and step out into the cool night air. There are two plastic chairs set apart, a planter of struggling flowers, and a full ashtray on the low parapet that runs around the roof wherever there's an edge.

Massimo Colonia closes the door and faces me. He is magnificent in the moonlight, feet apart, coat lapel whipping in the breeze. He's not that much older than I am, but he seems weatherworn, worldly, as ancient as the city itself.

A curl of hair escapes from my bun, and I flick it behind my ear so my view isn't impeded.

I shouldn't be here. I should be safe with my family, but I chased him across the wedding hall and wound up caught in his web. I will live or die tonight, but I will not run away this time, even if he demands it.

"Sit," he says, coming forward to pull the chair back.

"Why are you sorry?"

He lets go of the chair and puts both hands on the head of the cane, covering the eyes of the brass cobra at the top. Below us, the wedding music thrums through the kitchen door.

"Because I decided I was going to see you again, hell or high water. But I didn't ask you first."

"You are forgiven." I lay my hand on the back of the chair, but I don't sit. Not yet. "Why did you decide to see me?"

"I needed to see if you were okay."

"I am."

"You are."

"Did I not look fine when you saw me at Don Orolio's?"

"You looked beautiful. But maybe fine, maybe not. There's a difference between 'fine' and 'undamaged,' and I can't tell which is which across a table that long."

"And now that I'm up here with you, what do you say? Am I fine?"

He steps toward me and bends a little as if he's sniffing my throat. I swallow and stand my ground as his energy engulfs me. I am under a spell that makes my mouth dry and my underclothes wet.

"You are not fine."

This is as close as he's ever been, and Holy Mother of Our Lord, he is glorious. I am torn between the stunned silence of a mere human in the presence of divinity, and the breathless moans of a woman overcome by carnal desire.

"I'm not fine." I mean it to come out as a question, but I don't have room in my brain to do anything but make statements.

"You're miserable."

The offense cuts through the thickness of desire. How dare he make up such a story about my feelings? It doesn't matter if it's true, he has no business saying it. But I'm not going to hold his assumption up to the light by dignifying it with a response. No. I came up here of my own free will. I didn't agree to be psychoanalyzed by a man my people barely tolerate.

"And what about you?" I cross my arms. "You're here, in Napoli. Obviously you don't want to be. You're the one who's miserable."

His smile turns into a short burst of laughter as he steps away and looks over the edge of the roof at the street, then at the short distance to the building across it.

"Yes," he says. "I'm miserable. Is it wrong to hope for better for you?"

"No. It's kind of… better than I expected, I guess."

"You expected me to be… what? Just mean? Nasty? Not a decent bone in my body?"

"Something like that."

"And you followed me up here, knowing I was the worst man in Naples?"

I shrug. I didn't know anything of the sort, but I also know that's part of what attracted me up here in the first place. The other part is that he is foreign—from a faraway land where things are different. I want to touch that. Know the width of the gap between us like I know my own self.

"If it were up to me, I'd let you go," I say. "If you wanted to leave, I'd kick you out and tell you to never come back."

"I wish you were queen."

"Do you?"

"I might even like this hellhole."

I have lived here my entire life, mostly behind the walls of my father's house. Even then, when I walk out in the Quarter, I know that I am home. As much as I long to leave, I know I will return. So I don't like what he's saying at all.

"This place is special. I'm sorry you can't see that."

"How would you know unless you've been someplace else?"

Of course he's right in one sense. In another, he's acting as if I've ever had a choice in where I go.

"I feel sorry for you," I say.

"You're one of one." He points over the side of the building abutting *Via Pignasecca*. "You see that pointed roof over there?"

"Yes. That's where the fish store is."

"Two doors down, the produce lady finds one soft tomato to throw at me. And right there, where the corner building is painted white?"

"Via Liborio."

"I live there, on the third floor. Over a butcher."

"Oh. I know where that is."

"There's an old guy on the floor below me. He sits on the balcony every morning, and when I walk out, he throws wet espresso grounds on me."

"That's terrible!"

"There's the spitting when I'm walking and the *malocchio* and this afternoon, a sunflower seed shell. I'm learning how to dodge most of it."

I sigh and sit on the chair he'd offered before.

A raven lands on the edge of the roof, triangulating between us, flicking its head to see me from the side of its head, then Massimo.

"I wouldn't allow that. I'd release you only after people

were nice to you for two weeks, then you'd be able to make an informed choice."

"You'd make a wise leader." He sits on the low parapet on the edge of the roof and lays his hand on his cane. "All I was taught was every ancestral line in America."

"Every one?"

"The ones attached to what you call the System here. Useless information."

"Was that your job in America? Useless information memorizer?"

"I was supposed to be the capo. My father was before me. He was murdered on the toilet. The entire organization was destroyed before I could take charge. All our spaces, all over Manhattan, are boarded up and empty. It's a mess."

"So, you're an exiled king."

"Something like that." He flicks his arm toward the raven, shooing it away. It jumps and flies to the top of a satellite dish.

"What's it like in New York?" I ask.

"Like here, but newer. Not as packed. More expensive."

I look over the edge, considering the word *packed*. This side is opposite the little smoking area we crossed, and much closer to the next building over than the *Via Pignasecca* side. The walkway five stories below is no more than a meter wide and partially blocked with garbage bins.

"What about the people?" I ask, wondering if America would tolerate an alley so narrow.

"They're all rich but live like they're poor."

The sounds of the Spanish Quarter push into my attention, because they're the sounds of poverty. The open windows letting out voices and words as if I'm sitting in a dozen strange kitchens. The engines. The music from somewhere I'll never place.

"I'd take you there, if I could. Show you all the places the tourists don't know about."

I have so many questions about the size and scope of his kingdom and its exact location far, far away from here. I want to dream of going there with pinpoint accuracy.

"I wouldn't mind being a tourist." I shrug and look at the wedge of buildings where he said he lives over a butcher shop. "Go someplace for a day or two. Wear white sneakers and a Patagonia vest. Take pictures with a glass phone instead of getting a postcard of the same exact thing. I'd go to New York without you even. I'd go alone."

"Would you now?"

When I look at him, the sounds of the city add a long, loud mewling, like hungry demon babies. I get up and peer over the edge of the narrow alley, where two feral cats circle each other. He stands next to me, watching them.

"I'd ask why rich people pretend to be poor." When I turn, he's so close to me that I can smell his cologne. "I'd tell them to bring me to their king."

He smiles and faces me. "If you came to New York when I was king, I'd know you were there before you had to ask."

The way he looks at me crackles, breaking through the shadows. It's unnerving. I shouldn't be here. If I'm caught with this man unchaperoned, he will be blamed for luring me away and I'll be blamed for everything else.

It's intolerable and exciting. The pressure of it forces my attention back down to the ground. The cats are gone, or hidden in some private place under the trash.

"In New York, does the garbage sit too long in the alleys?"

"We don't have as many alleys as you think. And they're not narrow enough to jump from roof to roof."

"Well, you can't jump over this."

"Of course I can."

I scoff. "I don't think so."

"Why not?"

This seems radically obvious to me, but I can't say it. I'm

not trying to insult his bad leg, but here we are, making a dare for a dare.

"I'd have to start at a good run," he says. "Probably at that other chair."

"You're just being crazy."

"You can spot me."

"Spot you?"

"Catch me."

"You'll fall to your death." I put my fists on my hips and check him from toes to head, making sure this insane man is not a figment of my imagination.

"You're looking at my leg?" he asks.

I turn away. He's right. I was looking at it.

"It was shot, not amputated."

"Who shot it?"

"My sister." He hands me his cane. I take it, but I don't know why.

"What did you do?"

"Why does everyone always ask that first?" he calls over his shoulder, walking back to the chair. He turns, assesses the space between chair and edge. "I was trying to save her and she didn't want to be saved." He crouches as if he's going to run. "She apologized."

He runs.

"Wait..." I cry with my hand out as if that'll stop him, but it doesn't even slow him down.

He steps on the parapet and launches. I squeeze my eyes shut, but can't keep them tight when I hear a scuffle. I have to know if it's from the opposite roof or the ground below.

I catch sight of him landing on his ass a good meter from the edge of the roof across the alley. He sits there laughing, then turns to me and waves.

"Are you all right?" I ask.

"Hundred percent!"

He walks to the center of the building, favoring one leg, before he turns and crouches for another run. I can't stop him, so I get out of the way.

This time, I keep my eyes open, and my God, for a guy who limped through his run, he's flying. Jacket whipping behind him, feet pumping, arms wide as his leap covers the distance and then some. He lands on both feet this time and turns back to me on the ball of one foot.

"See?"

"I want to try." The words come out of my mouth before I think them through. He seems as surprised as I am.

"Delfina, I was just showing off."

"Yeah, now I want to." I shove his cane into his chest.

"Hold on…" He starts to follow me to the chair, but stops when I get there first and face him.

"You have to spot me."

"Shit," he murmurs, looking at the edge, then at me. "Take off those shoes."

Good idea. I kick them off, then gather my skirts high enough to run, leaving my legs bare to the tops of my stockings. When I lift my foot, the surface of the roof pricks the bottom of the nylon.

"Ready?" I call.

"I don't like this." He's standing against the parapet, cane on the ground so both hands are free. He'll catch me. I'm sure of it.

"I love it," I say too low for him to hear, then before I have a second to doubt myself, I run.

CHAPTER 14

DELFINA

Two steps from the edge, I realize I'm going to be half a step short of the actual edge of the parapet, but I'm going too fast to stop.

Massimo's eyes widen, and he crouches with his hands out, and his lips make the word, "shit."

The last full step to the ledge lands too far on the other side of it, and at the wrong angle. I'm thinking I should have planned this better and let myself get talked out of it. Also, I should have been nicer to my sister at her wedding.

Then I feel his hands on my hips, lifting me but not catching.

If he was catching me, he'd be stopping me, but that's not what's happening. My velocity is increasing. I'm going higher, faster, turning so my feet are behind and my head is first in line to the opposite side.

I am flying.

It's not the same flight as Massimo's. I do not walk on air. I soar, weightless, still as a single moment in time, gliding for a split second before the earth realizes I'm aloft, then, like a half-empty sack of flour, my stomach flops on the opposite ledge while my feet hang over the drop. I scrabble up to the roof.

"Holy shit." Massimo clutches his shirt at the chest as if he's ready to rip out his own heart.

"I made it!"

"You gave me a heart attack." He steps backward to the chair. "No more jumping for you. I'll walk you down and around."

"You can throw me again!"

"No fucking way."

He runs and leaps over the alley, landing on one foot right in front of me, but with too much energy to stop, he's forced to take another lurch right into me. With an *oof*, I stop him from falling on his face and fall onto my back, under him.

"Are you hurt?" he asks, even as I laugh at the slapstick of it.

"No." I keep my arms around him. "Not at all."

"Are you sure?" He gets up on his elbows.

His face is the world, blocking out the sky. The hard surface under me is a mattress and the stars overhead are a ceiling. There's no sound outside us.

"I am fine." I don't know how to prove it except to lurch up as much as I can to kiss his cheek, then drop back down.

"You're a dangerous woman."

If he means it as a compliment, it lands dead center in a place I didn't realize wanted recognition.

"Do you think so?"

"A man could lose himself in you."

"Just any man?"

"Me," he says, hoisting himself up. "I'm the man."

He offers me his hand and I take it.

"Thank you for coming to my rescue last night." I smooth

my skirt. The wedding music calls. "I hope you don't end up in trouble."

"It was worth it to meet you."

He turns away from the gap we just jumped and starts for the stairwell, then stops, indicating I should go first. I barely get a step before his hand lands on my shoulder and stops me long enough to murmur hotly in my ear.

"You're a goddess trapped in a bathtub shrine."

"What?"

"You glow. Has anyone ever told you that? Your father, who keeps you hidden behind a wall... did he ever tell you it was because you cast your own light? That if you got out, you'd be a danger to the darkness?"

"The darkness? You mean... you?"

"Maybe." He smirks and slides his hand away, lingering on my bare skin long enough to leave a trail of electricity. "Probably."

"Definitely." I say it with a smile, because his darkness is appealing.

"I'd gladly be the shadow following your light."

"You have a golden tongue, Massimo Colonia."

"It wants to taste yours."

For a moment, I believe he's going to kiss me. My reaction is a deck of cards shuffled into a bridge. All equal. The same size and shape. All the same from the back, moving too fast to observe. Ten of desire. King of need. Five of panic. Ace of fear. How am I supposed to know whether my fear trumps my lust if it all happens this fast?

Without another word, Massimo leans down, placing two fingertips under my chin and tilting my face toward him. My heart pounds against my ribcage as if it's trying to break free and submit to him without the complication of my mind.

Then his lips meet mine. This is wrong, and this feeling of sudden stillness is why. It's too big. Too full. This heat in my bones expanding to my skin is wrong. The quiet of mind is wrong, because it has everything, and this screaming of body because it wants so much more.

His tongue touches mine just a little. A swipe. A tiny taste before he pulls it back into his mouth and runs his lips along mine.

This is why God invented sin. I'm sure I'll never be able to breathe again.

My hands stay at my sides. I'm afraid to let more than my lips touch him. If I feel his realness—the space, the mass, the solidity of him—I'll burst into flames like a thousand dry Christmas trees in January.

What am I doing? Kissing a man? *This man?* Here, on the day of my sister's wedding? This is insane.

The hands so committed to staying at my sides fly upward. Without a thought or decision, they push him away.

Has the wedding music stopped? I heard nothing but the rush of blood in my veins until our lips separated, then the sounds of the world crashed in. My world is so thin, I can hear voices from the courtyard across the alley. The door slamming. A muddled conversation.

"It's my brother," I say, eyes darting everywhere for a hiding place or escape route. There's too much of both and not enough clarity.

Aris calls my name. The rest is garbage lost in the landfill of urban noise. He's with two, maybe three friends. I can't pull the voices apart.

"They're looking for me." I push Massimo again, but toward what?

"You're not there. You're here." He smiles. "Say you'll see me."

"If we hide behind the—"

"Say yes," he whispers.

"—planter. We can crouch low."

"Tomorrow."

"Fine! Tomorrow."

Voices louder, calling my name.

"Morning," he says, the stubborn ass. "At the Maradona shrine in Bar Nilo."

"No. Noon."

As suddenly as the voices appeared in the night, they're gone. They must have given up and gone elsewhere to look for me.

But Massimo tenses like a wolf hearing a rustle in the bushes.

"They're coming up." He pulls me to the stairs. "We can make it to the bottom if we run."

My feet are bare. Both of his hands are free.

My shoes and his cane are on the opposite roof.

"There's no time." I jerk my arm loose and dash for the center of the roof.

He's not at the ledge to throw me, but I'd miscalculated the distance. I won't this time. I know what a roof feels like under stocking feet. I know how big my steps are, and I also know how fast Aris can get up a few flights of stairs. He cannot find my shoes and Massimo's cane in the same place.

I gather my skirts. Massimo comes at me as if he's going to pick me up and throw me over his shoulder.

Now or never, and I'm absolutely in love with my now.

I run.

"Delfina, no!"

Four big steps, a leap right from the corner, and I fly, fly, fly, over the alley. My right foot lands solidly on the ledge and I launch myself to safety, dropping on my hands and knees, then rolling onto my back.

The stars above. The flat hardness of the tar roof. The sounds of the city. Scooters. Voices. The constant traffic far away.

But there's no wedding music.

"What the fuck are you doing?" Aris cries from the top of the stairs, where it's safe. He's afraid of heights and won't like even being up here.

I jump up and grab my shoes, then I sit in the chair Massimo's cane leans against. It falls behind. I kick it to the shadows, but the brass cobra head shines in the moonlight.

Scooting the chair and widening my skirt, I block evidence of the man who just tore my body apart with a kiss. He defended me once. I'll defend him now. If Aris spots the cane, I'll lie and say I didn't even notice it was there. I'll deny the kiss and the meeting tomorrow. I'll deny Massimo Colonia even exists if I have to.

I look over toward the opposite roof. Massimo isn't there, but he's not on this side either.

Aris steps forward into the moonlight, like a ghost from the shadows, with Franco and Enzo behind him.

"There you are," he says, scanning the roof to make sure I'm alone.

"I was just getting some air."

"And?" Aris asks, head tilted with suspicion. He's not searching the roof anymore. He's completely focused on me.

"And here I am." I shrug, dropping my shoes as if I'm going to slide them on.

"Delfina." My brother holds up his hands—showing me they're empty, as if he'd ever hurt me in the first place. "You don't have to do anything stupid."

"What?"

His two friends have moved behind me, to the edge of the roof.

"It's going to be all right."

Over Aris's shoulder, I see Massimo perched on the opposite roof like a crow. He will fly across that alley if he needs to, and I have to make sure he has no need.

"You're freaking me out, Aris."

"Enzo," he says to his friend, "can you not get so close?"

"I'm not gonna fall, you cabbage."

"I'm not either," I say.

Aris's demeanor changes. He drops one hand. The other runs through his hair. "I thought you were going to…" He shakes his head. "Never mind."

"You thought I was going to what? Jump? Why would I do that?"

"Do you not know?"

"Know what?"

"The letters came."

"For us? For Armistice Night?"

"Yeah."

"Am I favored?"

"Let's go down. Papa will tell us what to do."

"Aris! Am I favored?" My voice comes from the depths of my fear. "Tell me now."

"Will you come down if I do?"

The answer is clear already. If I wasn't being forced to marry a stranger, he'd just say so. He wouldn't be making entreaties for me to not kill myself.

"I'll come down either way, you idiot."

"You are favored, Delfina. But Papa's not gonna fix things for everyone but you. It's going to be okay."

Easy for him to say. My life will be over or just beginning in a few days.

"It is. Maybe."

Maybe maybe maybe?

Maybe means nothing. What should I want? I knew this was coming. Didn't I make a plan about how I should feel about it? Was I supposed to? I don't know whether to be terrified or hopeful. I feel kind of blank. Like a wall with pasted-on ads and graffiti and a mass of chaos and color all over it that gets scraped and painted right down to the nothing.

Following Aris to the door, I don't glance up for the shape of the man who just kissed me. That matrix of possibilities is closed. I felt something a minute ago, but now I can't even remember his cologne. His voice sounds like wind in my head. He's been scraped off and painted beige. He may as well be a ghost to me now.

CHAPTER 15

FOUR DAYS TO ARMISTICE NIGHT

MASSIMO

Two hours after falling asleep, I wake with a shooting pain in my leg from jumping roof to roof twice, with that panic gripping me. I can't catch her on the first jump. She falls. Before I can even get to the edge to jump after her, she's already on the ground, broken like a stick.

Then she falls again on the way back. This time, I catch her but poorly, and we both drop over the edge.

Last night, across that roof, waiting in a crouch with my leg aching, as still as a piece of furniture, listening to her brother deliver the news about the letters, I couldn't stop feeling the panic of her jumping off that roof. My dreams were clothed in chest-seizing panic.

She will not fall, because I'll be there. I won't let it happen.

The Montefiores can burn down everything they see. I don't care. It's been too long since a woman was so beautiful, men would destroy a city to have her.

I have to reassure myself that her safety isn't some fantasy I made up to cover up the reality of her fall.

It's early enough to leave the apartment without having espresso thrown on me. In these early morning hours, I can pace the streets relatively unmolested, telling myself I'm wandering randomly, but my feet know exactly where the fuck I'm going.

Her house.

Generations of Gargiulos live in a huge building with a courtyard in the center. It can be accessed from the street through two huge metal doors on either side. It can be entered through the tunnels under the city. There's one roof close enough to the next building to jump.

There must be windows. Service entrances. Fire exits. A trellis.

I walk around the perimeter, checking everywhere.

Gentile Gargiulo is a rich man with the money to seal the doors. I visually check each entrance anyway, putting more miles on my father's cane in one night than he did in his adult life.

The Colonia were the same. In the middle of one of the most cosmopolitan cities in the world, we locked our women away, where they'd be safe.

They weren't safe though. Not from us, and not from the outside world. Once that containment shattered, everything fell apart.

On the westernmost side of the building, I stand in front of an unmarked door that looks as if it was sealed shut during the Black Plague and has never been opened since. The Colonia had doors like that. They opened fine.

The falling feeling comes again. She kicks on the way down.

What if she didn't fall? What if it was all fine? Lots of people have lives that don't collapse.

We don't have to live here or New York. There must be a third place somewhere on this planet where no one will bother us. Where our children can run through fields or streets, skinning knees and causing their own trouble, instead of dealing with the trouble caused by their grandfathers.

I hear a man singing to himself about the mountain of fire and death. It's a protest song drunken students are known to belt out in the night streets.

I've stopped here too long.

It's just a Tuesday night drunk, so though I step into the shadows, I don't hide.

"Fucking saw you!" the drunk man sings when he's halfway to me. "Who's making hideys?"

Aris stops right in front of me and stares in my direction. A fuss or fight would suggest I don't belong here, so I come out of the shadows.

"Ah!" he cries when he sees me. The jacket is gone, and his tuxedo pants and shirt are soaking wet. "Walking the streets to find more little ladies in distress?"

"Water and two Advil, Aris. Sleep it off." I try to walk away, but he grabs me by the elbow and almost falls down. I have to catch him. He stinks of salt water and gasoline. "What happened to you?"

"What? This?" He spreads his arms. "Boat ride."

"Your boat sank?"

"My boat? Shit. Rich guys. They sit there eight months at a time. I just borrowed one."

"And sank it?" If he's stealing boats and putting holes in them, that's more trouble than I want to be seen walking around with.

"Nah, man," he laughs. "Hey, I seen you once playing carom, like, four months ago and now you just keep showing up. Where's your little minder?" He pokes my chest weakly at the last three words. His breath stinks of wine. "Where is my cousin? Cosimo oughta dock his pay."

"You're drunk as a monkey."

"Fuck you, man." He yanks his arm away and tips backward. He's too far away to catch. "Nobody likes you."

He's right, of course. My journey to see where Delfina lives is over and nobody likes me.

"Then I'll be on my way."

I start down the street, but check over my shoulder. Magically, he's on his feet and practically unconscious. He retches.

Jesus. If he collapses face up, he'll choke on his vomit. The Colonia wasn't a house of drinkers. Anything that dulled the ability to defend the group was discouraged, and as the future First Chair, I had to keep my wits. But I often sneaked out with my friends to drink coffee and watch the crowds around the clubs. One time, we came up on a guy leaning against the base of a streetlight on Second Avenue. He was our age, in a collared lavender shirt and gray slacks. One shoe, two socks. His head was tilted toward the light and his mouth was open casually, as if he was breathing through it, but a soup of vomit was pooled up to his lips, drawn down his throat by gravity.

Aris stumbles back and hits the wall, then breaks out into song again.

Lavender shirt guy was already gone. Aris isn't. And even if I leave him sitting, all he has to do is go unconscious with his head back and that'll be it for him.

"I wished you killed Rafi," Aris shouts to me, pushing himself away from the wall. "Half a job. Next time, you and me load his body onto one of Cosimo's cabin cruisers. We throw him overboard. Maybe he went to get cigarettes and never came back. Who can say?"

I'll hang around long enough to make sure he loses consciousness with his mouth facing the ground.

I go back to Aris. By the time I get there, his cheek is against the wall he's pissing against. Amazing that he got his dick three-quarters out.

"I'm glad I didn't kill him," I say.

"Pussy. Put you in a boat and—"

"You're pissing on your shoes."

"He's stable. Pig is gonna walk. Make you run."

"I'm not afraid of Rafi."

"Maybe I kill him. Overboard. *Poosh* and splash."

"You're done."

"What?"

"You're not pissing anymore."

He grunts, steps back once, twice, bangs into a light post so hard his exposed dick swings. I'm not sure I'm going to be able to leave him alone at all.

"Did you know," he says, putting his dick away and trying to close up his jeans with all the concentration of a toddler, "when the game's over, the king and the pawn go back in the same box?"

"Did I know nothing means anything? Yeah, I knew that."

"No, you fucking cabbage. That's not… it means fuck my dad. You done more to protect Delfie than he has, so…" He either thinks he has his fly buttoned or has stopped caring. "I don't know."

"You should call someone to come get you."

"I don't know!"

A light flicks on above us. He woke someone.

"Aris." I hold out my hand. "Give me your phone."

"I lost it." Half his face is lit by another lamp behind a balcony.

"Where?"

"I don't know!" he shouts louder, then louder again. "I. Don't. Know."

"Okay, calm down."

"*I don't know anything!*"

"Aristide!" A woman's voice comes from above. "What—?"

She stops. I stop. We see each other at the same time, and I am at once relieved someone will come for Aris and elated to have her in my sight. He could be choking on his own vomit right now and I wouldn't be able to help him. She is the only thing that exists. She is the rising sun, washing away the dim light of a jealous moon.

"I don't know!" Aris chants again.

"I was just walking…" I say, a piss-poor explanation for standing under her window at this hour. "And I stumbled on…" I can't finish the lie. She deserves better. "I kept having this dream you were falling off the roof and I was hoping I'd see you, just to—"

"I'm fine," she says. "What did you do to him?"

"Almost killed him but…" Aris ends with a spitty raspberry. "Fail."

"You didn't say yes." Getting closer to the balcony doesn't put her in my arms. "Will you meet me today?"

Aris sings his song again, bouncing from wall to wall as if he's stuck in an old pinball machine.

"It's complicated."

"Yes," I say. "Yes, it is. But… you and I don't have a lot of time before it gets more complicated." She watches Aris, and I fear she's forgotten about me. "He's not going to remember this in the morning."

She shakes out of her fugue. "I don't know how to think clearly right now. It's too easy to make a mistake, and I'm scared."

"Make it me. I'll be your mistake. I'll be the least scary mistake you ever made."

She laughs. "You make promises you can't keep, Massimo Colonia."

Suddenly, the door that looks as if it never opens swings open. A man walks out, gives me a dirty look, then tracks Aris, who waves hello before putting his cheek on my shoulder and leaning on me as if I'm an inanimate object.

"Nunzio," Delfina calls, leaning over the ledge, "can you bring Aris inside?"

The man bends down and throws Aris over his shoulder like a sack of rice. At this point, it's a habit to look inside a man's right elbow to see if he has the scar, and this man does not. He shoots me another dirty look before gazing up at Delfina. She smiles and waves. Nunzio goes inside with Aris and shuts the door.

"Go!" Delfina says in a breathy shout, shooing me with both arms. "He'll get more of them. Leave. Get out of here."

"Will you come?"

"No! I will not! Now go!"

She goes inside and slams the door.

The answer was no. I won't chase her further, but I'll be at the counter at Bar Nilo, waiting for her.

CHAPTER 16

DELFINA

Aris is sprawled on the bed, immobile but wide awake.

"I'm not undressing you." I pick up his ankle. "But you're not putting your dirty shoes on the bed."

"Sorry I woke you."

It's funny that he thinks just because he hustled me home and told me to go to bed that I was able to fall asleep, not knowing the barest outlines of my future.

"Jesus, your feet stink." I drop his foot. "And you're soaked. Whose boat was it this time?"

"Cosimo's sloppy."

"You're going to get yourself killed if you keep doing that."

"Papa bought me and Cesare out of the System."

"Can you pick up your other foot please?"

Massimo's taste has faded from my tongue. The touch of his lips on mine went from a thing made of explicit moments tied together with less precise milliseconds to a handful of memories too short to hold in my head. They became smaller and smaller while the worries over the letter, what it said, what it meant, and who else got one rattled around, smashing Massimo to bits.

"He rushed Liliana's wedding to keep her off the line."

"Yes." I pull off his shoe.

I'll be the least scary mistake you ever made.

"He'll figure it out for you. He has to. It's only fair."

"If you throw up again..."

"I mean it, Delfina. If you're not taken care of, none of us ever were."

"Aris." I place his feet together, straight, so his body is one continuous line. "There's a towel by your head."

"If he doesn't, I'm going to go work for Cosimo."

"You will do no such thing!" I bark.

"I bet he figured it out for Serafina."

I can't argue about that. Everything is always easy for the Orolio princess.

"Just stop. You're not cut out for that life. I mean... look." I sit on the edge of the bed. "When things aren't right and even, you don't feel right and even. But nothing's fair in the System. You'd be miserable. You know it. I know it. Papa knows it. That's why your arm has no scar."

"Mm." He makes the sound as if he means something very definite by it, but his eyes are closed, and no further noises come to clarify.

I turn out the light, go to my room, and step onto the balcony. The first mopeds of the day zip under me. The morning workers trudge to their jobs. I'm not checking for them. All I see is absence.

Massimo is not there. Those last words were a gift that was not meant to be kept.

By the sink, I redress the knees and heels of my hands where they got bruised and scraped from flying. No, not from flying. From landing. The sting of antiseptic contrasts with the soft memory of Massimo's kiss.

I already told him no, and it was the right thing.

Forget him.

I have to forget him. I have problems that aren't my own. He's a distraction. I am summoned by monsters. I will never taste him again.

At midmorning, I decide that staying in my room feeling sorry for myself isn't helping anyone. Grabbing a basket, I go to the courtyard garden to be alone, with all my questions and concerns taking a back seat to the thrum of desire I can't shake.

The tomatoes are flowering but not fruiting. I cut two romanesco bunches free, snap a few *taccole* from the vine, find a ripe artichoke, and put them all in my basket. It's too early for a real harvest, so there's not enough for a real meal.

Not enough of anything today. Not enough kissing, or touching, or laughing.

Not enough options to make a real plan.

Plenty of weeds though. On my hands and knees, I pull them, tossing the dandelion flowers while adding their leaves to the basket.

Packs of children run in every direction, their cries and demands the backdrop of any day in Gargiulo Palace.

"Delfina!" Liliana cries from across the yard, waving and smiling.

The wedding moved, but the honeymoon didn't, so she and Paolo are holed up in a less-used section of the estate. She picks up her skirt and rushes across the stone path to me, her light brown hair waving at the sides of her head.

"Hey, Mrs. Alessi."

She takes me by the shoulders, bending a couple of inches to look me in the eye.

"Del. Fina." She really means it. "Sex."

"I've heard of it."

"It. Is." She shakes me. "Amazing."

"No, you are."

"Not as amazing as you." She shakes my shoulders.

"No, you."

"Neither of us come close to being as amazing as *sex*." She yanks me to her. I'm a laughing rag doll in her hands. I hold her arms and put my forehead to hers.

"I miss you already."

"I miss you too. But—"

"I know. Sex."

"Even if you have to marry into the Montefiores, there's gonna be sex."

I stand straight. My sister is older than me but more naïve than I was at half my age. "I'm not sure that always works out great, Liliana."

"It will for you." She loops her arm in mine and we walk. "I have faith."

Great. She and Papa both. I'm not sure I can live up to their devotion.

"What are you doing out of bed anyway?" I ask.

"Paolo had to run off to meet people. I don't know. And anyway, Papa told me to find you. He's in the office."

"Hi, Papa." I walk into his office with my basket.

"Delfina." He approaches with his arms wide, places a hand on each of my arms the way Liliana did, and kisses both of my cheeks. "Sit. Please."

He takes my basket and leads me to a chair by the window.

He shakes the basket. "This is a measly harvest." He plucks out a few string beans.

Leaning back in his chair, he bites a string bean. I can hear him crunch on the beans. My father is a mannerly yet loud eater, even with his mouth closed.

"What happened to your hands?" he asks.

I pull my sleeves over my scraped wrists. "I fell playing *acchiapparella* with Mariana's kids."

Lies, lies, and damn lies.

"They are terrors. Like you were, *capretta*."

"Am I not still?"

"No." He shrugs and takes out another few beans, eating them one by one in the pauses. "Or maybe I stopped worrying so much. Of all my children, you're the one who will use her troubles to make herself stronger."

"We'll see," I murmur.

"When you were five, you fell and opened up your knee. Big cut."

"I remember." I touch the scar through my skirt. There was blood everywhere. Aunt Lina sat me on the kitchen counter and dressed it while I cried.

"It took months to heal, and why?" He shrugs and tosses the stringy ends of the beans into the garbage pail by his desk. "There was no infection. The other cuts that day closed up fine. It wasn't some disease or a curse. It was just the knee kept opening no matter how tight she bandaged it."

"Then Aunt Greca stitched it, which hurt."

"She did, because you kept pulling it open."

I sit back in the chair and sigh. A handful of kids rush past the window. I did reopen the wound over and over, before it could even scab. I'd forgotten about that part the way we all try to forget pain.

"She told me scar tissue is stronger," I say. "Then she told me not to let it open again because I'd have a bigger scar on my knee. I mean…" I stop to see if he's with me, and he's watching me with soft brown eyes. "Who wouldn't keep it open as long as possible?"

"See? I have faith. In you above all, I have faith."

"Is that why you sent me home with Rafi? Because you thought I could fight him off if I had to?"

"That was a mistaken judgment." With an exhale, he leans back to slide an envelope off his desk. It's old-fashioned paper, tea stain brown, with a cracked red wax seal—like something you'd see in a movie.

"Is that the summons?" I ask.

"My whole life," Papa says without answering my question, "I've run my business and paid into the System, but I've never participated in it. I have been clear that I will never be a king or a pawn in their game. I am respected for this. It works. When Orolio came for Cesare, to make him a soldier, I said no. He's not obligated to serve in any army. I paid them, and he went to university. They came for Aris when he was fifteen and I paid again. Liliana is walled off in time. But now, the System has come for you, and there is no price." He hands me the letter. "I tried, Delfina. I tried."

I hesitate, waiting for him to look at me. All he does is wave, encouraging me to open the letter while he gazes out the window to the courtyard.

The wax seal is crisp and brittle. When I put it together, it makes the shape of a bird with pebbles of red missing where it was snapped. I unfold it to find a short note in ancient-looking cursive written in ballpoint pen.

"It's Italian but…" I look closer. "Not normal."

"You don't need to analyze it," Papa snaps.

He's right, I guess. I can understand it well enough.

To the master, nay father, of the daughters Gargiulo,
   I greet thee well after many years of my colony's absence.

It is known you have prospered from your participation in the System, but the city suffers from decadence and lost tribute. Thus, we must resume the customs that have ensured the steady power and growth of our great and secret System.

Be it known to you that we of the Montefiore colony have decided to take our brides from the greatest of the families of what was once known as the one unified Kingdom of Sicily.

This taking will occur at the Night of Peace and Armistice at Castle Ovo on the Twentieth of June this year. We command you to come to the aforesaid place with your unmarried daughters dressed in the color of surrender, as candidates for marriage in accordance with our rituals that they may be brought into our colony.

You shall presume to send them with no other provisions, as all will be provided in luxury as befits ones chosen. We command this in general, but in specific, your youngest daughter, named Delfina Anjelica Gargiulo, shall be equipped with documents necessary to travel abroad.

See that you show no negligence if you desire to have our favor.

Carmine Montefiore IV

I close it.

"I always wanted to go to Armistice Night." Out of habit, I'm putting a positive light on the trouble for Papa's sake. "But we aren't in the System."

Now that we are equals in knowledge, Papa looks me in the eye. "The last time the Montefiores lived in Naples, we were. So—"

"So it is what it is." I run my finger along the edge of the paper, trying to cut myself. "Who else in the house?"

"Your cousin Rizzo."

"Ah." I shake my head. I shouldn't be surprised. Her father works for Cosimo, just as his father before him did.

"You're not the only favored one." He takes my hand over the table, then pulls the letter away. "There's a good chance you won't leave in a wolf's mouth."

"I told you, Papa." I stand and take my basket. "I don't gamble."

CHAPTER 17

DELFINA

When I left Papa's office, a deep, cold sadness filled me. I thought I was choosing whether or not to be with Massimo, but I was kidding myself. Now even the playacting is over. There's no point.

I could still get Rizzo to escort me to Bar Nilo though.

But then what? Meet Massimo at noon and tell him it's all pointless? Or beg for him to save me from my odds? How would he even rescue me?

I need a sign. Some message from the heavens to tell me what to do.

Either enjoy every moment I have before I'm in the line, or avoid temptation, play it safe, and pray I'm delivered.

"Bright side," I whisper to myself, "it may be fine. Maybe I'll travel all over."

Dreams of escape are no comfort.

I pace the circumference of the courtyard balcony imagining Massimo kissing me again and again, promising to take me out of here, which he can't even do for himself, or marry me, which isn't possible. There will be no more weddings in Naples until after Armistice Night.

Massimo can't save me this time. His power comes from every inch of him, but here, in my city, he's been stripped of the ability to exert it. It takes every bit of my energy to circle again and again, knowing he's waiting for me.

There's no sign from the heavens, and that's its own sign.

Just before noon, right after I've decided that meeting Massimo at Bar Nilo would be both pointless and painful, Rizzo catches me circling the veranda around the courtyard.

"Hey," she says, "we should—"

"Dammit, Rizz!" I throw my arms around her. She hugs me back for a moment then peels me off. "I'm trying not to go somewhere and I'm so preoccupied I didn't come and see you."

"Where?"

"Nowhere. Forget it. Papa said you got a letter. I'm so sorry."

"Why? It could be cool. Honestly, it sounds like a better arrangement than staying here and getting promised off to someone terrible. And if I don't get picked, it's whatever. And anyway, I was asking… where are you trying not to go?"

I rub my eyes. I've been self-involved and terrible. I should have gone to see her right away to make sure she's all right. "Is it just us that we know?"

"Serafina."

"Right."

"And Fabia, Dina's sister. The rest are from outside the Quarter, I guess."

My mind flips through every girl in school. So many not chosen. The letters are almost surgical in their precision.

"Lucky them."

"We have to get white dresses. There's an account at Nicia's for us and we can spend whatever we want."

Dresses. The whole ordeal never seemed so innocuous.

"Fine." I loop my arm in hers. "Let's go."

"You were trying not to go someplace?"

"You're such a pest!"

"If I ask again, you have to tell. It's a rule."

I want to tell her about Massimo so badly I can taste the words on the tip of my tongue, but I hesitate, because once spoken, they belong to her.

"Delfina! Rizzo!" Luna calls from the balcony across the courtyard. *"Aspettare!"*

"To wait? What does that even mean?" I whisper.

"She's been making my mom crazy asking how to boil water and arrange an antipasto."

To her mother's dismay, Rizzo has taken no interest in learning how to cook. Luna might be a relief. Cosimo's American guest whips around the balcony and arrives, freckles glistening with sweat.

"Ciao, Luna. Come va?" Rizzo says.

"I... um... *compare ves...?"* She hand signals putting on clothes.

This poor human. Not being able to communicate seems like torture for her. She takes out a scrap of paper with a word written on it. *Nicia's.*

Rizzo and I exchange a glance. That's three from the Quarter, but this strange foreign girl in the line makes no sense. Is her family even in the System in America? She must be, but her inclusion puts doubt on the surgical precision theory.

"Sì, come." I let my body language express my acceptance, looping one arm in Luna's and the other in Rizzo's.

Together, we go to buy white dresses.

We can leave my father's palace because we're in a group. Once we're on the streets, we can't link arms for long, unless we want people crashing into us. When we do separate, Luna walks as fast as she talks, stopping at street shrines and windows with her mouth agape like a tourist, which I guess she is, missing turns and whipping around others as if she knows where she's going. We have to call her back too many times to count.

"So where were you thinking about not going?" Rizzo asks when Luna's not close enough to hear.

"It doesn't matter, pest."

"I didn't ask you if it mattered."

"It's someplace I shouldn't go…"

"Oh, this is getting interesting."

"If I get a sign, I'll go. Then you'll know."

"You're waiting for a sign? Sheesh, I can make one." She holds up one finger while the other hand digs into her pocket. "I have a euro here." She shows me the coin. "Heads, you don't go and tell me everything, tails is a sign you should go, then tell me everything."

Heads, I tell her about Massimo and avoid meeting him.

Tails, the angels send me to him, and I tell her later.

"Okay. Yes." I'm more eager for her to flip that coin than I realize. The relief of knowing the will of the heavens is priceless. "But then…" I twist my fingers to my lips, buttoning them shut and throwing away the key.

"Deal." She stops walking long enough to toss the coin. It spins in the air. She catches it and slaps it on the back of her hand.

Heads.

There is no sign from the saints. I should not go to Bar Nilo to meet him. I have to stay strong and do what's right. Fulfill my responsibilities. Leave Massimo at the bar.

My nose itches. My eyes sting.

"Oh." My voice cracks.

"Delfie?" Rizzo pulls me to a shady bench against the wall and sits me down. "What is it?"

"I can't now. Later, okay?"

I want to see him. I want it so bad that since 12:01, life has been a hazy blur of things happening to me.

Rizzo pantomimes pulling something out of thin air, putting it to my lips and turning it, unlocking my mouth. "Tell me."

I take a big sniff and wipe my nose on my cuff, making a mess of the shirt I wore to hide my scrapes. Now I really can't go. With another big sniff, I laugh at the thought that a little snot on my sleeve will stop me.

And if that won't stop me, a coin flip won't either.

Or a letter. Or giving myself to save the entire Quarter. There's nothing they can do to me, really. I'm actually more free than I've ever been.

"Last night," I say, with one last big sniff. "At the wedding, I saw Massimo and he almost kissed me."

"Massimo Colonia? Almost? What?"

"He almost kissed me, then…" I don't want to admit this, but I'm going to. "I kissed him all the way."

"Delfina! Anyone but him. He's so much *trouble*."

"No. Everyone's treating him terribly."

"Everyone?"

"The old ones are. They're spitting where he walks and giving the horns. There's a guy who dumps espresso on him from his balcony. It's not right."

She lowers her voice to a well-articulated whisper. "A man that hot can take care of himself."

"It's embarrassing. I'm ashamed. I wouldn't like him if his people were acting like that."

"Wait… you *like* him?"

It doesn't matter what I feel. It's pointless.

"We should just go get these dresses and be done with it." I look away finally, and curse under my breath. We followed a tourist around a wrong turn and now we'll have to backtrack. "Crap. We're going the wrong way. Where's Luna?"

She appears, skipping back in our direction, all smiles and slowspeak as she pulls out a ten-euro note. "Coca-Colas?"

She points behind her at the café where she intends to get the drinks, and it's not any café. No. It's a lightning bolt. A choir of angels. A coin flip landing on tails.

Bar Nilo.

I'm an hour late, but it's definitely a sign.

"Aris!" Luna says, pointing at the brooding man coming our way.

Crap. In my head, I curse Aris being anywhere in a twenty-meter radius of where I'm supposed to meet Massimo.

"What are you doing here?" he asks.

"Getting dresses for the…" I find I can't say it. "The thing."

"What about you?" Rizzo asks. "You lost?"

"I'm doing your brother's job." He shakes his head, scanning the street, eyes landing on a flower shop. "That Colonia fuck's a slippery guy."

My fingertips go cold. He's looking for Massimo, and I know how close he might be.

"Well," I chirp, "you better get to it. I'm going to check out the flowers."

I brush past him to pretend to look at the buckets of bouquets in front of the shop right across from Bar Nilo. In the window's reflection, I can see the rectangle of the café window, but what's inside is hidden in the shadows.

I turn to face the doorway. It's still too dark to discern one thing from another, but he's in there. I know it.

CHAPTER 18

MASSIMO

Corrado usually shows up in the morning to tell me what I'm doing for the day or accompany me to whatever trouble I'm hired to cause. He knows who I'm shaking down, what bags of money go where, how I'm working like a day laborer.

But I got out early, climbed to the roof and jumped, walked across buildings, jumped again. I hid in corners and stairwells, then headed to Bar Nilo knowing he'd be pissed, but he'd live.

Now, the sun is comfortably settled in the morning sky. I go down to the street. Less recognizable without Corrado in front of me, I still get a few dirty looks and shots of spittle, but I've learned where I'm hated and where I'm just another American who speaks decent Italian. I keep my gaze to myself and walk as if I'm thinking about something else.

That's the easy part.

My Lucretia will be with me soon. Her kiss was a sigh in a storm. A single pure act in a city built on sin. She is goddess and woman. Light and mystery. History and future. She's none of those things and potentially all of them.

And she is brave. She flung herself off a roof last night. Twice. I catch myself smiling as I walk into Bar Nilo and sit at the counter across from the shrine to the late, great soccer player, Diego Maradona. His face is all over the Quarter, but in this bar, his smile covers every surface. I smile back, because I'm happier than I've been in a while.

Delfina and I just met.

How many times should I have to meet the woman I'm meant for before I'm allowed to admit she's meant for me?

One more time.

That's how many.

This time, if she shows, I'll know.

I'll wait for her in this little sandwich shop all day. The barista is free of a generations-long grudge, so she's always been friendly to me.

"Where's your friend with the—" She taps inside her right elbow, referencing his System scar. Corrado. I don't think she's ever seen me without him.

"Probably sleeping in. Late night last night."

"On a Tuesday?"

"Wedding."

"Wow." She crosses the bar to take care of a customer.

At noon, I watch the tourists come in for the Maradona shrine and leave with a cold soda.

At twelve fifteen, I think I see her looking in from the street, but it's someone much older.

It's twelve thirty, and I've convinced myself I can save her from this lineup. She won't be favored by anyone but me. She'll resist. But if she comes this one time, she's undeniably mine.

At close to one, I order another Coke with ice. When I finish it, I'll accept defeat and go.

But I don't finish it, because she's there.

In the glare of the sun, she stands across the street, bathed in light. A moped whips by, flinging her hair to one side. She is luminous, framed by the doorway in front of her and the flower shop behind. Pots of carnations bloom at her feet.

Grown men don't have feelings like this. Even as an adolescent, my emotions were muted. Real, but manageable. This though? I can't even get my arms around where it begins and where it ends. If those edges even exist, I intend to find them.

She's coming this way. A woman with short dark hair walks next to her, holding Delfina's arm as if she needs to be steadied. A friend or cousin. Another man's daughter who's too valuable to walk the Quarter alone.

I stand, ready to meet her.

Another young woman with freckles and curls around her face steps in front of Delfina, waving a ten-euro note. There's chatter among the three women. The euro note changes hands a few times.

Then Delfina stops. Turns. A little of her light dims as she talks to a man. Like her, he has a Greek nose that bends for neither god nor human. Aris. Her brother. Her escort, the woman, makes some kind of joke and laughs. Aris smiles.

Delfina turns to come inside. I grip the head of my cane and calculate quickly.

If Aris leaves, we're fine.

If he remains outside, she won't be able to stay with me more than a minute.

If Aris sees me, suspicion will fall on Delfina. He may not realize we're meeting here, or he may be smarter than he looks.

I can't take that chance for her. I need to leave. Slip out the back. But I'm frozen in her sights. Over her shoulder, I see Aris turning to follow.

Move.

Get out.

I can't. I'm angry at my paralysis, but not angry enough to shatter it.

The woman with the short dark hair grabs Aris's arm and points at something in the flower shop. The freckled girl follows.

Delfina enters alone. The light that made her glow cuts out, bringing her down to the shadowed earth. I stand as if royalty has entered the room. I don't even think about it. My body is in charge.

"Signorina Gargiulo," I say when she's in earshot, keeping my voice and syntax formal. Behind her, Aris is distracted by the women.

"Signore Colonia." She holds her chin high, nodding and smiling to the barista, letting her know she's fine.

"It's a nice day."

"It is." She turns to the bar and orders three bottles of Coke.

"Let me pay for that." I tap my dwindling pile of euros, nodding to the barista. Beside me, Delfina looks like a queen, showing me her magnificent profile. I stand as close to her as I dare. "How was your sister's wedding?"

"Lovely. Thank you for asking." She puts her hands on the counter, watching the barista get her sodas from the fridge.

"I'd like to go to a wedding again someday." I put my hand near hers on the counter.

"Maybe your own."

"I hope so." I flick my pinkie to the right, touching the side of her hand.

Her skin must be made of life itself, because when she shifts her hand into the touch, I am suddenly alive with purpose. I want more than an escape from my circumstance. I want an escape with her, into her, through her. There's nothing for me without the rest of that skin.

I put my fifth finger on top of hers, and she loops hers around mine, embracing it. My eyes close with the enormity of it, so I only hear the bottle cap pop off and clink to the floor. Then there's another, and I'm reminded she did not come alone. I force my eyes open.

She's looking at me. I hook my pinkie tighter.

The barista puts the bottles on the counter and announces the price before sliding the euro note from under the pile.

"You're mine," I say. "I just want you to know."

"I'm sorry," she says. "I came to tell you I can't see you again."

"Why not?" I sound like a child in an ice cream shop being told he can't have chocolate. Or that he can't wear his canvas sneakers in the rain. Or that his mother left and is never coming back. The answer isn't relevant, and it's going to hurt.

She can hurt me with a thousand knives. I don't care. I'll abide by her decision, but not without finding out why she made it.

"Come with me." I take her whole hand and pull her behind the bar before she can object.

I catch the barista's attention for a moment and hold up one finger, ready to alienate the one person who doesn't hate me, and push Delfina through the door. The desk in the tiny office is a deep shelf and the chair is a stool shoved under it. There are papers tacked to the wall like giant, broken butterflies.

"Massimo!" Delfina scolds, leaning against the desk edge.

"Listen to me, because I will listen to you. Okay?" I pause to give her a moment to object. She's annoyed, but she doesn't tell me to stop. "Good. I'm going to kiss you now. And that kiss—it's not going to be just a kiss. My heart… my soul is going to be asking you a question that you can't answer with words. Your brain can talk later. I need what's inside of you to talk to what's inside of me."

She should slap me. Maybe tell me to go fuck myself.

Instead, she nods, arms crossed. Permission granted on a probational basis.

I take her face in both my hands. "Are you ready?"

"Is that the question?"

I smile so hard I can barely make the shape of the word, "No."

"Ask it then."

Leaning down, I fill my head with the music of Delfina, Delfina, Delfina. My lips to hers, I construct my name in her voice. When I inhale through my nose, I let the scent of her perfume linger there. Her mouth opens for my tongue, and I let it drift along the side of hers, meeting at the tip before continuing the slow dance of a question that cannot be twisted into words.

Her reply has no qualifiers, no maybes, no longing *if onlys*. She is as open as a flower in full bloom, opening sweet petals to reveal the depths of herself. She doesn't hide anything from me, and I reveal myself to her with that kiss.

We separate.

She slides past me and goes out into the bar, grabbing her bottles of Coke just as Aris is about to walk in looking for her.

She was smart to end the kiss when she did.

The question has been asked and answered.

Leaving the rest of the euros on the counter, I slip behind the bar and out the back.

The alley leads up a stone stairwell. Quickly, with my cane tapping against the cobblestones, I make my way to the raised walkway over the street.

The bar and the florist are below. Aris accompanies Delfina and her friend down the street, in my direction.

She glances up when she drinks her soda, as if she knows

I'm up here, watching. I step away from the edge. I can't be seen here, watching her as if I'm the only supplicant to this most graceful of saints, but I wait for her to pass, then I pace the Quarter until my thigh aches.

When I first got here, I did the same thing, but with a fresher wound in my leg. There was nothing I could do as a trapped animal but learn the map of my cage.

I pass a store I've passed a hundred times. It's dark inside, and it has the same objects in the little window it's always had. I've seen the white plaster stature of Lucretia before, but never noticed it. I go in. The old woman behind the counter makes a point to ignore me while I scan the bric-a-brac, old books, repaired radios, clothing racks.

My attention lands on a box of postcards. The top one has a picture of the Empire State Building.

Funny. I come all the way here for a postcard of home.

I flip through them and try to sort my thoughts.

A few days ago, all I could think about was finding allies at Armistice Night. Who would I know there? What argument for my freedom would land on sympathetic ears? Could I plead my case to the entire room, all at once? If they demanded the knife as a trade, would I relinquish it? Or just pretend to long enough to go home, then betray all of them?

Today, I feel the loss of her touch in my very bones.

Now, my opportunity to plead my case has been stripped.

Now, my desperation to get out of here has been whittled down to a thread.

Now, I am redirected to Delfina Gargiulo, a woman I barely know, who I've only barely touched, but whose touch has changed the composition of my skin. Between moments of panic and fear, we've shared a few words that have created deep channels in my mind.

I'm only a pariah within the System. I can find a woman if

I want one. But I only want Delfina, and she's off-limits to me. Forbidden.

If I ask her father if I can see her, he'll refuse me. I am not good enough for his daughter.

He may be right, but that's not going to stop me from seeing her again.

I choose a random postcard. The back is clean, with a little blurb about a New York softball rivalry I never knew about. It's never been sent or stamped. The front has the Washington Square Arch on one side and on the other side of the red diagonal slash, a pic of the Cooper Union clock. The text says WEST VILLAGE vs EAST VILLAGE.

How did this rivalry develop right under my nose without me knowing or caring? I know the arch and the clock at Cooper Union, and nothing else about a rivalry deep enough to inspire a postcard. I want to know, and I never will.

I am too desperately, embarrassingly homesick at the sight of this card to keep it, so I put it back and look for another.

But that homesickness isn't just a shameful weakness. It's who I am, and I want to share it with her and only her. As weak as this sadness makes me, she is the only one who can make me stronger.

This postcard will be a place-marker for all the conversations we'll never have, and a message that I will do anything to make the impossible happen. Or maybe it's just a piece of card stock to hold enough longing for the both of us.

CHAPTER 19

DELFINA

It seems as if half a lifetime has passed since we left for the dress shop, but here we are, outside of Nicia's on *Via Toledo*, shopping for a gown, shoes, bag. I can barely keep my mind on the project. I feel filled with him.

"What happened?" Rizzo says, looking in the store's window. "Was he there?"

"He was."

"And?"

"Just a kiss," I say.

"You shouldn't be doing that, but I can't say I blame you."

Luna looks at the dresses with us. I can't read her expression. Not being able to talk to her about the simplest things is getting frustrating. That's what it'll be like if I run away with Massimo—discovering an entire planet of people I can't talk to.

This is all a bad idea, but there are no good ideas.

"I wish I could get a dress that makes me disappear," I say in a deeply pleasant melancholy.

"You look too good in white."

"Maybe Nicia can make us something from used garbage bags."

"Or just a sign on a chain that says, 'Can't cook.'"

"Yes!" I elbow her in agreement. "Or, 'Hates kids.'"

"'Infertile.'"

"'Lousy in bed.'" I don't know what that means, and I'm probably bad in bed, but whatever.

"'Not a virgin,'" Rizzo suggests. "That's the marriage-killer."

"Oh, my God." I take a deep breath. "It is."

"Really is." She looks at the hot pink and bright blue dresses in the window. "We should go in."

"Rizzo. Are you thinking what I think you're thinking?"

She turns to me with eyes wide. "Delfina. No."

"Of course not," I backpedal.

Luna touches the window with her fingertips. I'm glad she doesn't understand a word of what we're saying. She's American. She's probably had sex already and won't get chosen because of it. Lucky her. But also, I don't want to seem backward. I try to hold all the thoughts and opinions and judgments in my head at the same time.

"We're probably not going to be chosen," Rizzo says, opening the door. "And then what?"

"Exactly."

"Not worth it."

"True, true. So." I step through the shop door. "Ready to sew up some garbage bags?"

"Absolutely."

Rizzo ended up with a satin, high V-neck dress that flares at the waist and stops two inches below the knee. I got something off-white, which is allowed. Once it's in the bag, I can barely recall what it looks like. Rizzo and Nicia said it's perfect. I just believed them and bought it. I was too deep in my thoughts to discern whether I looked good or not.

Not a virgin.

"Rafi said he was saving me from the line," I mutter. I thought he was making excuses, but obviously he was trying to do something. Was it an excuse to take what wasn't offered? Or would it have worked?

And, why?

"If he wanted to help you," Rizzo says, "he could have explained and asked. But it's not like the word 'virgin' is in the summons at all, so I think he's probably what we thought he was."

She's right, but all the women who get letters are young, unmarried, and probably never bedded. Wouldn't that keep me off the line? And why is this thought living so closely with the memory of Massimo's lips and hands? If we hadn't been pressed for time, would he have taken me right in that little room at Bar Nilo? Touched me everywhere with his mouth and fingers, entered me with whispers and breaths, making me safe and free.

"Don't you think?" Rizzo asks.

"Yeah," I say, bag bouncing against my leg.

"Come on." She stops us in the middle of the narrow street. "You just agreed that osso buco should be stuffed with bees."

"I'm sorry."

"Wake up." She snaps her fingers in front of my eyes. "Where are you?"

Before realizing she's not asking for a physical place, I look up for a street name and see we are in front of a butcher shop. The second floor has a balcony with a café table and chair.

"I'm here."

An old man could drink espresso up there every day. If he

wanted to make a newcomer feel unwelcome, he could dump the leavings on him.

I'm offended all over again, but more deeply. It feels personal.

The insult is mine. I am the one being insulted because it's Massimo with the grinds on his shoulder, and I'm the one doing the insulting because it's coming from people in my home city. The hatred is in my name and I cannot tolerate it.

The stairway is next to the butcher, and the door is open.

"Delfina?" Rizzo says from the world of ten seconds ago.

I walk through the doorway and up the stairs. There's a skylight at the top of the squared-off spiral. I climb to it. On the first landing, I remember that Massimo said he lives on the third floor. I could skip the old man with the espresso entirely. Go up to three. Knock on the door. If he doesn't answer, I could wait there for him to come home and beg him to take my virginity. I could make what I desire be my salvation instead of my ruination.

"Delfie!" Rizzo calls from outside, her face a moon in the sunlight. "Where are you going?"

"Stay out here with Luna. Don't let her wander off."

"But where..." She fades as I climb with a bag in each arm.

When I'm at the second-floor landing, I stand at the apartment that would lead to the balcony, holding my knuckles up to the door.

If I want Massimo, I should just climb another flight of steps and do what needs to be done. This old man is irrelevant to that.

But he's not. He's insulting and degrading and... I knock on the door hard, as if I have every right to be here. A part of me hopes he isn't home, buying me time to talk myself out of it.

"What are you doing?" Rizzo says from the bottom of the

stairs. Luna's right behind her, looking up at me with a knotted brow.

"I'm teaching manners to someone who should know better." I knock again, harder this time.

"I don't get it?"

"Just wait for me outside, okay?" I hold up my fist, ready to swing it at the door so hard the hinges rattle, but it opens and my fist flies past it, touching the old man's shoulder. I gasp and pull it back.

"Signorina?" the portly man says, clearly baffled. His bright brown eyes are pushed into the tufts of his face like buttons in a cushion. He's wearing olive green trousers under his belly and a white shirt washed to gray. I can see all the way through the one-room apartment to the balcony. The TV is on to a soccer game.

"Signor." I suck a deep breath and stand as tall as I can. "My name is Delfina Gargiulo."

"Ah, Gentile's daughter. I went to your mother's funeral." The revelation is disarming. "Everyone did." He shrugs.

Behind him, a woman his age stands at the stove, facing us, smoking a stubby cigarette. There's a *caffettiera* pot for espresso on the burner.

"I understand you take your espresso on the balcony every morning."

"*Si, si.* Does Gentile want something from me?"

"No." I swallow hard. This guy wants word from my father, not me. My authority has been built up in my own head, but doesn't exist outside it. "I want something from you."

"Who is it, Vito?" the woman calls.

"Gentile Gargiulo's daughter," he replies with a half turn into the apartment.

"What does she want?"

"I don't know."

By the time he's fully facing me again, my confidence has shrunk to the size of a coin. But I'm here and I'm committed.

"Signore," I start. "Do you consider yourself a good citizen of the Quarter?"

"You need some money for the Saint Magdalena? Let me see if—"

"Signor, please. Answer the question."

He stands a little taller. I notice a crumb in his moustache. "Of course. Now what is this about?"

"Garbage collection has been under control for fifteen years. There is no reason for you to throw your coffee leavings into the street."

His wife scoffs from the kitchen. I can't read the purpose or meaning of the sound, so I ignore it and continue.

"You may hit someone with them. And if that someone isn't from here… if they're new and they don't know us… they might think you're throwing it at them. They might tell the world we're animals, and we're not. Are we?"

He stares at me, eyes narrowing as if the couch cushions are being pushed together.

"Are we?" I lower my voice and make it less of a question.

He crosses his arms.

My power here is all borrowed, and the moment I have to return it is approaching fast.

"Does your father know you came to me with this?"

He could tell Papa what I'm doing. Then what? I'll be in trouble.

No. This is a power play, and I will not lose. I have what I take with both hands.

Mirroring his posture, I fold my arms across my chest, letting the shopping bags swing from my forearms. "Do you want him to know? That can be arranged."

At first he doesn't answer. The only sound is the scraping

of slippers on the wood floor as his wife approaches from behind him.

"I told you," she scolds, slapping the back of his neck. "Stupid old man."

"Enough, woman." He tries to maintain his dominance.

"I told him, 'the Montefiores can carry their own water,' but his grandfather poisoned his mind."

"Enough!" he yells so loud she starts a little, then her eyes go steely.

"Excuse me?" I ask. "What do the Montefiores have to do with it?"

"You're talking about the man upstairs," she replies. "The Colonia? With the cane?"

"Yes." That was too much of an admission. I was supposed to be keeping it vague. I'm helpless against taking unnecessary risks here.

"The oldest insult was between them before Italy was even Italy. My husband was brought up by morons who think the devil moves the ball offside for Inter Milan." She goes inside, shaking her head, and stamps out her cigarette in an ashtray.

Whatever I'm witnessing right now isn't about me, or Massimo, or coffee grounds.

"*Grazie.*" I step away.

The husband slams the door closed and I clamber down the stairs, outrunning the echoes of an argument that must have been raging since the day they were married.

I did it. A thing. I don't know what, but I did it for him, to make his life a little easier. I am drunk with power when I loop my arms in Luna's and Rizzo's.

"What the hell?" Rizzo says when we're halfway down the block.

With a smile I cannot control, I'm a ball of energy, pulling the girls along so fast they can barely keep up.

"Listen, can you do something for me?" I ask, then press on

without confirmation. "Can you talk to Corrado? About Massimo. About… I want to see him."

She stops short. "Have you lost your chickens?"

"Just tell him if it was arranged, I'd show up."

"It's not tense enough right now?"

"Please, Rizzo. Please."

"Absolutely not. Delfina. No."

She walks away so fast, I lose her in the crowd. I wait for Luna, who takes my hand and runs next to me. When we catch up to Rizzo, she will not entertain any further discussion.

I'm going to have to figure this out myself.

CHAPTER 20

THREE DAYS TO ARMISTICE NIGHT

MASSIMO

"You want to get into Gentile Gargiulo's compound." Corrado puts down his empty espresso cup and repeats my request with far fewer words. "To see his youngest daughter, who's completely off-limits."

"Yes."

He lives in the Gargiulo compound with his immediate family, but his grandparents on his father's side have a *bassi* that opens right onto the street, and we sit at a little table just outside the kitchen, where his grandmother chops something.

"Now?" he confirms. "Right after the letters come and she's favored?"

"Now. Tonight. Tomorrow. Yes."

"*Altro caffè?*" Epifania, who looks too young to be Corrado's grandmother, stands over us with a tin pot. She used to hate me, like everyone else, but I think I've grown on her. Sometimes she even smiles in my general direction.

"*Sì, grazie*. This is a nice blouse," I add in my shitty Italian.

"Don't sweet-talk me, Colonia."

"I can't help it around you."

"*Stronzo.*" She smiles and shakes her head as she pours. "You should leave Delfina Gargiulo alone until the line breaks." Pulling out a chair, she sits with us. "She's one of the favored. The System may depend on her to keep the Montefiores in their hole."

"They showed up, by the way," Corrado says. "Big line of cars rolled into their villa. The one that didn't get burned down, obviously."

"Don't change the subject," I say.

"Nonna doesn't want to hear about your little conquest."

"I don't need protection." She reaches back for a cup and places it in front of her. "Every eye in the Quarter will be on Delfina Gargiulo." She picks up the pot, swirls it, and pours herself a *caffè*. "You'll wait until after Armistice Night."

"That's what I was about to say," Corrado adds.

"Then it's too late." I wave away the idea.

"I've been on the line." Epifania plops two lumps of sugar in her tiny cup. "Favored are not always chosen, and the chosen do not always line up as favored."

"*Grazie,*" I say with deep sincerity. "I appreciate the advice, but you don't understand me. I have to see her before I'm freed."

She scoffs and downs her espresso. "You're not going anywhere without the knife."

"*Nonna,*" Corrado objects, seeming surprised that she knows anything. "Please. Go back inside and finish the dishes."

But she continues as if he hadn't said a word. "Cosimo Orolio thinks old trinkets can make him live forever. You can't fight his fantasy of immortality."

"So you agree I shouldn't give him what he wants."

"What do you want with a stupid knife? Just give it to him.

He'll let you go, and in the end, God will decide when he's fully cooked. Give him his lies and go home."

"Forget it, Nonna." Corrado sighs deeply, sliding down his metal chair and throwing an arm over the back. "They're both stubborn. And here I am. Stuck." He waves in my direction. "Maybe I should marry you instead of Angela. We can wipe the Colonia name off the map."

"I'm not changing my name." I turn my cup ninety degrees, deep in thought. "You are."

"There can only be one man between us," Corrado says. "It's not you, *stronzo*."

Once I give up the knife, I have no more power. They can just shoot me. Another ninety degrees. I can't give up the knife, but the *promise* of the knife is a wedge. I just haven't had anything to leverage it against.

"I know you love me, Corrado." I turn it again, unscrewing my old will from my new desire.

"Fuck off."

"But I have to see Delfina Gargiulo."

He laughs to himself. "Fantastic. Good. You go get yourself killed, I can go to Abruzzo and chase Angela properly. Everybody wins."

"Except Cosimo," Nonna says, pouring herself more coffee. "No knife for him."

"Fuck him," Corrado and I say together.

I lift the cup as if it's been fully unscrewed to reveal a prize underneath, but there's nothing there but a band of coffee inside the ring.

"Can you give this to her?" I hand him the New York City postcard. East Village vs. West Village.

"No." He doesn't even look at it.

Epifania picks it up and flips it over.

"It doesn't say anything." She puts it back down.

"It can say whatever I want, once you agree."

This must pique Corrado's curiosity, because he finally looks at it. He looks away as if averting his eyes, then drops them again, picking up the card to inspect it.

"Fuck!" He flicks the card into my chest, and I catch it. "Fucking fuck!"

"What?" I start to slip the card into my jacket.

"Give it to me." He holds out his hand, waggling one finger.

"You just threw it at me."

"Fuck you. Come on." When I hold it out, he snaps it away and tucks it into his jacket pocket. "I'll do it, but only because it's a fucking sign and I'm not tempting the saints, okay? They don't like sending signs in the first place."

"What sign?"

"I'll get you there with her. You're on your own for the rest." He gets up. "Let's go."

"What sign, you fucking cabbage?"

"You'll know when you know."

Epifania stands and collects the cups. Coffee is over.

CHAPTER 21

DELFINA

He touches me. Massimo's hazel eyes pin me where I stand. His hands are all over my body and where they touch, I melt away. My breasts drip down my belly and inside my thighs. His caress on my throat breaks solids into liquid. He's going to touch me everywhere. I won't exist anymore. My arms dissolve into molten electricity. I want this annihilation. I need to be a nameless puddle.

"Delfie." Rizzo's voice pushes against the membrane of the dream. I want him to finish my calves and the bottoms of my feet. "Come on." She bops my nose with a piece of cardboard.

"What?" I wake in simultaneous panic and arousal.

"I have something for you."

I rub the sleep out of my eyes. "What time is it?"

"Late." She bops my nose again. "Corrado brought me this."

She holds up an old postcard. New York City. Massimo's kingdom split in two with a vs. between them. Each side has a name printed in English.

"What does it say?"

"Corrado says it's East Village vs. West Village."

"Tell Corrado we're too old for games."

"It's from Massimo Colonia." She says his name in a whisper.

I snap it away and stare at it with clear eyes. Massimo was half a world away when we played that game. I flip it over. The other side is blank. There's no message.

Squinting, I look for more subtle meaning besides the two cardinal directions. Nothing comes to light. The words on the card are a coincidence, but him sending it is intentional.

"How would he know about East Village vs. West Village?" I drop it in her lap and lie back down, fully awake, wishing I could walk wide-eyed into the molten dream.

"Apparently, the saints sent him a sign."

All of the Spanish Quarter has tunnels connecting basements. Under ours, there were always locked doors my young body didn't have the strength to open, but they all had names. The Scary Door. The Room On The Other Side. That Curvy Hallway Behind The Rusted Iron Gate.

The East and West room—which both the East Village and West Village teams used for home base—is where I chased my brothers and cousins in a daily game of *acchiapparella*.

I am supposed to meet Massimo there at noon for *riposo*, when everyone goes home until three. It will be quiet enough to be with him alone. Three solid hours to do what I want before Armistice Night. No permission. No regret. I feel as if I'm expanding past the limits of my skin.

When I get there, I find what used to be an unused, seemingly secret room has changed. For one, it now has two light sconces on each side of the two doorways.

Shelves have been built against the walls and filled with

smaller wood crates. Larger crates have been stacked in high rows so that there are paths between them. They're all stamped with numbers. Some have an eagle clutching a bundle of sticks stenciled on them.

Some things haven't changed. The frescoes announcing the EST and OVEST are above each doorway. The smell of men has overwhelmed the stony musk and the boxes make a lie of the size of it, but I know it. I came upstairs filthy with this exact grime.

Feet crunch on the other side of the OVEST arch.

We are alone. He isn't in a long jacket this time. Just a gray, long-sleeved Henley and black jeans with boots. And the cane. Always the cane. He's too straight for it. Too tall. His face isn't made sickly in the flat, yellow light, but dangerous and otherworldly.

He came here with a purpose—to see me. Only me. We are each other's reasons.

He stands on the other side of a short row of crates, staring at me as if he can't decide whether to worship me or devour me.

"*Ciao*," I say, then clear the nerves from my throat.

He looks around the room and breathes a "Huh," as if what he sees solves a puzzle.

"Welcome to the center of the compass."

"When I showed Corrado the postcard, he said it was a sign. I still can't figure it out."

"We played in these tunnels. East Village..." I point at the EST fresco above the arch, then OVEST. "Against West Village."

"Ah." He follows my attention to the fresco signs. "That explains a lot." He turns back to me. "Did you beat him? Were you the champion?"

"Nobody really wins *acchiapparella*."

"What are the rules of *acchiapparella*?" He paces the length of the row, voice echoing as he tries to get his tongue around the Italian word.

"Kids chasing each other around until they're tired." My eyes follow him to the end of the row, where he stops with his feet apart and the cane planted between them.

"That's a long word for tag."

"Tag? So short, with two hard consonants. It sounds like a spitting game."

"We could have worked in some spitting." He comes down my row, cane barely touching the ground. My breath quickens with each step. "Kids have ways."

A meter away, he stops. My heart is trying so hard to punch through my chest that I can barely breathe.

"I stopped playing a long time ago." I look away before I explode. "I don't know what they play now. This room didn't have all these boxes."

My voice is sticky and soft with thoughts that don't match the conversation.

"What child wants to run through an old man's fear of death?"

"Uncle Cosimo just likes old things." I rub my hands together.

"Am I making you nervous?"

I smile, letting my gaze linger over the rows.

"No." I hold out my palms. "They're dry. See?"

He leans his cane on the crates and takes my hands from the bottom, running his thumbs over my palms.

"Dry as a bone." He lets them go. Unsupported, my arms drop like a trapdoor, revealing a cache of disappointment. "You're very brave."

"Why?"

"Because you don't know me. You've experienced what can happen when you're alone with a man."

"You'll protect me, I'm sure."

"Against myself? Yes. I will. Until I can't."

Imagining the moment he lets himself go with me, my heart's pounding turns into a high-speed flutter.

"When I first got your postcard," I say, "I thought you were going to pick me up and whisk me away to New York."

We both smile at the foolishness we share.

"Is that what you want?" he asks.

"I want you to want to, even if you can't."

"I do want to. And also, I want to kiss you again." He leans forward to turn his words into reality but stops a few centimeters from my upturned lips. "And more. But I won't take what you don't offer."

"I offer."

He keeps a breath away, close enough to soften the lips he won't touch. "I can't accept."

"You must, Massimo. You have to."

The craving for consummation is painful. Just a kiss, then an agreement to do the wrong thing for the right reasons. Without the inspiration of a part of his body touching mine, I won't be able to lose my mind. I need to lose my mind.

My head jolts toward his, looking to meet his lips, but he's quicker and pulls back. With no kiss to stop the motion, I fall forward. He catches me. I'm so annoyed I push him away.

"Something changed for me. Before I kiss you again, you have to know it's not just a kiss anymore. I'm not just going to touch your lips or taste your tongue. It's more than that now. You're in my blood. You run through my veins. I can't get you out even if I want to."

Despite his promise to both of us, he leans down.

"Wait." I put my fingers on his lips. I want him to kiss me, but not like this. "This is so fast, Massimo. I'm scared. And I'm so worried about everything, and then you're there and I'm not worried anymore. What is that?"

"It's real. It's the only real thing I've ever felt."

"For me too." My fingertips brush the roughness of his chin as they drift away from his mouth.

"I can't stop thinking about you. Meeting you in that alley, I lost any chance at getting my life back, but I don't care. I fall asleep with your name on my lips. I dream of your touch. I wake up with your voice in my head. Every cell in my body, every drop of my blood calls your name." He presses my hand to his lips. "Delfina, Delfina."

On the second chant of my name, I slide my hand to the back of his head, pulling him into me just as he's doing the same thing with his free hand. In tandem, we pull one into the other, smashing our lips together as if we are, and always were, connected by some invisible elastic that's retracting after too many years of stretching.

He pushes me against a pile of crates. I clutch his shirt as if he's falling off a cliff and I'm pulling him to safety. He holds my face with both hands like a man afraid to lose what he treasures most. His tongue touches mine, and we are inside to inside. Viscous and ugly, open bodies, soft flesh, pink and glistening.

His hardness presses against my thigh, and it's so new and unexpected—so much more thrilling than I ever knew possible—that the curtains of my consciousness start to close. My vision blackens into a groan.

Closing his lips, he pulls away, holding my head a few centimeters from his, where I can still taste his breath and see the webs of his eyes.

"Am I assuming too much?"

"Can you ever assume too correctly?"

"I'm a stranger to you."

"You aren't."

"I'm reckless." He puts his forehead to mine. "I'm a monster. All I'll do is wreck you, but I don't know how to stay away from you."

I feel him pulling away, and I can't allow that.

"Don't." I hold him tight. "Please don't."

"I don't know what we're doing."

"Me neither," I whisper. "But it's real."

"It is real." He repeats my words as if he's telling himself something he didn't know already.

"Before you fall asleep, do you have these flashes of a different reality? You're still awake, but suddenly your mind puts you someplace else. You're reading a book, or dialing the phone, or choosing between two fruits at the market. And there's a whole history behind you. A purpose to your actions. A whole other life that's so real. But you don't know what they are, and as soon as you—the awake part of you—tries to grasp the purpose, it disappears. All the past and purpose are gone, and all that's left is the book or the phone or the fruit."

"What are you comparing this to? A half-dream?"

"We have a purpose. We just have to understand it before we wake ourselves up."

"You mean it." His lips brush mine.

"I mean it."

His next kiss is as earnest as the first, without the questions. Without the probing or wondering. There's no doubt in him.

His kiss tells the truth, and my kiss is the rock we're carving that truth into.

My hands explore his shape and his find mine in the planes and curves of my back and waist. He pushes me against the tall crate behind me, then he lays me down over a shorter one. I pull him on top of me. We kiss gently enough to learn where we begin and end, and hard enough to wish those boundaries away. I hold him to me with my arms, and when I am in the thoughtless throes of lust, I wrap my legs around his waist and press him close.

"Oh…"

"What?" He kisses my neck.

"I feel you."

"That's good or bad?"

"Good." I tighten my legs again. "It's so..." His erection pushes against layers of clothing, causing an unexpected, overwhelming burst of pleasure. "Good."

"Good." His hand finds its way under my shirt, brushing electric fingertips against my skin. "I don't want to hurt you."

"You're not."

"You'll tell me if I do."

"I will." I push his hand up to my breast, over my bra.

He bends his head away as if he can barely stand his own rush of desire. We are physically detached from one another, and linked by the same desire for physical attachment. We are different, and the same. The astonishment at the coexistence of our connection and disconnection flows down my spine.

We kiss as if we're trying to burrow into each other. I want more. I want to see how close we can become. Experience purpose and pleasure with him.

My skirt is hitched to my waist to free my legs, so when his fingers run along the back of my thigh, my skin crackles. He jolts the shape of his erection against my soft center with intention, as if he knows exactly what he's doing. My jaw clenches and a groan escapes my throat.

"You like this?" He pushes side to side, rubbing up against me.

"Yes." I can barely breathe.

"Open your legs wider." He pushes one knee away, untwisting my ankles. Beneath my underwear, I am open like a flower. He pushes right into me and I shudder under him. "I can make you come right now."

"But..."

"But what, beautiful?" He moves as if he's inside me. This

is what my sister was talking about. I'm never listening to Nonna again. "I'm not going to fuck you. Not yet."

"I want to. Yes. No buts."

"Good girl."

He leans back on his knees and pulls my legs apart. He must be able to see how wet I am when he kisses inside my thigh, but the explosion of sensation is more than my brain can process. It's too big for the size of his mouth. When he sucks the tender skin, he's sucking the pleasure from my core. I grab his hair, back arching, eyes closed.

"Hey," he says into a soaking wet strip of fabric between my legs. "Eyes on me."

"Huh?"

I look down at his beautiful face as he pushes that useless, stupid fabric aside and looks at the gift he just unwrapped, then at me, the woman exposing herself to him.

Even the shame is arousing.

"Eyes," he says, dipping down between my legs, pressing my knees apart.

With a single flick of his tongue, my eyes close, and he stops.

"On me," he says again. "Yes?"

"Yes."

I'd say yes to anything. His tongue touches the tip of my nub and circles. My mouth opens to scream in pleasure but nothing comes out.

"You're really close."

"Uh-huh."

"You're swollen right here." He sucks my clit, stopping before sending me over the edge. "And you're soaking wet for a cock, right here." Eyes on mine, his tongue enters me, circles, and snaps back. "If I was the first man to fuck you, I'd do it when you're this hot. No sooner."

"Be him."

"No, little lovely. Today is for you."

"Please."

"Just keep your eyes on me."

Slowly, he licks every part of me, coaxing me slowly to the edge of orgasm.

He reaches up, points two fingers at his eyes, then at mine, letting me know I have to keep us connected, and when our stares are locked, he finally lets me come, and it's like rolling waves. A storm in the middle of the sea, so high, and a drop, with his gaze an anchor tying me to place and time. There's no land, no point of reference but him as I ride wave after wave of exquisite pleasure.

Just when ecstasy flips over, threatening to drown in itself, he pulls away with a gasp. The world floods back in. My spine hurts from being pushed into a wooden crate. My legs ache from tensing around him. The air is stale and the light is flat and dull.

Men's voices echo down the hall. We've been here for over an hour.

Massimo leaps off me, pulling down his shirt.

"I'm sorry," he says, helping me up.

"It's fine," I say in a half-whisper. I pull down my shirt while he crouches to straighten my skirt.

"I couldn't stop." He wipes his chin with his fingers.

"Me neither."

Fully dressed, we stand before each other as the voices get closer. My face feels raw and burned.

"I need to see you again." He kisses me. I taste myself on his tongue.

"Yes." I step backward. EAST. "Here."

"When?"

"I don't know." The world is encroaching. The voices will turn hard. They will defend me and curse Massimo. He caused my heart to pound, but now all I feel in my chest is a twisting pain. "Thank you."

"When, Delfina?"

"I have to go."

Without another word or a single glance back, I run.

CHAPTER 22

MASSIMO

We had another few seconds, but I don't blame her for running. I pick up my cane and walk out the opposite door, making a left so I won't cross the men coming back early from their afternoon break.

Corrado's sitting at a café table near the exit onto the street. It's a few steps to his table, and with each one, I miss Delfina more. There's so much I don't know about her, and I want all of it. Every moment. Every wish, desire, and fear. A minute ago, I felt as if I owned her, but now she's a half-dream I can't capture. I'm left with her taste on my tongue, and none of her present or future.

"I didn't expect you to spend an hour and a half," Corrado says, putting down his thick paperback.

"Sorry." I sit across from him.

"She's my cousin, you know."

"I do know."

"Part of me thinks I should cap your other knee."

"Her honor is intact, Corrado." I can't tell if he's reassured. "I swear it."

"I don't like you." He rubs his upper lip with a faraway expression. "I never did. So I don't know why I trust you." He flicks his wrist at the waiter, then down at the table in front of me, ordering a coffee. "I'm supposed to watch you but not hover, because I got other things to do. And now I'm asking myself, when I took my eyes off you just now, did I take my eyes off my cousin too?"

"You're supposed to watch her? That's your job?"

"She's my fucking cousin. What part of that don't you understand? I wouldn't leave you alone with my sister either. And fuck the saints if they told me to." He waves in my direction. "No more signs."

The waiter comes with a tray and a pot of espresso, then leaves me to do the pouring.

"The guy upstairs didn't throw coffee grounds on me this morning."

"Delfina told him to stop." He's still distracted and annoyed. "Rizzo told me. It's like you got my cousin working for you."

My shock must be as big as a neon sign and twice as bright, because Corrado doesn't seem to blame me, even before I say a word. The denial needs to be made anyway.

"I didn't send her."

"I'm thinking…" He shrugs, flicking away a speck on the table. "We hire her as muscle. She's the first one to go in and convince the freeloaders to pay up. Soft warning."

"I'd rather have coffee on my shirt."

He shakes his head. "There's a way we do things here, okay? And you're just… you're disruptive. I never heard anyone think they're gonna plead their case at Armistice. You know why? Anybody else would be dead already. They'd have lead in the brain and a new home under the *Triangolo*."

I sip my coffee, carefully considering the next thing out of my mouth. Every word is true. Each one is unwise in its own way.

Yet my caution is wasted. I will say every word.

"I'm going to marry Delfina."

He laughs derisively. "Like fuck you are."

"If she consents."

"What makes you think her father doesn't have his own plans? What, one guy stops throwing shit at you and suddenly you're one of us?"

"I love her, Corrado."

"You don't even know her."

"I want to hear the stories about how she became who she is, but they're just stories. She speaks to my heart."

"On Maradona's fucking hair," he swears in frustration.

"Listen. I don't believe in signs and omens, okay? But you do. Forget the postcard. Why was I there that night, when Rafi went for her?"

"And what are you going to do about Carmine Montefiore? What if he wants her?"

I hadn't considered that thoroughly, but do I have to? What difference does he make, really? None at all. He can't have her. She's mine.

"I'll throw my entire body at him, and if he kills me, I'll make so many friends in hell he won't be able to get out of bed without stepping on pitchforks."

"I almost believe you." He waves at someone coming down the block. I recognize the swagger. It's Aris, Delfina's brother.

"Almost?"

"I think if anyone could have gone to the Armistice and gotten his freedom without giving Cosimo that knife, it would be you. But... here we are." He stands to greet Aris. "That's not happening."

"What's not happening?" Aris asks, his hand on his cousin's arm.

"This guy." Corrado jerks his thumb at me then tips his chin to Aris. "What are you doing here?"

"I got an hour to kill." Aris pulls a chair from an empty table and sits backward.

"Before what?" Corrado scoffs and takes out a pack of cigarettes. "Big job doing squat?"

Aris shrugs, left leg bouncing like a piston. "Cosimo wants to see me about something."

Aris averts his gaze. The inside of his arm has no scar. He's not in the System, but he's being summoned.

"The other night?" Corrado offers him a smoke and he takes it. I decline.

"Fuck off."

"What other night?" I push my coffee toward Aris. I don't want it. I'm not ready to wash her taste away.

"None of your fucking business." Aris leans forward to let Corrado light his cigarette.

"So, he knows you stole his boat and went swimming in your tuxedo?" I ask.

Corrado laughs and lights both cigarettes. "Whole fucking neighborhood knows."

"We brought it back," Aris says.

"How much of his wine did you drink?" I ask.

Corrado laughs again and slaps his cousin on the shoulder.

"Those boats are sitting out there, never getting used," Aris says sullenly and pulls my espresso toward him. "It's stupid."

"Tell him that to his face." Corrado flicks his ash. "See how far that gets you."

"Fuck it." Aris shrugs again, looks away, takes a drag, then a gulp of espresso. "Everything is fucked. It's upside down. People busting their asses seven days a week and living in shit so Cosimo Orolio can buy another fucking cabin cruiser."

"Hey." Corrado takes Aris's arm, revealing the scar inside his elbow. "You're gonna stop saying shit like that. You're not cut in, so there's nothing stopping you from getting cut out."

"Sure." He flicks his ash. "Telling the truth is all it takes. Some guy comes—maybe you, Corrado. Maybe this bag of dicks here to tell me to stop telling the truth. But why? Why does saying what everyone can see mean I'll end up in Rafi Scanga's old hospital bed?"

"He's not in it?" My spine straightens involuntarily. "He's out?"

"No." Corrado stamps out his smoke. "He's dead. Good job."

"How?"

"Shit." Aris shakes his head. "You're a murderer now."

"He was stabilizing." My objections come from a reality that died five seconds ago.

"He got unstable." Corrado throws down some orange money and checks his watch. "It's time. Cosimo wants to talk to you about it."

Aris gets up and twirls his chair so it fits back under the table he took it from. "I guess we're all going to get chewed out together."

CHAPTER 23

MASSIMO

The little curve of docks is a ten-minute walk and a twenty-minute drive. My leg doesn't start bugging me until I'm out of the Quarter, and even then, I'm so much lighter for being out of that prison that I barely notice.

Rafi weighs on me. I killed him. Thinking he was going to fight out of it put the guilt on pause, but now I'm responsible for his death, his mother's tears, the loss of any good, decent thing he might have done.

The six-lane boulevard that separates us from the sea has one place to cross, so we wait there. Corrado takes out his pack of cigarettes again and offers it to Aris and me. I haven't smoked since I was twelve, but I consider taking one. Then I taste her in my mouth. She's lingering there like a cloud, and the cigarette will be a strong wind across the sky. I wave a refusal.

Will she love me now that I'm a murderer?

I can't think about this yet. I have to survive first—for her.

"If he tries to kill me—" I start.

"File it with the complaint department," Corrado interjects.

"—I'm taking him out," I finish, directing my words to Aris. "And I'm gonna have to run. I want you to know I'm taking Delfina with me. If you try to stop me..." I shrug, expecting him to get pissed; instead, he laughs, which is worse.

"You're gonna take care of my sister?" he scoffs. "You?"

"I am. Not here, but I am."

"For how long?"

"Forever."

"The Scangas are gonna find you before forever comes."

"I'm not leaving her."

The light changes. Eventually, enough drivers stop their cars, and we cross.

"You got it that bad for her?" Aris asks at the slim opening in the median, checking for rogue Fiats before we step into the road again.

"Yes. I do." We finish crossing. "And it's real. So you don't have to act like a dick about it."

"It's not Cosimo or us you gotta worry about," Corrado says. "You killed Rafi Scanga. That's a blood debt."

"Fair is fair." Aris leads us along the short wall to the pathway to the docks, because nothing is a straight line here.

"Fair would have been you taking your sister home."

"Fuck, Massimo, why?" Corrado murmurs in frustration while Aris spins around with one finger jabbing in my direction.

"You think I don't know that?"

"Just walk," I say. "For once in your life, get out of the way."

"You think I don't feel that weight on my head? And Rafi dying? And this entire fucking conversation about you and Delfie and forever? Now when the Scangas get you, if she feels even this bad about you getting hit? That's on my head too. All of it is my fault because I didn't want to walk my sister home. I'm shit and there's not anything in this world I can sacrifice to fix that one stupid decision. Happy now?"

Corrado's rubbing his temple as if he's heard this a thousand times in places more private than the middle of the street.

"I won't be happy until I know she's safe." I say it as reassurance, but it doesn't seem to work.

"Well, me either," Aris says. "So if Cosimo comes after you, fucking kill him, okay? Is that fair? No. But do it anyway so I'm not worrying alone."

The way this guy worries is to take a dive off a stolen boat. I can't imagine what it would be like to have to keep his head out of his ass.

"You want to stop worrying about her?" I come close to Aris so I don't have to do more than murmur. "Get her out of the line."

"How am I supposed to do that?"

"Armistice Night is right there." I point toward the deserted-looking castle at the end of a long land bridge where the event will be held. "Surrounded by water on three sides."

His eyebrows tense and his head tilts. He hears me. "I think I know a—"

"How about no?" Corrado waves his hands between us. "What you're suggesting"—he pushes me back—"is going to get me killed even if I have nothing to do with it. Okay?" He nudges Aris away. "And you, my dear dumbass, take this to heart. There will be no secret stolen boat rescues. You're going to apologize to my boss for joyriding his yacht."

"It was a cabin cruiser."

"Then you're going to go home and find another hobby."

Turning away, Corrado paces along the concrete berths. Aris and I share a glance and a shrug before we follow.

Corrado stops at a thirty-footer named *The Second Crown*

and talks to a huge man who looks as if he's casually standing around, but who is apparently there to stop random residents and tourists from going any farther.

"I'm rooting for you," Aris says under his breath. "If Cosimo hasn't made a deal with the Scangas to save them the trouble of killing you, I'll put money on you making it out of here before summer's out."

"I go with Delfina."

"Not taking odds on that."

"Before the line," I insist in a harsh whisper.

The big man steps aside.

"Are you listening? If you live that long, you're not going anywhere until they all decide what to do with you. What's the point of seeing her if you'll be sent to hell the next day?"

"Massimo," Corrado calls. "You're on the boat. Aris, you're in the office, talking to Dino." He indicates the big guy.

Aris goes a few shades of pale.

"Is he going to be all right?" I say before I step onto the metal gangway.

"I'm going with them to make sure he understands. Now fuck off," Corrado says.

The two of them go past a short gate, but Dino walks backward until I step onto the metal ramp. The boat is forty feet long—a small yacht, give or take. Aris probably knows the exact type, but I can't ask him right now. Cosimo has a bigger one—the *Dragon Bones*—and his daughter Serafina must still be on it. He likes to show off. That's all I really need to know.

My leg throbs. Once I pass to the other side of this thing, I might not be able to get out.

Then Cosimo appears, grinning as if he knows as well as I do that I'll be trapped.

The gangway rattles under my strong, excruciating steps.

I will not limp to my death.

CHAPTER 24

MASSIMO

ONCE I STEP onto the deck, the ramp is lifted and Dino unties the boat. The engine roars and spits exhaust.

"Okay," I yell over the motor. "Here I am."

"I wanted to talk somewhere private. Just us and the fish."

The captain waves to me from the upper deck. Not that private. I'm not sure if his presence as a witness is a good thing or a bad thing, considering he may be a man of many talents, including throwing bodies overboard.

Cosimo pats my shoulder and guides me to the front deck, where a table is set up between two leather-covered lounge chairs.

Seconds later, we're motoring into the open sea.

Everything in the Spanish Quarter is worn where humans have touched for hundreds of years, cracking at the seams and layered with stories. I haven't been out of there in so long, my eyes don't know what to do with this boat. It bears the marks of its owner's effort to appear worthy of a better place. It is pristine. Clean enough to soil with a breath. White enough to blind.

I step over an upturned plastic fire truck with *Vigili Del Fuoco* painted along the side. Doll-beige hands and legs stick out of the back, as if a giant Barbie got stuck bobbing for firemen.

It's the only sign of life here. I pick it up.

"You have grandchildren."

He takes it with a smile and an embarrassed shrug. "Kids are kids."

Will Delfina say that about our kids? Will they be unleashed Italian urchins or overscheduled American neurotics?

Cosimo puts the truck inside a bin and points me toward the leather seating area, where the table is set with two glasses of something fizzy and red with a bright yellow half moon of lemon at the edge. I sit, looking back to find Naples getting smaller in the distance, and before us, a faraway line of docks before the open Mediterranean.

I'm not a great swimmer. I actually can't swim at all. I won't last five minutes out here.

"Salute." He raises his glass.

"Grazie." I tap his with mine, but I do not drink. Delfina's sex is still on my tongue. If he's going to kill me, I'll die with Delfina's taste in my mouth. That's mine and I'm not giving it up to be polite.

Cosimo drinks with big gulps, finishing half the glass with a loud *ah* of refreshment.

"Perfect." He shakes his ice and drinks more. "I love coming out here. I've got seven boats, but *The Second Crown* is perfect. It's big enough to feel good." He punches his chest. "But not too big. When they're like the *Dragon Bones*, it's a pain in the ass with the crew and fueling and stocking. There's no spontaneity. You know?"

We pass the last of the docks and head out of the Bay of Naples.

I don't trust him. I fear his single-minded pursuit of his goals and the hold he has on the people surrounding me. I am frustrated by his ability to keep me in smaller and smaller boxes, and I don't know how I'm going to get out from under him and keep Delfina at the same time.

But my father taught me that a king must enter negotiations on his own terms when he can, and the adversary's terms when he must—but he must enter them. Otherwise, he won't know how to crush him.

This is why I sit with Cosimo Orolio on the deck of his boat as it trundles into the setting sun, but I don't care about the importance of spontaneity when choosing a boat and I don't know why he called me here.

"To what do I owe the honor?" I ask.

He takes his time, facing the sea, ankle crossed over knee to reveal a sharp white boating shoe and a lower calf sprouting a bumper crop of dark hair.

"I looked into buying your building on Fourteenth Street," he says.

My blood crackles with ice, but I try not to show it. Under that building, we dug out the Dome, the Gallery, the places where our children are taught our ways. That's where we committed our worst sins, and that's where we keep the objects that make us who we are.

"New York real estate prices make your nose bleed?"

He scoffs, sips. "I could sell half of what I got in storage and buy that entire block."

"Would you though?"

"If it was for sale."

"Manhattan's being bought up by hedge funds. You think you got enough stolen shit in those crates to win a bidding war with billionaires?"

At first, his expression darkens at the accusation, then he laughs and takes a bit of his drink. "It's still in your family trust. The taxes are being paid outta some lawyer's office. No liens. It's sitting there, that knife, in the basement."

He's looking over the water, not at me. It's hard to tell what he's thinking, but I know what he's doing.

He's telling me he knows where the knife is.

No. I shouldn't attribute knowledge where none has been proven. He's prodding for a confirmation I am under no obligation to give.

"Is it though?"

"Yes. I'm sure it is."

"Then steal it."

"That, my friend, would be illegal in New York."

"Breaking and entering." I shrug. "But only if you get caught."

He puts his empty glass on the table, then notices I haven't touched mine. "It's not poisoned. If I wanted you dead, I'd just shoot you."

"I've noticed the drinks in Italy… the prettier they are, they more they taste like shit."

He chuckles and switches our glasses. He tips the full one toward me. "Salute, Colonia." He downs half of it and sets it on the table. "I know my limits. Here, where the pretty drinks are made for a man's taste…" He makes a circle on the table, setting the boundaries of Naples. "I can do what I need to do, no problem. Over there." He jerks his thumb over his shoulder, to an imaginary New York on a backward map. "I'm looking for the *Mona Lisa* with a bag over my head. So, here's how it is. You're gonna—"

"No." I push the empty glass toward him a few inches. "I'm not."

He turns to profile again, crossing the opposite ankle over

his knee. He keeps his hand on his leg to keep it up. "I hear you been making eyes at one of our women."

At some point in this conversation, I underestimated him, because this catches me like a tripwire in a dark alley. I pause, trying to find clarity in Delfina on my tongue. She's fading already. I taste more salt than anything.

"You do have very beautiful women, and I've been looking at them for six months already. I'm still a man."

A huge yacht passes us, racing into the open sea, leaving a widening cone of waves behind.

"Yeah, I get it." He's playing a cartoon of casual, letting the breeze whip his thinning hair. Twisting in his seat, he makes eye contact with the driver and draws his hand across his throat.

Cosimo won't shoot me and spray blood on the shining white fiberglass. Not when his grandkids might find it in the seams between the floorboards. He's going to do it clean. It's going to be me fighting not to get thrown overboard. I'm glad I didn't take a drink or a cigarette. I want the last thing I put in my mouth to be her.

Instead, the engine cuts out. The boat drifts a little and I realize not only how loud the motor was, but that a hand across the throat means both *kill this guy* and *kill the engine*.

"You all right?" he asks.

"Yeah." The wake from the big boat hits us, and we rock to the rhythm.

"Not seasick or nothing?"

"No."

"Because you look a little pale."

He knew exactly what he was doing with that gesture. It's rarely as clear as it is right now, exactly how such a mediocre person gets to be so powerful.

"It's the light. You look like you need a transfusion yourself."

He laughs and waves to the galley. A middle-aged woman with a low bun at the back of her neck pokes her head out.

"Bring our guest a... what's good for you people? A Coke or something?" he asks.

"Sure." I won't drink it, but she can bring it.

"*Si*," she says and disappears.

The waves slap against the hull, but the cadence of the wake is gone.

"Now," Cosimo says, leaning into me as if he's done with the bullshit. "We were talking about a woman."

"You were." It sounds more like an agreement than a correction.

With a smirk, he continues as if we're on the same page. "I've known that Gargiulo fuck my whole life. His father worked for me. When he was a kid, he saw a guy and his wife get hit in front of a grocery store. Big fucking deal, right? But he saw the guy who did it, and that put people in a position. You know what I mean?"

"No, but yes."

"Another one on the high horse. Fine. Same as you, that cabbage grows up thinking he's too good for us. Doesn't want his precious babies in the System. No matter how expensive I made it for him to walk, he pays. What was I supposed to do? Can't shoot him, because his brother's one of my top guys. Can't force him, because he 'slips' to the wrong ear and I'm stuck answering questions. You get it? I have to make it worthwhile to shut up."

I get it. He doesn't want to answer questions. There's got to be more to it.

"Who shot them?" I ask. "The grocers."

"Jesus. What did I just say about questions?"

The low-bun lady comes out with a can of Coke and a glass of ice on a tray. She opens the can and pours it for me.

Cosimo and I watch each other across the table and say nothing.

"Grazie," Cosimo says. "Get Nedro to take us back, yeah?"

"Yes, sir." When she turns to walk away, he checks out her ass, then turns to me.

"So," I say. "You want me to pay my way out the same—"

"No, no. You got it all wrong. Drink your Coke and listen. That night, when you busted in on the cabbage's daughter getting the business from Rafi?"

"Yeah?" I figure this is it. This is where he throws me overboard so Fedele Scanga doesn't have to avenge his son on Orolio turf.

Man, I really didn't want to die drowning. And Delfina's going to think I just walked away after she told me she couldn't see me again. I don't want her to think I gave up.

"Nice job on that by the way." He raps a knuckle on the table.

That must be the sign instead of the hand across the throat. They come when he knocks. I stay calm, trying to be aware enough of my surroundings to know when his men are coming. But they don't. Not yet, at least.

"You didn't walk in on a horny moron," he says. "The minute good old Papa Gargiulo heard about the Velletri letters, he made a deal with Scanga. His son, Rafi, takes Delfina and makes her unsuitable for the line. Just to get it done."

The implacable mask I've been trying to keep up slips away, and I'm left with a pounding heart and a face burning with rage.

"What?" I hope I heard him wrong.

Cosimo is better at this. While my entire body and mind are at war, he maintains the casual, just-two-guys-on-a-boat-talking demeanor.

"The method was up to the boy. The man, her father?

Couldn't even say the words. Ask for her hand or rape her. That coward didn't know what he was paying for." He scoffs when he sees my expression. I must be an open book. "Right? You see it. That man will do anything, pay any price, to keep those brats from fulfilling a single fucking obligation. What a *stupido*. Now he's got a daughter on the line, favored no less, and Rafi's dead for his trouble."

There are questions Cosimo may answer. They exist. But I can't formulate a single one. All I can do is look out onto the horizon, listening to the hush of the water and the slap of waves on the hull. What the fuck did I interrupt that night? Not her rapist but her savior? A guy doing a job? Her only chance out of a forced marriage?

Delfina will never hear about this from me. I'm not destroying her over hearsay from a man with complicated motivations. His word is shit, and I'm not going to work at disproving it at the risk of proving it instead.

The engine starts up again and the boat turns around. Maybe they'll kill me on the way back. I don't even know if I have the mental space to care.

"You're confused," Cosimo says.

"No, I got it."

"You don't know how to feel about it."

Pushing my hands against the table, I stand, leaning into him. "You my fucking therapist, Cosimo? Or my jailer? I don't need either and you can't be both."

"Easy does it, Colonia. You're gonna bust a blood vessel."

"Just murder me now or tell me your fucking *point*." I slam my hand on the table. The ice rolls and clinks in my glass.

"Oh, you wanted 'the point.' Well, let me get right to it. Sit, please, take a load off." When I don't sit, he holds out his hand. "Please."

I fall back into the chair because I'm trapped on this fucking boat anyway.

"You're not a bad kid, you know that? I had a hothead in the house, what a shame that was..." He shakes his head. "But you? You're just a little smarter."

"The point."

"Okay, the point is, Gentile Gargiulo owes me, and when the Scangas do an Armistice petition to have you taken out, his contribution to his daughter's trouble is going to become public knowledge. I've done that cabbage favors and I'm keeping his secrets. He owes me."

Somehow we went from me at Armistice Night, petitioning to go home, to a family from Velletri petitioning for permission to murder me. Maybe this is why Cosimo hasn't thrown me overboard yet.

"And once you're dead, I'll have to—like you say—get into a bidding war with hedge fund guys."

"You want the knife." By now we're passing the far piers where we can be seen. Too late to toss me. I somehow lived through this.

"I want to offer a carrot. It's been all stick and you haven't budged. So if you want Delfina Gargiulo, she's yours."

I can't speak. Can it possibly be this easy? I get her? Everything? What else can there be to want?

Can't be. There's a trick. If I say yes, will a trapdoor open up under me?

"Once I have the knife," Cosimo continues, "you can go where you want, but you have to figure out the Scangas yourself. I don't give a—"

"Yes." The agreement bursts out of me. The word yes has never felt this good coming out of my mouth, so I say it again. "Yes. *Yes*, when do we leave?"

"After Armistice."

"That doesn't work." I drop back in my chair. I didn't even realize I'd gotten up.

"I won't cross the Montefiores. I have obligations."

"It has to be before."

"What's the rush?" he asks.

"If she's chosen, the deal is off."

"Then I gotta figure out how to get that knife before the Scangas put a hole in your head."

I rub my eyes until they spark orange and white. Two steps forward, one back is still a better position than the start, but somehow it feels worse.

CHAPTER 25

ONE DAY TO ARMISTICE NIGHT

DELFINA

I wake to the sight of my Armistice Night dress hanging on the back of my bedroom door.

I don't want to think about this. All I want to do is memorize Massimo's tongue, the weight of him, the way I could only see one blissfully closed eye when I opened one of my own. I want to memorize the pleasure I gave him. For a little while, I was the center of his world.

Packs of cousins run around the courtyard in front of my bedroom window. They're always up early, eager to play in the vastness of my father's palace with the exuberant confidence of people too young to understand how hard it is to be happy.

What would it be like to have Massimo's children? Would we raise them here as the heirs to a merchant's fortune, or in New York as princes and princesses, or some faraway land I can't even imagine?

The dress is a simple pillar of off-white. I chose it for Massimo, even though I won't be wearing it for him. I want him to see me in it, eat me up with his eyes when I present myself. But he won't be there.

I'll save it. When I walk away from the line unchosen, I'll pack it away and wait until he's free, or I'm free, and slip it back on with nothing under it, for his hands only.

Aunt Etta's in the kitchen, standing on the counter, with Luna looking up at her. The contents of the upper cabinets are laid on the counter and my aunt has her arm deep against the back wall. They seem to have a rhythm going without much speaking. Luna smiles and waves, giving me a cheerful *ciao*.

"If you want breakfast or..." Aunt Etta says from inside the cabinet. "Lunch at this point, there's bread on the table. This one made it. Tell her it's good."

"How am I supposed to do that?" I unfold the cloth napkin from the brick of bread and break off a corner.

Our guest watches me swipe some butter from the pot and eat the bread as if she's up for first prize in a baking contest. She's not going to win with this crumbly mess, but I give her a thumbs-up anyway.

Aunt Etta pulls herself out of the cabinet, and Luna takes the dirty rag she's handed, then passes up a clean one.

"Did you hear about Rafi?" She jumps down with Luna's help.

I stop with another break of bread halfway to my mouth. "No."

"Died early this morning." She wipes the tops of the cans and Luna gets the hint and does the same. Meanwhile, my heart fills with a growing sense of dread. "Personally? The world's that much better without him."

I put down the bit of bread. I can't stomach it. I can't even swallow my own spit.

"Delfina?" It's Luna.

I look at them, hands stilled mid-wipe, big eyes and knotted brows.

"Why do you look like death itself?" Aunt Etta asks.

Because now Massimo Colonia is a murderer. There's going to be a blood price on his head. The Scangas are going to kill him if he stays here, and chase him if he goes.

This has to be stopped.

Papa will fix it. He fixes everything, and I've never asked him for a favor. If I ask him to do something, anything to pull Massimo out of this fire, I can say it's because he did the right thing in that alley and shouldn't be punished for it. I won't have to admit anything yet.

I need to talk to Papa.

"I'm going to the garden."

I walk out, but Luna catches up before I can get a real running start, stands in front of me, and looks me in the eye as if she's reading a book. I push her away before she yanks my fear and sorrow into the light.

"What?" My question is an accusation.

"*Mi dispiace.*"

I sigh. It doesn't please her. Good job. She's sorry about it. I understand, but I don't feel like being a practice partner for the language learner right now.

"Thank you," I say the one English expression I know, then take off at a run as if I need a private place to throw up.

Papa isn't home. He's out at the docks all day, running his business. Preparing dinner with my aunts, I hold in the entire world, chopping, boiling, frying.

"Why are you so quiet?" Aunt Silvia asks me, giving Emilia some walnuts to crack.

"Just tired, I guess."

Actually, I'm pretty sure that if I open my mouth to speak at all, my panic over Massimo's fate will come spilling out in a deluge, then I can't take it back. I'll never have the chance to talk to Papa before someone else does.

But at dinner, his chair at the head of the table remains empty. My worry flows toward the hole in the meal like the heat running out a window into the winter night. The rest flows to Aris, who's sullen and silent, looking straight ahead as if his gaze alone could burn the artichokes.

I don't ask him what's on his mind. He might say something that will cut a hole in the bag holding me together.

In the middle of cleanup, Aunt Etta enters the kitchen with a half-empty bowl. "He's back. Let's set him up a plate."

She means Papa.

"I'll do it," I volunteer, trying to sound casual.

It works. No one questions me as I make a plate of the things Papa likes best. More meat, fewer vegetables, only the brownest potatoes. I place them on a tray and rush out as if Papa's comfort is my only motivation, hustling over the cracked tile floors to his office. The door is closed. I raise my hand to knock, but stop myself when I hear Aris's voice.

"It's not fair."

Papa's voice is lower and his words run together. I lay the tray on the floor and put my ear to the door.

"You paid to keep me and Cesare out of the System. You made sure Liliana was married before you got the letters."

"I did what was possible."

"You're hiding half his hoard of shit under this house!" The sentence increases in volume. By the last word, he's so loud I have to move my head away.

"That was part of the deal!" Papa never yells, but here he is, shouting at his favorite son. "Don't you dare question what I've had to do for all of you. She is favored. If I keep her off the line, all our lives are forfeit. This family is my life. We are already responsible for Rafi."

"You can at least go with her."

"I cannot!" The door shakes with his voice.

Papa isn't moving any mountains for me; he's not going to move a grain of sand for Massimo.

I'll have to move it all myself. I've waited all day for nothing.

Leaving the tray at the door, I run.

CHAPTER 26

DELFINA

I KNOW BETTER than to try to get past Nunzio.

If Massimo taught me anything, it's how to get past someone who's watching you. So instead of running down to the street, I run up to the roof. From there, I jump to the closest building as if I've done it a million times and down an open stairwell.

I'm two streets deep into the city when the sound of a nightclub alerts me to the fact that I don't belong here. It's night. I am alone. I don't slow down.

Unescorted through the streets of the Quarter for probably the first time in my life, I am free to run fast for my own reasons. I'm not led quickly or rushed by anyone but myself or anything but my desire to see Massimo. People greet me with a wave or a word, and I give them the same in return, but not enough to slow me down. My feet burn and slip on the uneven cobblestones, but still, I run to his building. The man on the second-floor balcony stands when I approach, but I do not stop to wave then, or at his door when he opens it.

"Signorina!" he cries as I pass.

I'm too breathless to reply.

At the third floor, there are two doors. One isn't closed all the way. I go through it, and between heaving breaths, I squeak with despair.

The apartment is empty. Only a table pulled away from the wall, a chair by the open closet door, and a bed with a thin mattress. The balcony doors are open, and the curtains flutter in the breeze. The doorway to the little kitchen has a pull-up bar across it.

"Signorina." Espresso Leavings Man stands in the doorway, his wife behind him.

"This is his apartment? Not the one across the hall?" It's my last-ditch effort to maintain a scratch of hope.

"Sì."

"Yeah." Massimo appears behind him. His hair is wet and his sweatpants stick to him in spots. A white towel is draped over his shoulder, only partly covering a muscle-hardened bare torso.

The bathroom is down the hall. Of course it is.

Caught by surprise, Massimo looks from me to his neighbors and back to me, but all I can see is the fullness of his shoulders and arms. "What's going on?"

It's then I realize my fears are unfounded. There's an electric clock on the short, mismatched table at bedside.

"Gentile Gargiulo's daughter does not belong here, alone with you," Espresso Man says.

"It's fine," I say. "I have a message from my father." The lie is too fast and can't be backed up. The only thing to do is barrel through.

Massimo passes me as if I'm an annoyance and throws his towel over the back of the chair. It hid nothing, but he's that much more naked. My stare drifts to the arrow of light brown hair from his navel to the edge of his low-hanging waistband.

That leads my gaze down to the bulge. Damn. My entire body tingles with heat at the sight of it. I turn back to the neighbors before I melt right in front of them.

"I have to deliver it alone," I say.

"It's not appropriate." The neighbor gives Massimo a look of disdain. He may have stopped throwing coffee grinds on him, but he didn't like it.

"Take it up with my father. Now, please excuse us."

Massimo crosses his thick arms and doesn't say a word. He's letting me lead, as a gentleman would, but he's not putting on a shirt either.

The wife taps him on the shoulder, and the husband obeys, as he always does. They file out.

I close the door and bolt it, then turn to Massimo, who hasn't moved a single inch.

"You're going to get me killed," he says with a smile, as if he'd relish just that.

"I'll send them flowers tomorrow."

He uncrosses his arms and leans his hands on the edge of the windowsill. There's only a small room between us, but it feels like a chasm has opened up since I let his lips touch my private places.

Have I made a mistake?

"I do have a message," I say.

"Do you?" He's terse. What happened in the last day?

"Rafi is dead."

"I am aware."

"They're going to petition to punish you for it."

"You mean kill me?" he asks.

"I thought they couldn't do that to a birthright king."

"They can do what they want if enough of them agree it can be done."

"Do you even care?"

"I care." His shrug is so slight, it's as if he doesn't really.

"So why aren't you... I don't know... reacting?"

"Because you're here, in my room, and you're not mine. I have to live with that for the rest of my life. It doesn't matter if that's two days or a hundred years." He steps away from the window, coming closer to me. "Any time I have left will be empty. But all I want to do right now is take you. I want to rip this dress off you and make you come."

"What if I'm not chosen?" I put my hands on his forearms.

"You won't be mine before they end me."

I slide my hands to his, and he grasps them loosely. "What if I'm yours tonight?"

"Excuse me?" He lets me go as if he's not strong enough to hold me.

"You and I... right here." I point at the bed.

"Then what?" He spits it out like an accusation.

"They won't hurt you if I belong to you."

"This isn't some transaction, Delfina. I'm not taking you to this shitty bed in this shitty room so we can walk out of here with a little change in our pocket."

"Why not?" I cross the distance he opened up. "Why can't we make each other safe?"

"Fine. Take your clothes off."

"Just like that?"

"Strip. Now. Then get on the bed and spread your legs." He pulls the tie on his sweatpants. "Let's get this done."

He told me exactly what to do, but I stand there as if I didn't hear him.

"Do you know how to take your clothes off?" His tone is demanding and hard, but his face is collapsing as he says it. "Do you?"

"This was a mistake."

I turn to the door. When my back is to him, he finally speaks.

"I can't even save my own life. What makes you think I can save yours?"

"So you don't want me?"

The silence that comes after is filled in with the sounds of the Quarter. People. Machines. The scaffolding of nature fighting to be heard.

"Do not ever say that again." He's right behind me. I can smell his soap and feel his breath on my ear. "I want you more than I've ever wanted anything. I want your body, your heart, your life. I want your next breath and your last one to be my name. To want you this badly is to want to save you, and that… it terrifies me, because I don't know how."

I face him. He doesn't move back but keeps his face to mine. He's clean-shaven, all fresh skin and soft invitation.

"Want me now. Just do that."

Tilting his face down, he strokes the edge of my collarbone with the reverence of a prayer, stopping where my dress begins. He's not sure of my full consent, and I'm past words. I release two buttons, and he traces down, following as I undo the third and fourth, to where the placket ends and the attached skirt begins.

"This can't mean nothing," he says.

"How could it?" I unhook my bra in the front and push his hand over my breast. He immediately takes charge, bending my pebbled nipple and sending a jolt of electricity down my spine.

"Little lovely, your next breath—"

I know what he's going to ask.

"Massimo." It's a whisper of desire. "Massimo."

We kiss with a hunger that's desperate, frantic, and feral as he pushes the top of my dress back over my shoulders. I slip out of the sleeves and shrug away the bra. His hands touch every inch of exposed skin, then push into the skirt. I suck in a breath when he grabs my ass.

"You all right?"

"Yes." I run my fingers through the hair on his chest.

"You're turning red." He kisses each cheek.

"I just don't know what to expect."

"Expect a war." He pushes down my skirt and underwear, bending to get the dress past my calves, kissing my belly and thighs. "Your arms and legs will be my first battle." He kisses my thigh, up to the inside of my elbow, then picks me up and lays me on the mattress. "Your breasts will be conquered next." He fondles one while sucking the other, blinding me inside a desire that vanquishes my every thought. "Your mind is going to fight itself, and your pretty little cunt is going to be broken and subjugated."

He stands at the foot of the bed, sweatpants hiding nothing, eyes burrowing under my skin to see where I am mindlessly aroused. I drape my arm over my breasts, but he shakes his head and pushes it away.

"Don't hide yourself." He pulls down his pants, exposing a member that seems so much bigger now than it did when it was pressing against me through his jeans and steps out of them. He takes one of my knees in each hand. "Open these."

Gently, he pulls them apart. That alone sends a shot of sensation strong enough to arch my back, but when he touches my wet lips, the vibrations get deeper. I don't have any control over myself.

"I think..." I start, then stop myself for a moment to consider what exactly I want to say. "I feel like I'm going to leave my body."

"You're really close. Too close."

"Is that bad?"

"Only if I was the kind of man who wanted you to come once." He pushes my legs open so he can see, then spreads my labia to expose my hard nub. Under his gaze, I am a gasping, near-blind mess. "Relax, little lovely. Breathe."

"Okay." I un-tense as many muscles as I can, letting out a long exhale.

"You're too sexy to rush." He slips two fingers inside me, and my bones explode, pushing hot against the muscles. Extracting his wet fingers, he slides them up to the very tip of my nub, barely touching it. My bones are dust and what's left of me is a bomb. "Stay still."

"Okay." I didn't realize I was writhing, but the control it takes to stay still only makes me feel every stroke more explicitly, with every future shard of myself mapped in fine detail.

"I love seeing how beautiful you are when you come. Now I want to see it when I'm inside you."

"Please. I'm going to burst."

"What's my name?"

"Massimo."

"I'm going to fuck you. But not to save you. I'm going to fuck you because you're the only beautiful thing I've ever wanted to get so deep inside."

"Do it."

"Relax. I'm going to go slow."

I'd gotten tight with expectation again, but the effort of loosening my muscles makes my face tingle with sobs. "Please."

He moves his fingers only slightly faster, touching only slightly harder, and that's all it takes, thank Maradona, because the detonation of my orgasm would light the sky over every horizon. He draws it out with the lightest touch, making it last an eternity, and after the crest of it, but before it's over, somehow, he pushes inside me, stretching and breaking, filling and heaving, fucking me deeply and gently as he said he would.

The pain is over before it even begins, and now it's just him and me, together. He kisses my face and neck, watching my reaction whenever he pushes harder and when he rolls himself against my clit, pressing hard against it until I'm sure I'll explode.

Rolling onto his side, he leaves me on my back and drapes my legs over him. He's inside me again with his fingers between my legs, gently stroking. All his attention is on me as he draws tight circles, bringing me so close to orgasm I can barely breathe.

He rolls on top of me again.

"Look at me," he whispers. "Let me know if this is too much."

"If what's too—"

He thrusts hard, pushing the air right out of my lungs.

"This." He does it again. "And this." Again. "I don't want to hurt you but… I might."

"You won't."

He grabs my wrists and pins them over my head. "Don't tempt me."

When he thrusts hard again, I inch even closer to the edge, and the place where he's holding my body down becomes the center of the pleasure. It's a buoy against a stormy sea. An anchor holding a roiling boat in place as he gets rough, and like a little boat far from land, I let him, because I am where I belong, and I trust him, and the harder he goes, the more I am truly known. It feels good. He feels good.

Just before I come the second time, he lets go of my wrists. I breathe his name and run my thumb with the grain of his short beard, twisted together with him in a pleasure that grows to unimaginable heights and bursts in the sky like a flower made of light. Then a bouquet. Then an entire field of them.

With one last thrust, his eyes close and he yanks himself

out, pressing his pulsing erection between our bodies. He loses himself so much, I am sure I can see the darkest and most hopeful corners of his heart.

After the east-west room, I thought I'd never need another orgasm in my life. I thought I was used up. But now that I know what it means to not just feel blind pleasure, but to give it to someone , I want it again.

My belly is sticky and warm, and it's all going to be fine.

I am safe from the line, but more importantly, I am safe from a life without Massimo Colonia.

CHAPTER 27

FIFTEEN HOURS TO ARMISTICE NIGHT

DELFINA

To the sounds of the Quarter we make love until I'm too sore to take anything but his tongue, which he gives me with gentle enthusiasm. He wipes me off with a warm towel every time.

"I don't think I can have another orgasm as long as I live."

"We should put that to the test."

"No, no," I laugh. "Tomorrow."

He presses his lips together and looks away. A minute ago, there were no more Montefiores. No Scangas. No more threats hanging over us. No obligations. No line.

There was only Massimo and me.

Tomorrow is today by the clock. Armistice Night. We may put my theory to the test soon, but not tomorrow.

"I'm a terrible host," he says. "I haven't offered you water or anything."

He gets up, fully naked, beautiful, messy-haired and barefoot, to get me a glass of water.

"Do you think," I ask, "we can be together after all this?"

He makes eye contact through the mirror over the white sink. "After all what?"

"The line." I shrug. "Even if I'm not on it." The water overfills the glass.

"Delfina." He twists the faucet shut and puts the glass to the side. He leans both hands on the sink, bending into the mirror as if that will get him closer to me. "Your father will never approve."

"So?" I don't understand why he seems to be getting upset when I was only asking a question I'm entitled to ask.

He stands, picks up the glass, and brings it over to the bed. I take it and drink, looking at him over the rim. Same. Gorgeous. But unhappy.

"Why did you run all the way here?" he asks.

"I came to tell you Rafi was dead, but you already knew."

"Why?"

"Because I was afraid they... someone... the Scangas maybe, were going to call in the blood debt. And maybe you'd have a minute to run." I put the empty glass on the side table. "Or defend yourself. I don't know what you System guys do, but you needed to know and do it. Why are you making me explain this again? It isn't obvious?"

"Delfina." He sits at the foot of the bed with his back to me. "You ran across the city to tell me something I didn't want to hear. That was brave."

I lay my hand on his spine and trace the line down and back up to his shoulder blade. "It was kind of fun."

"You also ran here to lose your virginity."

"So? Are you trying to make me mad?"

"I'm trying to say, neither one of us is in a position to decide if we can be together. Between your father, the line—"

"Which I probably don't have to do now."

"And the blood debt? How can we even talk about a future past the next hour?"

"I misunderstood you." I sit up, holding the bedsheet over my chest.

"You came here to lose your virginity. You can just say it to me... to yourself. Instead of trying to shoehorn this in where it can't ever fit. Just say it. I won't think less of you."

"I will not."

"You're building castles on a swamp."

"So you want me to tell you it all means nothing? Why? So you can feel better?"

He laughs dismissively.

"It would hurt. That's all. It would hurt if you came here to use me, but I'd appreciate the hurt now. If I just knew... if you just told me... I'd know what I can't have. If I'm going to be alone, unmarried, no family, whatever, for the rest of my life, I'd make decisions accordingly."

"What? Massimo. You think I'd do that?"

"You're human. It's fine."

"It's not fine." I get off the bed. "I'm not that way."

"No, no..." He turns to me, waving his hands to dispel a mistake he thinks I'm making. "I'm not calling... saying... it's not what you think."

"You sure?" I pluck my clothes off the floor. So many pieces came off so quickly and they can't be put on with the same speed. "Because you'd have it all wrong. Any self-respecting *puttana* isn't going to run across town to fall into bed with you." I put my legs through the underwear. "There are men all over the place I can impale myself on." I wrestle into my bra. "I chose you, because you're you." I hook it. "The one who beat a guy to *death* to help me. Same one sitting here telling me how much I hurt him."

My anger is diminished with every change in his expression. High offense that I'm calling myself a *puttana*. Jealousy for all the men I could have let inside me. A kind of shame at being my choice.

I sit next to him on the bed. "And just… no, but yes. I'm glad if this gets me off the line. But also, I want to be here. I would have done it anyway, because it was you."

He rubs his eyes as if clearing his mind.

"I'm sorry." When he puts his hands down, his eyes are ringed with red. "It's been a fucked up twenty-four hours, and everyone wants to trade on someone else's trouble." He takes my hand. "Except you."

I lean my head on his shoulder. "I just want to be with you."

"Well, if we're going to get you off the line, you'll have to tell your father about me. He'll either have me killed or demand I marry you."

Option two doesn't come with an opinion one way or the other. So maybe he wants to marry me, maybe he doesn't. It's definitely too soon to consider it, but we also just did something I'm supposed to wait for marriage to do.

"He's not going to take it well. And Aris." I pick up my head. "Aris could get really mad at me."

"I'm the one he's going to come for."

"Please don't hurt him." I'm only half joking.

Massimo puts his arm around me, pulling me onto the bed. We stare at the ceiling together.

"I'm a murderer," he says. "I killed someone."

"You did." I turn to his profile. "Do you feel bad?"

"I think I should. But when I think about what he was about to do to you…" He faces me. "I'd murder him again."

"That's so sweet."

"Come with me." He twists sideways and drapes his arm over my chest.

"I already did." I turn to him and draw his arm tighter around me.

"We'll go to North Africa. Or Greece. Spanish is close enough to Italian, so maybe Madrid?"

"How long before you want to go home?"

"And how long before you want to?" He runs his fingertips over my cheek and across my lips as if learning my face by touch.

"I just want us to be away from all this."

"What about your family?"

"What about your kingdom?"

"The only thing I want to rule over is your body. We'll be king and queen of the bed. Sovereign over our house. First and last of the Colonia birthright, whose father and whose father before him did the same things in their own beds."

I laugh, closing my eyes and exhaling slowly. We are quiet together. I'm going to accept this offer. If we can do this, I want to be with him on the silent waters, with horizon all around, and no one to demand anything of us.

A wail cuts the undertone of noise. I stiffen and wake from a dream that there's a red wax raven at the window sill.

"What's that?"

"It's just the alley cats."

The wail rises again. It's the exact pitch of a knife through the soul.

"It's a baby." I get up on my elbow. "They're like little clocks."

"Lie down." He pulls me close. "It's cats in heat. They're at it every night." He kisses my shoulder. "I used to be a little jealous, but not now."

Again, the squealing comes. He may be right and they're just alley cats, but the sound is too close to what I hear from my cousins across the courtyard.

"No. It's someone's morning feeding." I sit up and blink the half-sleep down to a quarter and pull away to turn around the bedside clock. "*Cazzo*. It's almost four thirty."

"Hour to sunrise." Out of arguments about cats, he's

already standing by the dresser and pulling out a pair of pants. "We can make it if we walk fast."

I get my dress over my head, and he's there, still barechested, shirt in hand, taking me by the back of my head and pulling my lips to his. The kiss is urgent, as if it's our last chance.

"So, I have to tell my father?" I ask. "If I want out of the line."

"I'll go with you."

Imagining Massimo next to me as I explain that I cannot go to Armistice Night because I'm not a virgin doesn't seem wise. Papa and Aris will look for someone to lash out at, and if he's right there? I shudder. The situation is already uncomfortable. Protecting me puts him at risk.

"No." I button the bodice of my dress. "I'll do it."

"Are you sure?"

"Absolutely." I've run out of buttons but not buttonholes. Crap. I have to undo all of it.

Massimo shoos my hand away and does the job, unfastening then doing it correctly.

"If it goes wrong, can you send one of your cousins for me? I'll come over and Aris can beat the shit out of me while your father demands I marry you." He smooths down the placket.

"What would you say if he did?"

"I'd say, demand all you want, sir. I'm a king by birthright, and Delfina was born to be my queen. Now." He leans down to let his lips caress mine. "We should go."

CHAPTER 28

MASSIMO

At a brisk pace, Delfina and I take the back alleys and empty streets where the gangs of teenage boys gather to smoke and haze each other. There are risks in walking her home. She's not supposed to be out at night and especially not with me. So even though we keep to the least populated streets, I don't hold her hand or put my arm around her. If we're seen, we need to be able to deny it all.

"If anyone sees us," I say. "Tell them you got lost and I'm walking you back."

"Me? I lived here my whole life. You don't even know where you are right now."

"Sure I do."

"Where are you then?"

"Next to you."

She smiles, facing forward as my cane clicks against the cobblestones. Above us, TVs churn out the early news. Half a mile away, a scooter revs and a boat blasts its horn. Even knowing how soon it's all going to fall apart, I have never felt so content.

"What if we go back to New York?" she asks. "Is it weird living far from your family?"

"They're dead or in hiding. But you..." I nudge her. "You have family there, too."

"How? Who?"

"Uh..." I picture the diagrams of descendants Ivy made me memorize. I had to practice pronouncing Gargiulo until I got that -y- grace note in the middle, even though none of them were Colonia and were, for all intents and purposes, just shy of irrelevant. "There's a third cousin living in Canarsie. Marie. So there's a third aunt and uncle, and a few cousins by now."

"Really?"

"Really."

"Do you know them?"

"Not yet."

She walks next to me, matching my pace with shorter legs. I slow down, but she speeds up, and we're jogging and laughing by the time we have to turn. I stop at the corner and kiss her. She'd do fine in New York. I'm just not sure I will at this point.

"Do you even need the cane anymore?" she asks when we're walking again.

"It comes and goes. Always when I'm tired."

"Like now?"

"I'm not tired with you. With you, I'd live the rest of my life without closing my eyes."

"Big talk." She turns into an empty alley. "Shortcut."

I follow with an unearned confidence. Nothing will stop us. No one will hurt her as long as she's with me. We're in a fortified steel box.

That's what I tell myself, but we're in a soap bubble blown by a child.

The figure that stands on the far side of the alley doesn't move. The streetlights are bolted into the buildings at an interval that leaves spaces of darkness between them. That's where he stands. His silhouette suggests a suit and shoulder-length hair. His stillness, with hands folded in front of him as if he's been waiting for us, contains more menace than any gun. I grab Delfina's elbow.

"What?" she asks as I pull her behind me.

Even closer than the first, a second man with short hair appears.

"Stay there." I rest my hand on the cobra head of my cane. I've killed one man with it. I'll beat ten more to death if I have to.

"Massimo Colonia!" The voice comes from behind.

Shit. This isn't a random mugging.

I reverse directions, turning toward him while pulling Delfina to my side so I can protect her from both threats.

The man who called my name is taller, and if it's possible for him to be more still, more menacing, and more imperious, he is all those things.

"Who are you?" I call, getting a little in front of Delfina. The guys at the other end are a threat, but this man is the one in charge. "Do I know you?"

I'm holding on to some hope that they're here for a reunion, but that hope is too slippery to keep for long.

"You do not." He steps into the light. He's in the penumbra between his twenties and thirties, but in a suit and tie, he carries himself like a man old enough to have conquered the world. "And that's unfortunate." He stops at a polite distance. "Signorina Gargiulo. It's a pleasure."

She says nothing. I look down at her. She's wide-eyed and slack-jawed, not the woman being attacked in an alley the first time. Then, she was Lucretia, fully conscious and clear in her motivations. Not now. This is different. She's frightened into some kind of fog.

"Answer me," I growl. "Who are you?"

I hear footsteps behind us. Two or three men. Shit. Did another one appear? I can't watch them all at once and I can't get between them on both sides.

Stepping forward, he keeps his gaze on Delfina. "I am Carmine Montefiore."

So, this is happening earlier than I'd hoped, in a circumstance I was too stupid to fear. I thought he'd be older. Much older. This Carmine is the son or grandson reclaiming lost power.

"What do you want?" I ask.

"What's mine, of course." He reaches for Delfina. He's going to touch her and I won't allow it.

I shove her against the wall and get in front of her. She clutches the back of my shirt as if it's the only thing keeping her from falling to her death, and I face three unsmiling men I've never seen in the Quarter before.

Jesus, we are fucked. I'm about to die and leave her utterly fucked.

"Delfina Gargiulo," Carmine says with a voice as smooth as silk. "Come."

"No," I bark loud enough to be heard over the blasting TV on an upper floor.

He raises an eyebrow as if I've done something curious and strange. "Why would I hurt her?"

"Hurt her? If you hurt her, I'll kill you. If you so much as touch her, I'll just break your face."

I mean every word of the threat, and I need to, because we're outnumbered. Me against four. Delfina isn't going down easy, but when he said *Come*, I felt her move. It was probably nothing, but I'm too close to losing control of this to waste time kidding myself. She's inclined to do what he tells her.

"I believe you," Carmine says. "But Raffaello Scanga was a piece of shit. Do I look like a piece of shit, Massimo?"

"You look like a guy who spent seven thousand dollars on a fucking suit. That doesn't make you anything. Do you *act* like a piece of shit?"

Slowly, with lips pressed tightly in regret, he nods. "I'm afraid I do."

Without warning, two of the three silent men are on me. I jerk my cane upward, smashing a bearded guy's chin from below. He falls back, but when I turn to crack the second guy—the one with the shoulder-length hair—in the head, number three sweeps my legs from under me, and I fall to the cobblestones, cane flying and clattering. My hands are pulled behind my back and a sharp knee presses into my kidneys.

Sideways, from below, I see Delfina standing against the wall as if she wants to crawl into it, watching Carmine, who stands with his feet apart and his hands clasped in front of him, thumb rubbing palm, staring at her.

"Ario," he says, to someone above me, "hold her."

"Don't—" I spit the only word I can get out with the little breath I have. It melts into the noise of the Spanish Quarter, unheeded and unheard.

"Viaro, hold him, would you?"

A foot is pressed to my neck, keeping me down as the man with the deep black beard grabs Delfina's arms. She fights, but he's too strong. I fight, but I am too weak.

Blackbeard pins her arms behind her back. She lets her legs buckle under her, but he holds her up.

"You are a lovely one," Carmine says to the most obviously lovely woman on the face of the earth. "I'm sorry I couldn't wait another few hours to meet you. The lineup can get... fraught."

She swallows. Panic, submission, and rebellion in a single undulation.

"What do you want?" Her voice has the husk of a throat closed in panic.

"Leave her—" The shoe's pressure on the bottom of my face increases until I can't finish.

"What any man wants." He shrugs. "Security. Order. A home I recognize. Rituals that make sense. Not this chaos of gods and shrines. Neglecting tradition makes men stupid." He looks at me from above. "Don't you agree, Mr. Colonia?" Carmine steps out of my sight and comes back with my cane. "Isn't that why you carry this?"

When he leans down to talk to me, his face blocks Delfina. She has to try to get away. Now. While his back is turned and she only has one guy to deal with.

"Isn't that why you're not giving up 'your' knife?" he asks.

Behind him, Delfina's leg moves just a little, as if she's preparing to make a move.

Good. She has to get out of here as fast as she can. People will be in the street soon. Will they do what they intend to do in front of a crowd? I get the feeling Carmine doesn't give a shit, but if she doesn't run, the consequences could be much worse.

The guy holding my head down loosens up just enough to let me move my jaw.

"Yes," I say through my teeth. I can't stop him, but I can stall him.

"Your people honored tradition. You're not stupid yet. This has value." Crouching in front of me, he inspects the cobra head of the cane.

Behind his shoulder, Delfina moves again.

"What kind of value?" I wish I had a longer, more interesting question to distract him.

"Miss Gargiulo." Carmine turns just his head. "I promise

you that if you kick Ario in the balls, you will not generate enough pain for him to let you go." Looking back into the brass cobra's sapphire eyes, he adds, "He hasn't felt anything there for a long time."

One of the guys above me laughs. Ario doesn't look happy with the comment or the laughter, but it's Delfina who's more affected. Her eyes cast down and she stops struggling. There's something unnatural about the completeness of her obedience, but there's a foot on my head. It's hard to think.

"Let her go," I say. "Please."

"Petition noted." Concentrating, Carmine puts his thumb into the cobra's mouth.

"You want the cane?" I ask. "Take it."

"You're giving up too easy."

I'm not giving up, I just don't care about the thing. But I can tell Carmine Montefiore needs to win everything. He is a man who doesn't choose his battles. He will defend every hill and he expects everyone else to.

"Just let her go."

"Adorable." With his thumb past the fangs, he twists the head with one hand and the wood with the other.

That's when I notice his right hand, right above the punching knuckles, at the base of the fingers—scars running across all four of them, but they don't meet at the seams.

There's a click and a snap from the cane, and the head comes off.

"Atta girl." He pulls the head from the stick, revealing a slim knife, like a rapier but shorter. He tosses the bottom part and it rolls to Delfina's feet. "I see from your expression your father didn't tell you about this? Or maybe he didn't know?" He stands.

All I see are shoes and cuffs. I can raise my head just enough to see him towering over me.

"If Cosimo wanted one of my knives, he could have done

worse than this one." He turns on the ball of one foot and faces Delfina. "Now, little one, let's see what you have for me."

He brings the blade close to her face while Ario leers. I swear Carmine's sniffing her.

"You fuck. What do you want?" I ask what Delfina asked a minute ago and get a different answer.

"Lots of things, Mr. Colonia. I want lots of things."

He puts the tip of the blade to her throat.

"No!" I growl from the bottom of my lungs, where I find either unknown reserves of strength or the grace of the saints, and fold myself backward, regaining the use of my arms to push up.

Neck-guy loses his balance. I throw the second guy off my kidneys, then leap for Carmine, who can just hold out the knife and stab me, but I don't realize that until I'm in the air and can't change direction.

Instead of stabbing me, Carmine moves to the side. My hand glances off his shoulder and my weight propels me forward, into the wall. I hit it with my other hand, then my head.

No. I can't black out. I stumble back. And back.

CHAPTER 29

DELFINA

When Massimo hits his head, the *thunk* is deeper than I imagined it would be. His face goes slack and his eyes roll to the whites for a moment. He takes two big steps back, finds his footing, wobbles, and is about to drop.

Oh, God.

How hard did he hit the wall? What if his head hits the stones when he falls? It's all happening so fast, and so slowly.

The serious man with the crew cut who stepped on Massimo's neck is the one who catches him. The other slaps his face to wake him up.

"Stop," I gasp. "Make them stop."

"*Basta*, Viaro," Carmine says casually, then draws his fingers across his neck. I'm sure that means Massimo's dead, until Viaro nods and steps back with a shrug.

My breath is even and shallow, but my eyes drop tears like a faucet. They tickle my cheeks and drop from my chin to my chest.

The guy behind me hasn't been holding me that tightly, I

just haven't been able to move. My muscles could work if my mind would allow it. I want to shake him off and run, but I need to stay still, and my instincts obey my needs. Even when the blade touches the flat space below my collarbone, I need to be completely still or I'm going to be the cause of my own death.

"A better answer to your question, Mr. Colonia, is that I want what you want. I want my kingdom back."

The blade drags across my skin. I am afraid and paralyzed. The tears flow without sobs.

"You can't... I..." Massimo isn't speaking clearly.

He can't protect me this time. The cane has been broken into blade and stick, and another man has it. Ever since Montefiore told me to come and I felt compelled to do so, I've been profoundly aware of this man's presence. I can feel the thrum of his blood between us, but I cannot smell him. The lack of scent isn't a lack of cologne or the results of a fresh bath.

He is nothing. He is a void. What my nose cannot detect is his humanity.

"You don't need to be afraid," Montefiore murmurs, watching the blade scratch me. He's not going to hurt me. Not now. Not tonight. But he may take me away, and I don't want to go.

My breathing loses its even pace, getting harder and deeper until I find the strength to speak.

"You don't want me," I say, gasping for air. "I'm not a virgin."

The revelation lands like a speck of dust in the desert.

"That's not my concern."

"You want me to kill Orolio?" Massimo shouts, a little clearer now, but held back by two strong men. I can't bear it.

"I believe you would," Montefiore says so Massimo can hear. "But I want more. I want the System to be as it was. I want the rightful kings on their thrones." With a sharp, quick pain, the blade opens the skin, and I bleed.

Massimo roars, twists, gets two of the men off him. When they try to get him down again, Montefiore holds up his hand, and they retreat.

What kind of man is this? Who holds such power over people?

His back to me, Montefiore holds up the bloody tip of the knife. Massimo stumbles as if he's drunk. He has a concussion.

"Don't worry." The man behind me, Ario, loosens his hold. I jerk myself free and touch the place he cut and my fingers come back bloody. "If he won't take you, I will."

"You fucking cut her?" Massimo puts his hand on the wall to steady himself. "I'll kill you myself."

"Hear me first," Carmine says. "I want you to go home and claim your birthright."

"What?" Massimo says what I'm thinking.

"Join me." He runs his thumb along the blade, cleaning off the blood. "We will bring this system back to glory. Make the world right again."

Massimo's brow knots. Processing this offer seems to take all his strength. "What about Delfina?"

"She is not your business." He considers the blood on his thumb as if he's never seen such a thing before.

"She is *my* queen!" Massimo points at me.

I wipe my eyes with my wrists, clearing my vision. Carmine's men stand away, but alert.

"She'll take her chances on the line. You will join me now or die in this prison of a city. Once they have a quorum to remove a king, the Scangas will kill you for Rafi. If you're one of mine, they can't."

He puts his thumb between his lips to clean the blood off it.

Massimo looks at me, back at Montefiore whose gaze is stuck in some absent middle distance, then me again.

He can't be considering this.

But he is. I can tell. His expression's already begging me for forgiveness.

"Massimo?" I utter his name, but I don't know him and I never did.

"This is a trick," Massimo says, but I'm not convinced he believes it.

Montefiore lets his hand drop away from his face, leaving his back to me. "Join me and ascend your throne, or I'll kill you myself."

Massimo's nod is slight enough to deny. I can pretend I didn't see it, and he can act as if it never happened. But I'm not a child. I am a woman and I am betrayed. The crack between what I feel and what I know gets wider and wider, filling with hot, molten rage.

It's all so clear now.

All I ever was to him was a path to his birthright.

I'm a fool surrounded by devils, but I'm not a weak fool. I'm not trapped, controlled, or limited. When I take half a step forward, I kick the bottom part of the cane, and my anger and foolishness find an outlet.

Carmine Montefiore senses the movement as I scoop up the thin wood, turns as I hoist it over my shoulder, and puts up his arm too late to keep me from smashing him in the face with it.

"Delfina!" Massimo shouts.

My name is lost in the rattling inside my head as I run away as fast as I can, toward the sliver of sunlight rising over the rooflines of the city.

CHAPTER 30

DELFINA

Running past Nunzio, who can take his questions and stuff them, I climb up the stairs and into my room, slapping the door closed. I push my back and palms flat against it.

It's okay. It's over.

Whatever it was, it's done now.

And Massimo? Are we done too?

I rush out to my balcony. I don't know why I expect to see him there, explaining everything. But I don't need him to explain. It's all right in front of me.

Can any woman blame a man who chooses to live, even if that means living without her?

Leaving the balcony doors open, I throw myself on the bed and stare at the ceiling. The cracks in the plaster make the shape of a bird.

Can Massimo be blamed for giving up on me for a city ten times the size of mine? Do I have to feel bad? Can I still love him? Between death, and New York, and me, why would he choose me?

The cut at the base of my neck itches. I haven't even looked at it. I should dress it so it doesn't scab. But I don't move. I let my mind wander. Let myself feel the sweet soreness between my legs that was supposed to keep me off the line and won't. When the memory of Carmine interrupts, with his void-scent and soothing voice, I crush him with the tenderness of Massimo's lips on my throat—the shape of his face against the line of his shoulder with the feel of this fingers stroking my cheek.

This can't mean nothing.

"You're still sleeping?"

I'm not dreaming, but remembering clearly with my dreaming brain.

I can't even save my own life. What makes you think I can save yours?

"Do you know what time it is?" Rizzo is shaking me now.

They're like little clocks.

"It's a cat in heat," my voice reaches my ears as if someone else borrowed it.

"What?" Rizzo asks, and I know I spoke aloud.

Sunlight explodes into orange clouds.

I want a man who chooses me. Or nothing. Alone is better than this.

"What?" I say with a gasp as if the sleeping part of my mind is unaware that I'm half-awake.

"Armistice Night is tonight." Rizzo is still shaking my shoulder as if my eyes aren't wide open. "And Luna learned just enough Italian to freak out."

"Stupid, stupid, stupid!"

I don't speak English, but it's the same word in both languages. The rest of what Luna rattles off in the courtyard, wringing her hands by a bench with an English-Italian dictionary on it, is too fast to catch. Luna spins to us, finger extended, and says something in fast English, then dives for the dictionary, flips around, then extends her pointer again. Her sweet, freckle-faced demeanor has morphed into one of angry, singular focus.

"Why reason no phone!" She spits on the ground with the venom of a native. "Uncle Cosimo!" She spits again. "Sim card! Hah!"

"Wow," I say. "What happened?"

"Seems like Cosimo told her a bunch of lies to get her here. Something about Armistice."

Luna hands me an envelope as if proof of the world's malfeasance is inside it. Gingerly, because the evil and carelessness of men seems to need no more proof, I open it.

It's a one-way plane ticket to Ontario, California, and her US Passport.

"The time." Rizzo points at it. "It's right after the thing tonight."

"He's sending her home without even a goodbye."

"No job!" Luna cries in Italian, using a full American accent and the wrong syntax. "Uncle Cosimo liar! I to kill!"

"I feel like I'm not getting the whole story," I say to Rizzo. "We need to call Corrado."

"I did. He's busy."

Luna hands me another envelope. It's similar to the one Papa showed me, with the red wax seal on it. "I to steal! Cosimo... ahh..." She shakes her hands trying to find a word, but gives up and pantomimes a flat surface and four legs, then a drawer.

"Desk. You stole it from his desk." I give her a thumbs-up. "Got it."

She then shows us another letter, typed, shoves it into the dictionary, slaps it shut, and gives it to Rizzo.

"Cosimo to send at me." She hands Rizzo a pencil.

Luna clears off the bench and pulls us both to sit on it. Then she sits on the ground in front of us, cross-legged like a child, and bites a corner off her thumbnail.

"I haven't even told you about last night." I open the summons.

"Do tell?" Rizzo sticks the pencil behind her ear and opens the dictionary.

"I heard Rafi died…"

"Sorry, but not sorry."

"And I ran to Massimo to tell him, but he already knew, so—"

"Hold. Stop." She slides the pencil from behind her ear. "How?"

"Rooftops. Not that hard. Anyway—"

"This should be easier." Rizzo squints at the dictionary. "No wonder she talks all wrong."

"Do your best."

"Mm-hm."

In tiny print under the line, she writes whatever she can translate. Eventually, I take the dictionary and flip through while Rizzo puts matching words under all the times they appear in the letter.

"We did it," I say with trepidation, but no shame. "Massimo and I."

"Did what?" Her hand stops moving for one second before she calls out the next word. We continue translating while we talk.

"It. The whole thing."

"Wow."

"Was it…?"

"Incredible? Yeah."

"That's why they don't want us doing it." She starts to write something then stops. "So you get out of the line? Right?

I mean, it'll be hard to tell Uncle Gentile, but he'll be kinda relieved, no?"

I sigh. "That's complicated."

"A-hem!" Luna makes a get-on-with-it hand motion, so we get on with it.

"How is it complicated?"

"What's the next word?"

She tells me. I look it up. This whole dictionary method is garbage. English is an absolutely impenetrable language, but besides hunting down Corrado, I don't know a better way. Also, I don't want to tell Rizzo what happened when Massimo walked me home. I don't want to tell her about Carmine. The fear. The danger. The betrayal. A lump of heart muscle blocks my throat and my lungs stop working.

"Delfina?" she asks. "What's going on?"

When I tell her about Carmine, she's going to be scared. I don't want her to be. Maybe I can skirt around it. Say it was fine! All fine!

"Nothing. Can we just finish this please?"

The work keeps my mind focused and my body humming along normally. Luna rocks back and forth, working on another nail.

Rizzo stops when about half of the words are filled in. "This sucks."

"Let's just finish."

"I don't think we need to." She slides the letter between us and I read the penciled letters.

"We have to be doing this wrong." I read it again.

"Sure." She snaps the summons from my lap.

I haven't bothered opening it because I know what it says and it's not mine. I'm in the habit of doing what I'm told instead of what's right.

"Look." Rizzo points at the name buried inside the summons.

"Serafina Orolio. Right. She's—"

"Do you see Luna's name in here?" Rizzo jabs her finger at the paper again.

It all becomes clear.

"He's sending her in Serafina's place."

"He told her there was a job. A glamorous job with opportunities. Damn."

I have problems, sure. I haven't even processed what happened last night, but what I see right in front of me is someone stuck in a foreign country, among strange people speaking a different language, who's now finding out she's not only unloved and unwanted, but trapped in a terrible situation.

"We have to tell someone," I say.

"Yeah. I have a great idea. Let's go to Mr. Orolio and slap his wrist real hard. Tell him he can't use this girl to replace Serafina on the line and he's either got to bring her back from, like, the middle of the Mediterranean Sea or wherever in a few hours or we'll tell on him and the Montefiores will kill them all. Or not, because it's all a farce."

Impossible choice, much like the one Massimo was given. He could lose me to death or lose me to betrayal, and in that case, what's the point of dying?

"It's not a farce," I say. "I met these people. It's real."

"You met them? When?"

"Last night."

Carmine Montefiore made a mistake. He was trying to separate Massimo and me, but he didn't give Massimo a choice really. The only chance Massimo has to be with me is to live, so he took the best odds. This isn't over yet.

"I no go!" Luna's fists are balled at her sides. "Me no go?" The questioning tone is about grammar, not the decision.

"Cosimo's going to make her go," I say.

"She's not going to get picked." Rizzo puts the letters to the side.

If Luna doesn't go, nothing good will happen to her. She has to choose between taking her chances with the line or some more painful unknown.

"She has to know."

In the deepest part of my heart—a place too deep for Massimo to occupy after such a short time, but does—I forgive him.

"Are you guys getting ready?" It's Corrado.

"Where the hell have you been?" Rizzo leaps off the bench.

"Busy." His reply is pensive—as if he's got too many of his own troubles to give a full accounting of his time.

"Do you know what your boss did to her?" She points at Luna, who's still sitting cross-legged.

"Yeah." He looks at Luna. "Sorry. She has to go tonight."

Then he says more in English. When Luna blinks, tears fall down her cheeks. They talk for a minute, and I can see from her reaction that he's telling her she has to go even though it's not her name on the summons.

Luna stands and points at us while talking to Corrado.

"She wants me to tell you what she's saying," he says before she starts an angry diatribe Corrado can barely keep up with. "She says you've been friends to her. She appreciates it. She's sorry she didn't learn any Italian before she came, but the letter came out of nowhere. From a lawyer, I think. It said there was maybe... ah... an inheritance? And a job interview at a... I think 'exclusive' is the meaning... party."

Luna puts her hand over her heart.

"She has nothing at home. Her boyfriend is a... vampire of emotions? She has no one. No family. No home. She lives in the desert. It's a... I don't know the word. It doesn't seem great. So she came because she was hoping to meet a real family and put down roots and *Dios,* she's going so fast... her mother died… and Aunt Etta and Sylvia were everything her mother wasn't and it was less than a week but… Luna…" He holds out his hands. "*Aspetta*. Hold on."

But she doesn't. She keeps talking and sobbing.

"It was a lie," Corrado translates. "It was all a lie."

Luna stops, throwing herself on the bench and putting her face in her hands. I sit next to her and wrap my arms around her shoulders.

"Did you know?" I ask.

"When Serafina never came back, I suspected."

"Well fuck you then." Rizzo punches him hard in the shoulder.

"You guys." He shakes his head with the sorrow of a man who has no control of the circumstances. "This is the least of it. Cosimo's gone."

CHAPTER 31

MASSIMO

My memory has holes in it. It's dark. That's all I know. I know what happened, but not how I got here. I know she ran away, but not if she was chased. I know that somewhere in this place, a man is in pain, because he's screaming.

I'm racked with nausea, and the taste in my mouth tells me I puked somewhere, at some point. I'm pretty sure it's not me screaming, but I wouldn't bet on it.

I've forgotten what I don't know and I don't know what I've forgotten, but the only thing I want to know is whether or not Delfina is all right.

The door opens. The light is like a bomb in my brain, setting off an unbearable headache. A man comes in and stands over me.

"I ain't your nurse," he says. "But here. Take these."

He holds out his hand and drops two smooth pills into my upturned palm. He walks out, leaving the door open behind him. The pills could be poison. They could be a mind-control substance. They could also be for the headache that's swelling my brain.

I take them without water.

Maybe I've just been roofied. Guess we'll find out.

I stand and shuffle into the light, tiny step by tiny step, limping a little without my cane, into a hallway with walls built from river rocks.

There are no rivers in Naples.

Jesus Christ. How far away did they take me from her?

One end of the hall ends in a turn left. The other ends in a stairway brightly lit from the left. That would be the sun. My head hurts thinking about it. The bend in the hall is dimmer. I consider it, but decide stalling pain is no way to end it, and climb the steps.

At the top, I hear water gurgling. Not the ocean, but a fountain. One more step up and the sun's relentless burn drops an entire cinderblock on my head.

"Sir," a man's voice says far away, "he's up."

"So soon."

That's Carmine. I'd know the way that voice carries anywhere. I hold up my hand to block the early afternoon sun.

"Massimo Colonia," he calls. "Nice to see you all in one piece." His English is crisp, without an accent I can identify. "Just follow the path."

Blinking, I see him in a shady area on the other side of the rosebushes.

"You speak English," I say.

"I thought it would be easier for you, since your Italian is so rudimentary."

"What did you do to me?"

"Do to you? You hit your head against the side of a five-hundred-year-old building. Did you think you were going to win against something that old?"

I follow the path around the rose garden. We are on the side of a hill. Naples spreads out beneath us, and above is a villa of white stucco and red tile. When I make the last turn, he's at the end of the path, under a trellis heavy with a grape vine. He's not in a suit this time, but slacks and a light sweater with a zipper at the neck. Last night, his cheek was cut from getting smacked with my cane and he was developing a nice bruise, but today it's all gone. Never happened.

"Where's Delfina?" I ask.

"Home with her family." Between him and the view of Vesuvius, an alabaster fountain gurgles.

"You let her go?"

"For now, but we'll all get to see her again tonight." He pulls a chair from under an iron table. "Sit, please, before you fall."

"Fuck yourself," I mumble but take the seat anyway.

"You have a way of surviving that I admire." Carmine sits with me in the shade. It's hot up here in the mountains, but he's not sweating. A young woman brings a pitcher of water with lemons, giving each of us a glass. "But that's not enough. If you want to rule, you don't need to be loved by the richest or most powerful. You need to be loved by the lowest. The poorest. Take care of them and you take care of your kingdom."

"And that's me? The lowest?"

"You're not exactly popular."

"I don't see them building shrines on streetcorners for you either."

"The advice is for a king, not a subject. You'll need it if you're going to go back to New York and claim what's yours."

The only thing I want to claim right now is Delfina. My birthright, my property, my people—they're all secondary. None of it matters without her at my side.

Carmine watches me as if he's reading every thought in

my head, and he takes a sip of water. The scars on the base of his fingers are not random. They're the end result of our marriage rite.

"What happened to your fingers?" I ask.

He turns the back of his hand to his face as if he'd forgotten what it looked like.

"Some conflict or other." He waves away what he sees as meaningless, smiles, and drops his arm. "You should see the other guy."

"Are you lying?"

"If I am, you'll never know it."

Maybe. His confidence is unrealistic for any human man. I'd like ten percent of it. Instead, I stall by drinking the lemon water. All of it. Nothing has ever gone down so smoothly.

I don't know what happened last night. I don't know why he cornered us in an alley or which of us was the target. I don't know what that little drama with Delfina was all about, or why he nicked her, or why that still makes me angry enough to murder him.

I sit back in my chair, spread my feet apart, and lay it all on the line. "I want Delfina."

"By this time tomorrow, you won't even remember her."

"Zero chance of that, but maybe you tell me what you want, since I already told you what I want."

He leans forward, elbows on the table, cold eyes that seem to change color every time the light shifts. "You will be my shadow tonight. There is an American on the line, and you will tell me everything about her parents, her grandparents, as far back as Ivy taught you."

The Colonia are scattered and destroyed, yet this man, who's been gone decades, knows what records the Colonia kept, what we taught each other, and who taught it. He wants to throw me off. I won't give him the satisfaction.

"So, what is this?" I ask. "Family gone for fifty years—"

"Colony. Family is something made up while we were gone."

"You weren't even born fifty years ago, now you're back asking about everybody else's ancestors? You trying not to marry a cousin?"

"I like that. It's a good story."

Great. There's only one thing I want but he got me sidetracked into helping him lie about something I couldn't care less about.

"Delfina." I say one word. Just her name. That's enough.

"I will guarantee my protection. She will get out alive."

"Not good enough. I want her off the line."

"Some things aren't up to me."

"Bullshit."

"Remember what I said about caring for the lowest among us? I am not the only one choosing tonight, so even if I promised I won't take her, which I will not do, I cannot take her off the line."

There's something deeply insulting about her being given to some lower level Montefiore as a consolation prize.

"Leave her alone or all bets are off."

"There are no bets, Mr. Colonia." He stands. "There's the trade. I guarantee her life in exchange for your service. Then there's the other thing."

I stand because I don't like looking up at him. "What other thing?"

"Not this." He holds up one finger to keep me in place, then goes into the house.

I don't trust anything this fucking guy says. He's as likely to kill me as keep up his end of the deal.

"It better be her leaving with me."

He reappears in the doorway with my father's cane resting on his palms. "Is that a threat?"

"Yes." I jab a finger at him. "Fuck with every boss in Italy,

America, wherever. I don't give a shit. But when it comes to her, don't fuck with me. I killed the last guy who touched her."

"You may eat the carrot, Massimo." He hands me the cane. "But never forget the stick."

The cobra head has been snapped back onto the shaft and the rapier knife that cut her is hidden away inside. My leg's better except when it's not and I'm tired of the worn scales under my hand and the way using a cane makes my shoulder ache. I'm tired of using it even when my leg doesn't hurt and tired of fingering the snake's blue glass eyes. But at this point, I miss it.

"There are no weapons at Armistice Night." He smirks, still holding it out. "You'll need it if you want to kill me, which you do."

He didn't have to be a mind reader to know that.

Pushing my thumb between the fangs, I press against the tongue. It snaps. I twist and pull the knife a few inches to make sure it's still there.

"Take her off the line."

"If I do that, how will it look for me? For her father?"

"He'll have his daughter, and you can just crawl back under whatever rock you came from."

From his expression, I can fully understand Carmine doesn't think I get how fucked up my situation is. But I get it just fine. I just know what's at stake.

"I want to show you something." He walks inside, expecting me to follow. "Come. Please."

Nothing's getting done out here, so I let him lead me into the house. It's sparsely furnished, and though every door is open to catch the summer breeze, there's something musty and old that the constant movement of fresh air hasn't dissipated.

Down a wide flight of white marble steps, I take my time, clicking my cane with each step, taking my time to favor my bad leg. The pain is as inconsistent as ever. It's decided to be that way and I'm not going to fight it.

More than that though, the descent brings the concussion whispering back. If I rush, I'm going to fall down these stairs. I go at my pace. The leg is the leg. My head is my head. Fuck him. If I can deal with it, he can.

From the bottom, Carmine looks up at me. "I can let Gentile go for marrying off Liliana. I hadn't sent the letters yet. She was promised already. It was timing. It was sleight of hand. I am merciful."

That last lie exposes the rest.

"You didn't want her anyway."

At the bottom, past a room with sheets draped over the furniture, he leads me to another short stairway down to a hallway built of river rocks. There's a bend at the other side.

"I hadn't decided, but yes, it turned out to not be a loss. Be that as it may, Cosimo's deceit is unacceptable." He stops at a door. "Sorry if the noise bothered you."

When he opens the door, it's obvious where the screaming was coming from.

The room is windowless cinderblock, like mine was, with a sconce on each side of the door. A man hangs naked and upside down from the center of the ceiling. Cosimo Orolio is bone-white, bloodshot-eyed, yellow-toothed. A strip of hair hangs from one side of his head. Though I can't detect more than bruises and a few cuts on his body, he looks dead. He looks at me, lips quivering, breath at the speed of a tiny bird.

Jesus Christ. Not dead.

My father wasn't above making an example out of someone, but not like this.

"Sir." A thick man with a crooked nose stands from his folding chair.

"Anything?" Carmine asks.

"No, sir."

"Thank you. I have it."

The man leaves.

"So," Carmine says. "I had to do this before we gathered obviously. I'll leave him somewhere they can find after. Where should that be, Cosimo?"

"'Fina."

"Cosimo Orolio thought he was clever. He found a distant niece in California and invited her to a trip. An event, in a castle, that could yield a lucrative job, while his daughter, who I called for specifically—as a favor, so he'd know my intentions—was where he thought I couldn't get her."

"On the *Dragon Bones*."

"There is nowhere on this earth I cannot go. Sorry to say, Cosimo, no one else on that boat made it back."

He killed the sister? Siena?

"The kids?" I ask. "Weren't there kids?"

"No. They stayed home, lucky for them."

"'Fina," Cosimo moans. "*Dispiace*." I can only assume he's apologizing to his daughter, Serafina.

"Now, once I've displayed what happens to fathers who make such efforts to break their promises, how can I let Delfina go without stringing up Gentile Gargiulo? And his son, Aristide? And you?"

I'm not worried about getting strung up. I've already tempted that outcome a dozen times. But if he kills her family, she'll be broken and alone.

"If you want to hang us all off a lamp post, you will. But you're not. Why?"

Instead of answering, Carmine leans down to look Cosimo in the face. "Signore Orolio. Where are my things?"

Cosimo's lip quivers. Spittle runs out the top and drops on his forehead. I look away. The humiliation is worse than the physical torture.

"Wait, did you say...?" Carmine asks. "The only reason you're not dead is because of 'the things'? Come on, pretty boy. Do you believe that any good will ever come out of stealing from me?"

Cosimo makes clicking noises in his throat. If he hasn't given the information already, he won't. He cares more about objects than his own life. Or maybe he's ready to die for an eternal life that doesn't exist.

Cosimo Orolio thinks old trinkets can make him live forever.

"You should just kill him," I say with a little sadness for the man who imprisoned me over a knife.

"Not until he tells me what I want to know."

That knife. Our knife. Is that what he means?

No. Carmine didn't say thing. He said *things*. Plural. More than one.

Corrado's grandmother warned us about the Capo of Naples.

You can't fight his fantasy of immortality.

I take a breath before speaking, giving a little voice that knows better a chance to speak up. Because maybe I'd like eternal life. Maybe I'd like to get my hands on whatever Cosimo's willing to die for before Carmine finds the things he's willing to kill for.

I could sell half of what I got in storage and buy that entire block.

Storage under Gentile Gargiulo's house, in the East vs. West room where Delfina used to play tag. All the crates Corrado counted out so none would get lost on the way there. Junk. Boxes of old, fascist junk. Maybe it's worth more than a man can count. Still junk.

"I could tell you," I say.

"'Fina!" Cosimo objects with more vigor than volume.

Carmine stands to his full height, coming toe-to-toe close,

looking down a full four inches. This got him. He's excited and trying to hide it.

"In exchange for what?" he asks.

"You know what I want, and you'll give it to me first."

"I can string you up next to him."

"Go ahead. Figure out the American girl for yourself."

He scoffs, then steps back. "You'll tell me to save your own life."

"I'll tell you to save hers."

"A little life advice, Massimo."

"From a guy who's… how old are you?"

"Women will always betray you. They're built for the job."

"Or maybe they turn on you because you're an asshole."

He scoffs then steps back. "You'll tell me tomorrow to save your own life." He leaves the room and turns to me from the river rock hallway. "Viaro is waiting for you. He'll show you where to clean yourself up. There will be clothes laid out for you. Be ready at sunset."

CHAPTER 32

DELFINA

Typically, Armistice Night is a celebration of peace, of treaties, of respect in the face of hatred. There's probably cocktails and dinner for someone, but not for us.

Corrado and Papa are in the back of the limo with Rizzo, Luna, and me. Corrado keeps looking out the window, then at his sister. Papa keeps rubbing his hands on his pants. He's not invited to the event, but he wanted to see me off. It's sweet, but I find myself angry at him anyway.

The car turns onto *Via Partenope*, a modern paved street with office buildings on one side and the Gulf of Naples on the other. Even with the limo windows closed, I can sense the sparkling wetness in the air. The road is strangely smooth under the wheels.

What if Massimo and I walk out of here? What will I do? Will I marry him? Now that Carmine has claimed him, will that take me inside the Montefiore corner of the System? Or the Colonia?

How funny now, after all Papa's energy spent staying out of the System, I'll end up inside it whether I win or lose.

The car pulls up to a short line of limos against the retaining wall between us and the sea. The door next to Corrado opens.

We have arrived.

The men slide out first. Corrado helps Luna out. Papa helps Rizzo. I am last.

Around the men in tuxedos, their partners in sparkling evening gowns, and the women in white dresses, life goes on. Italians rush home from their jobs, to their families or to dinner. They have things on their minds, skirting the tourists photographing the old castle fortress jutting into the sea and reading the plaque that tells the story of how it was built.

I've always wanted to go to Armistice Night to feel as if I was part of something, but I'm not and never will be. The Gargiulos are separate. We always have been. I had no chance to live in the world's noise or its silence.

"*Capretta.*" My father puts his hand on my arm and affectionately calls me what he always does when he's conflicted. Baby goat. "When you come home, we'll have a feast."

What an absurd thing to say. He thinks I'm the same person I was a week ago. I'm not even close.

"I'm not coming home."

"There's a good chance—"

"No, Papa. No talk of odds and risks, okay? It doesn't matter. If I'm not chosen, I'm still leaving."

"How? Where will you go?" He seems genuinely concerned. Poor Papa.

"Wherever Massimo Colonia goes." I take Papa's hands.

Now he seems baffled. A week ago, he blinked and missed my entire life changing.

"Papa, thank you for everything. For sending Cesar to

university and keeping Aris safe and getting Liliana married to a decent man. Thank you for dreaming we'd all be free."

"It was what your mother wanted."

"Thank you for loving her that much."

"But… Massimo Colonia?"

"I love him, Papa. When I dream of the best parts of my life, the ones that haven't happened yet, he's there. He fills my heart, and if I can ever be free, it's with him." He squeezes my hands, and I repeat, "I love him."

He's obviously still baffled. It may take him days to absorb this, and we don't have that kind of time.

I hug my father to the absolute limit of my strength. He puts his arms around my waist and hugs me back.

"You were always the one," he says into my neck, "who needed to leave to do great things."

"I will."

"You always have a home here, *capra*."

I laugh when he calls me a fully grown, adult goat and pull away.

"We have to go," Corrado calls to us.

"He can wait," my father barks and hands me a cloth hankie. I wipe my nose and dab my eyes. "You be good as long as you have to. Okay?"

I sniff, hand him the hankie, and step toward Corrado and my companions in white. "Tell Cesar to never come back. He should go everywhere."

"I'll tell him you said that."

"Tell him you said it."

"Good luck, Delfina. I love you always."

"I love you, Papa."

I turn away and join the procession to the castle.

Black cars double-park on either side of the entrance to the passage, which is a lantern-lined land bridge to the island where the poet Virgil put an egg in the foundation of the fortress, promising that the structure would stand until the shell breaks. Castle Ovo still stands, but what earthquakes and floods cannot crack, time will.

The castle jutting into the sea has deteriorated so much that it's closed to the public, but the System is the most private of public institutions.

Corrado is patted down for weapons. Our bags are checked and a woman lightly runs her hands over us. She feels the stiffness of my passport in the hidden pocket of my dress and moves me along.

Following Corrado, we walk across the bridge, three abreast, with Luna in the middle. She is the guest, the tourist, the most shaken of us, and the most likely to go home.

I turn my face toward the darkening sky to feel salty droplets on my cheeks. I listen to the slapping of the waves against the rocks as if that's all there is, imagining away the constantly present traffic and cars and voices.

We walk among men who absently adjust their jackets, as if they're naked without their guns, and their wives, whose expressions range from comfort, to boredom, to deer-in-headlights. Girls from other families walk with pride or timidity, white skirts flowing when the wind whips. We've giggled and gossiped with them in church, and school, and the streets, but today we just nod as if we've only seen them in pictures. On this night when the families in the systems of America and Italy declare peace, these women seem like enemies.

I notice all this while looking for Massimo, who is nowhere to be seen.

"Looks like about a dozen of us," Rizzo says from the other

side of Luna. "Some inside already, some not here yet, so I guess... double it."

"Good odds."

"Yeah." She gives Luna a thumbs-up.

The American nods. Swallows. She'll have a story to tell when she goes home, but who will she tell it to?

Corrado turns as we approach the entrance to the castle, stopping us from going farther.

"I have to go left at the door. You're going right." He points back where two sisters in white are being separated from their mother. The younger one holds her tightly, while her sister tries to tug her away.

"This is inhuman," I mutter.

The word in Italian must be close to English, because Luna nods.

"*Totalement*," she says.

I give Luna a nod of approval, then for some reason that can be excused away as chance but isn't, I look up the side of the building to the top of the wall where two men talk from behind a parapet.

One of them is Massimo.

He's here. Alive. On two feet. Watching over me.

I didn't realize I'd lost hope until it fills me again. Even when the other man turns and I recognize Carmine Montefiore, the hope runs through me just as quickly. Carmine is powerless against it, because Massimo is with me.

Part of me knows it's not going to be that simple, but the rest needs it to take another step.

Massimo and I lock eyes for as long as we can. But as I walk forward and the angle changes, he disappears behind the stones.

We are two steps from the front.

"You're going to be fine," Corrado says to all of us, keeping his eyes on Rizzo. "Yeah?"

She throws her arms around him. At first, he doesn't seem to know what to do with himself, but eventually finds the warmth he needs to hold her tight. She pushes him away violently, with a half smile.

"Tell Mom how brave we were."

"You tell her." He steps out of the way. "Now go."

And so we go.

CHAPTER 33

MASSIMO

From a high battlement of Castle Ovo, I can't hear anything but the roar of the wind and ocean, slashed through by the occasional car horn. A crow lands on either side of me. One shits a stream of white slop onto the top of the wall.

Far below, on my right side, rocking white boats are docked on the piers. The sea stretches to my left. The land bridge stretches in front of me, with dots of white and black making their way into the fortress.

How do I know it's her, walking behind Corrado with two other girls? How can I tell it is the center of my universe from this far away? At this angle? How is it possible to be sure?

The combination of her posture, her pace, and her shape are enough to contour her in my mind, and what my perceptions outline, my heart fills in.

It's her because my body reacts to her. It can't be anyone else.

Delfina has no good reason to look up here, but she does. As if she hears me calling, she turns to the top of this particular tower, where I must be as much of a dot to her as she is to me, and settles her eyes on mine.

Until now, I didn't wonder what she thought when I agreed to Carmine's terms. Her expression is too small to see, but the patterns of the people coming along the path, the sound of the wind, the shape of her body—all together, they spell a grace I didn't ask for and didn't know I needed, but for which I am grateful. I need to see her light in this world.

"You see her," Carmine says from behind me.

I stifle the instinct to stiffen and gasp with surprise. My cane rests under my hand. The knife comes out easily once you know how to snap and twist, but the blade it too narrow to do more than puncture. Killing him with it would take excellent aim and a ton of luck. But the cobra head's effectiveness as a bludgeon has been proven at least once.

We are up high, alone. Now is the time.

"Yes."

He stands beside me, smelling nothing but shadow. The parapet is chest-high. If I grabbed him by the legs, stood quickly, and pushed before letting go, I could throw him over.

Why do I feel like he'd land on the path like a letter K, then get up and walk away?

"Do you recognize her? To the left?"

It takes me a moment to realize he's not talking about Delfina but using her as a reference.

"No. Do you have a name?"

I can't attack from the front. He needs to turn his back to me for one second.

He's got his hands on the stone in front of him on a patch suspiciously absent of bird shit.

If I grab his legs and tip him over the side, he'll leverage himself against his hands and straighten his elbows. I'd have to be ten feet tall to make that geometry work. If I hit him in the back of the head and he fell forward—

"Luna Beneforte." He keeps the heels of his hands on the corner of the stone, tapping his scarred fingers on the top.

Crows caw and screech from the top of the tower.

I scan my memory for the Benefortes. I know the name. They weren't in our core book or the next concentric circle out. They came late. I see the name in new ink, printed cleanly in the writing of the woman before Ivy.

"Yeah. She's on the Cavallo line. Mother is Lucy Cavallo." I slide my fingers down the cane, to the metal below the head.

"From Altieri?"

"Antonio." Cane off the floor, casually resting the heaviest part in one palm.

"Good." Carmine claps me on the shoulder. "You can tell me more on the way down."

He turns his back to me to walk inside.

This is it. My one chance. I hoist the cane to hit him in the back of the head, but the cobra freezes in place. I can't move it —as if it's caught in a laundry wire or something. When I look back, it's caught in Viaro's hand. He must have slipped out here when I was looking at Delfina.

"I'll be taking this." He pulls the cane away and reaches for me.

That's all I will ever remember.

CHAPTER 34

DELFINA

The halls are cold and narrow, the stairs are hard, and the doorways are arched. Everything is made of stone. The walls and floors throw our words back at us as an unintelligible polenta blob.

We're herded into a round room with high arched openings looking onto the sky. The sounds of the sea smacking against the shore come through them. Rizzo counted right. There are about two dozen of us. Some are sitting on the stone bench built into the outer wall. I always thought Armistice night included the American families, but though I hear dialects from all over Italy, no English reaches my ears.

"Luna," I whisper, "are you okay?"

She nods, scanning the room over and over, landing on the tapestries hung between the windows, one above the other, stacked in pillars of two and three. Women. Single portraits. Groups sharing wine and song. Some with halos—worshipped and honored. Some cast in shadow with expressions of mischief and trouble. They are ancient, faded, spun with gold. The solo portrait with the least fading is catching the last of the day's setting sun, proving they were brought here just for this.

That's the one Luna's looking at when she squeezes my shoulder. She points at it, then at me, then back at the portrait.

"What?"

She taps my nose high up at the bridge, then points at the portrait.

"Yeah. Greek nose. You have it too."

She doesn't understand me. Maybe if I live through this and I finally, one day, leave the Quarter, I'll communicate as well as Luna does. Maybe one day, Massimo and I will speak English together. Or some romantic pidgin that has a syntax only we grasp.

Rizzo has left my side to talk to a couple of other girls with Northern accents. They all seem so relaxed, comparing their dresses, but another second of observation reveals the tapping fingers, darting eyes, fading grins.

I hate not knowing what to hope for. Quick death? To be left unchosen, only to see Massimo taken away with Carmine Montefiore? To be chosen so I can forever lie under the wrong man?

Luna stiffens, grabs my hand, and turns to the entrance right before the commotion of murmuring starts. Two audible gasps. A muffled cry. One last woman is escorted in and the gate is rolled closed again.

Her dress is crisp and bleached, but it's out of style and wouldn't fit even if the back zipper was closed. Her long, medium-brown hair is knotted, dirty. Her eyes are as yellow as twenty-four karat gold. There's a streak of blood on her cheek and when she rubs her tears away, she leaves behind another streak of blood. Her fingernails are black with it.

She is barefoot, and I know her.

It's Serafina Orolio. Cosimo's youngest who was out to sea on the *Dragon Bones*, and now she's covered in blood, looking as if she's been dragged through the streets by the hair. What happened? How? Was her sister, Siena, spared?

Why am I assuming everyone else is dead?

She sniffs, stands straight, swings her dark gold eyes past every other woman there. "What the fuck are you all looking at?"

The ones who came in with me are already facing the unknown, so they back up, unwilling to stand up to an unproven threat. I don't like her, which is one reason to back away, but I've also never seen anyone get the better of Serafina, and I'm struck by how beaten she looks.

"Do you want me to zip that?" I ask.

"No." She yanks the shoulders away and pulls it down, leaving herself fully naked, streaked with blood and grit. "I'm not wearing their costume." She balls up the dress and throws it. "They want to rape me?" she shouts, addressing the other women in the room, then the men on the other side of the gate, who ignore her. "I'm not gonna pretend it's anything but that."

Tantrum over, Serafina turns to her cohort staring at her and whispering. She didn't look intimidated while screaming at men twice her size, but she does now.

"Serafina," I say quietly. "Come sit with us."

Glancing around, she steps our way. "Hey, Delfina. What's up?"

"Busy summer."

"Yeah, sorry I missed Liliana's wedding." She looks Luna up and down. "Who's this?"

"Luna. She's American. Sit." I lead Serafina to a space on the stone bench.

Luna and I sit, leaving a space in the middle. Serafina

hesitates. I don't realize why until Luna spreads the fullness of her skirt over the space so naked flesh wouldn't face the discomfort of cold stone.

"Thanks." Serafina's about to sit when the gate clatters open again.

Everyone stands as if they're at church. I'm already standing, but the impulse to make sure I am makes me straighter and more formal.

Serafina stands to my right. She's also straighter than she was. Luna scuttles to my left, grabbing my elbow. Rizzo has somehow socialized herself all the way across the room.

Carmine Montefiore enters.

I've met him already, so I'm not surprised by how tall he stands or how commanding he is with his black jacket and white tuxedo shirt open two buttons at the top. He clears his throat and fixes a cuff.

"He's beautiful," Luna whispers in English, and the language is close enough that I understand her perfectly.

"Ladies," he says, voice carrying right to the base of my spine, where fear sits next to sex. "Thank you for coming."

"As if you gave us a choice," Serafina barks.

I elbow her, but she doesn't move. Carmine's pinned her in place with his eyes. With a sigh, he turns to the doorway.

"Ario. Viaro."

Two men march in. One has a thick black beard. Ario. The other has shoulder-length brown hair. Viaro. The fear rattles my spine harder.

"Put her dress on."

Viaro snaps up the ball of dress and Ario comes toward us. I step in front of Serafina. "I'll do it."

Ario pushes me out of the way so hard I land on the floor. There are gasps echoing off the walls. Someone cries. Rizzo tries to run across to help me, but Viaro holds her back with his free hand. Luna's already gripping my wrists and pulling me up.

"Let her do it," Carmine commands. Viaro hands me the balled-up dress. "Thank you, Delfina. Please go to the end."

He indicates the far side of the curved line we're making, away from Luna, who stares at him with such intensity she probably won't even notice I've gone. I hate the fact that he uses my name. I hate that it looks as if I'm helping him. I feel gross about it, but I don't think Serafina wants these men touching her, so to hell with him and everyone. I feel around the edges of the dress for the openings.

"You are surrounded by queens." He steps farther into the room. "From ancient times, women have been chosen to enter the Montefiore family as brides. It was an honor."

I glance at the tapestry Luna pointed out. The regal Greek profile. A queen apparently, but what about the groups? And if this happened every year, aren't some missing?

"They killed Siena," Serafina sobs quietly. "And her husband, his brothers. My friends… Elena…" I can tell there are more names, but she breaks down.

"We have been away for half a century, and in that time, it seems as if things have changed. Brides and grooms marry by mutual consent. Children are planned to a calendar, like cattle. They leave their families behind to pursue… whatever they want."

"It's okay," I whisper as I pull the dress over her head. "We're going to be okay."

"Much has changed. Much…" Carmine has a faraway look, as if he's thinking about all the disappointing ways the world is different. As I'm zipping the back of Serafina's dress, he snaps out of it. "But, my princesses, whose fathers and grandfathers have profited from our System, hear me when I say… I. Do. Not. Care. That's not how I want it."

"You're all set," I whisper to Serafina, squeezing her shoulders. She pats my hand, then I stand next to her.

Carmine takes a visual inventory of the line of women, landing on Serafina and me last. "Everything is in order. Yes, Princess Serafina?"

"Fuck you," she says softly.

He tilts his head a little.

"But yes," she adds. "Fine. I'm in order."

"Good. Everyone take one step forward."

It is done all at once, as if we are puppets and he is the stringmaster. He starts at the opposite side of the line, in the space between the curved line of girls and the stone bench, taking inventory by sight and flicks of hair. He leans in behind their ears as if he's sniffing them.

He did that to me from the front this morning, but it didn't affect me like that. I was just a preparation. He was tenderizing the meat before cooking.

"I hate him," Serafina says so quietly I can barely even hear it, but over Gala Ricci's shoulder, seven meters away, Carmine looks at Serafina, scolding.

He heard her. I don't know how. I don't want to know, but Saint Maradona save us, he heard.

Carmine places a hand on Gala's bare shoulder and whispers something in her ear. Her lips part and her eyes close. She's wearing a thin satin dress and maybe a cold wind blows through her side of the room, because her nipples get hard.

As Carmine moves past the potential brides, more attentive to some than others, each one seems to melt a little under his attention. When he reaches Rizzo, she is as brittle as a statue, looking forward without seeing a thing. He touches her neck, and I'm filled with boiling rage as he flips some switch inside her and she loosens, warms, gets turned on just for his amusement.

Don't touch her.

If I could march across this room and slap his hand away, I would. But I can't. I'm frozen in place like every other daughter who did what they were told their entire life.

I hate him.

Rizzo practically groans out loud, then he moves on.

I want to kill him for doing that to her. He barely touched her, and it doesn't matter. She's been violated.

What if he does that to me? Where's Massimo? Will he know? Will he be hurt?

Wait.

Where *is* Massimo?

He's supposed to be with this gang of animals. Two stand back with their hands clasped behind them as if nothing is happening here. Viaro watches his boss's progress with a half-smile. Ario stares at me like a predator. He licks his lips, and knowing he's doing it just to upset me doesn't make me any less upset.

I sense Carmine getting closer. My attention is on a knife's edge. I glance at Serafina. Her breaths are shorter, shallower. She has a million reasons to hate him, and this may be the worst insult to add to her injuries.

If he touches me the way he touched Rizzo… I will not melt or turn soft. I will be strong.

CHAPTER 35

MASSIMO

Everything hurts, but if I had to find the hub of the pain wheel, it would be the inside of my right arm. My head aches where it's resting on a stone floor, and one knee is bent so the entire leg has fallen asleep.

I hear a groan. I am not alone here, wherever this is.

I open my eyes. The last of the day's sunlight comes through the windows, casting a grid of illumination on the ceiling's chipping fresco. Some kind of war. Birds up there. No. Bats. This must still be Castle Ovo in all its under-maintained glory.

My mouth tastes like park bench and has the texture and heat of a sidewalk in summer.

Getting my right elbow under me, I try to sit up. Get dizzy. Pause.

This is worse than the worst hangover.

I hear another groan. I close my eyes to fight the spinning room and only open them when I'm sitting.

Bodies everywhere. Maybe twenty-five men. Tuxedos

jackets half off. Shirtsleeves ripped. Some breathing, shifting. They are all deadly pale. One guy looks inside his right elbow. There's a bloody gash. I know before I look that mine is the same. That pain isn't coming from nowhere.

So, we've all been inducted into the System?

"Massimo," a husky voice comes from behind me. Corrado is up on his good elbow, holding out the other. "Why? I already had it."

"I don't know." I get on my hands and knees slowly. I have to get my feet under me and find Delfina. "Did they start yet?"

"Fuck if I know. Wait, that's Nunzio." He points at an unconscious man with no tuxedo, just an arm with a gash. "He watches our west gate."

It's getting dark, but I remember the morning after Liliana's wedding. He's the guy who came out of the door under her balcony to drag Aris's drunk ass inside.

"He's not in the System, but…" Overwhelmed, Corrado stops himself.

"He's got the cut now." My wound isn't a scratch just enough to scar. It's wide and deep. It should be bleeding much more. "They want us to know they mean it."

"Mean what?"

Carmine said he wanted to make things the way they were. He can't conquer anything without men cut into his service.

"He's building an army." I scan the faces of strangers, conscious and unconscious, some confused, some still dealing with vertigo, and stop at one wearing jeans, lying with his cheek pressed to the stone. His shirt sleeve is ripped off.

"Aris!" I think I'm shouting, but I barely make a whisper. I crawl on one arm and two knees. Corrado is there with me. "Shit. He's not supposed to be here. He's supposed to be getting us a fucking boat."

We turn Aris onto his back and he wakes with a groan. More men are rousing.

"What happened?" Aris notices his arm. "What the fuck?" He leans back as if he's trying to get away from the cut. "Who did this?"

"We have to get out of here." I stand. The room turns sideways, and I hold onto a stone pillar. Is this from smacking my head last night? Or is it from what they did to all of us? I need to know how much time has passed and how close I can get to Delfina in whatever time I have left. "Aris, you have to get us a boat."

"My fucking head." He holds it with both hands as if he's trying to keep it from exploding.

"How do we get out?" Corrado's question is to me, Aris, the room, himself.

"One way." I point at the brass door, which looks impenetrable. When I let go of the pillar, the room tilts, and I touch it again, looking up at the sky. "Or out a window."

"There's no fucking way." Aris is right behind me, looking a little pale but otherwise awake. "They're too high." He puts up his arm. The edge of the opening is three feet past it.

"That's west," I say.

"That's a sheer drop onto rocks."

"You sure? Get on my shoulders." I go to the wall under the window, but letting go of the pillar sends me into free fall for a second.

"You can't even stand."

"I need you to go get the boat, Aris. Please."

The men are waking. Like us, they're all groggy and weak. This is going to be a madhouse in a minute.

"Fuck you with the boat already."

"The water's on this side."

"The water's on both sides and the boat's east. Okay? The other way."

"You have no idea what they're doing with her and you're —" Taking my hands off the wall, I quickly put one on each of his shoulders. "Aris, you didn't come this far to give your sister a fair shot so you can stand here and do nothing."

"It's too high."

The noise level in the room has exploded. Almost all of us are up. There's a lot of clamoring and banging on the door. It's extremely locked. Pulling the handle doesn't rattle or shake it. There's a lot of shit-talking and confusion. No one knows what's happening and no one's taking the lead. One guy sits with his back to the wall, head dropped to one side. Doesn't look good. We could all die here, or we could all end up following the next guy who walks in the door and makes an offer.

I know who that's going to be, and it's going to be bad.

I turn my attention back to Aris. "You're afraid of heights."

"Fuck you. And yes."

"Why didn't you say so?"

I have to hold onto him when I put two fingers against my tongue and blow. The whistle pierces the chaos. All eyes on me.

I have half a second.

Either I'm a pariah, or I'm my father's son.

Time to put up or shut up.

"There are two ways out of here," I project into the room, fighting dizziness. I point at the brass door. "That one isn't opening when it's a good time for us. They're going to open it when it's good for them. That's not gonna work. We're leaving here on our terms. You all got it? Our terms. Not theirs."

"What are our terms?" a guy in street clothes asks. He's half lying down, completely confused, but he's skinny enough to stand on a guy's shoulders.

"Paolo!" Aris helps him up.

Liliana's new husband stands and shakes the pain from his arm. "Check it!" He looks up, smiling, delighted he was cut in.

"Don't get attached." Aris shows him the gash inside his elbow.

I hold out mine. Paolo scans the room. Everyone has one. He's confused again.

"My boss isn't gonna be happy," Nunzio says. "Cosimo neither."

I won't tell him what I know about the fate of the boss of the System in Naples. Let him worry about who's going to be mad about what.

"Paolo," I say, "these can't be real. We gotta get out of here to figure it out, okay? You have a chance to prove you earned it."

"Who would do this?" Paolo turns slowly to get his eyes on every other man in the room. I don't know what he's looking for or what he sees, but he comes full circle to me. "We have to get out of here."

"Look out the window." I motion to Aris.

"Tell us how far the drop is." Aris gets it immediately and crouches under the window, tapping his shoulder. "Tell us if it's instant death or just two broken legs."

Paolo climbs on, and Aris stands as everyone watches.

"Wow," Paolo says, turning back to the men trapped in the room. "Someone's fucking fucked, and I think it's my brother-in-law."

CHAPTER 36

DELFINA

Carmine has reached my half of the semicircle. I can't see him, but I feel the pressure of him behind and to the left, while Ario's leering is a dead weight in front of me and to the right. I'm going to be smashed in between these men, and Massimo is nowhere in sight.

I need him desperately. If he was here, I wouldn't expect him to save me until my life was in danger, but he'd be an anchor. I'd keep my eyes on his, and with only my breath, I'd push my lips into the shape of his name over and over again.

"Luna Beneforte," Carmine says. *"Benvenuta."*

"Me to speak not Italian," she says with the usual butchery.

"Zitto."

She babbles nervously in her language. I catch "don't speak" in English, an apology, and nothing else I recognize.

"Shh."

"Oh." The noise she makes is sticky and thick.

He's touching her. At this point, I can't look forward anymore. I snap my head around to see him stroke Luna's throat as he presses his nose against her forehead, which he can only do because she's thrown her head back in a kind of ecstasy.

He pulls away as if he's been stung. I haven't observed him react that way before.

She straightens and rubs her neck, looking back at him, but he takes her head and forcefully points it forward.

"Open your mouth."

"*Non. Parlare,*" Luna insists, as if speaking more slowly in Italian will help an Italian understand her.

Pushing between her and the girl next to her, Carmine comes to the front—the first woman he's come face to face with—takes her jaw in one hand, and squeezes hard.

"Ow!" doesn't need any translation.

"Nod if you invite my fingers into your mouth."

She does not respond. He says something in English, and I gasp a little at how easily it flows from his lips.

She shakes her head against his hand, and if he just repeated his demand, I can't blame her. It's weird.

"Fine," he says, then puts his open mouth to hers. It's not a kiss. Both of them keep their eyes open as he sucks her tongue into his mouth. He does not linger, but lets her go as soon as he tastes her. "*Grazie*, Luna Beneforte."

I don't understand what happened, but I'm turned all the way around to see Luna watching him as she wipes her mouth with her wrist. He starts toward the next girl and a look of concern comes over Luna. Quietly, she utters a couple of words and he freezes.

"What?" Serafina whispers. I spin to her. "She just said, 'you're sick.'"

"*Scusa?*" he says, coming back to Luna.

And with softness and compassion, she says another thing.

"Oh, shit," Serafina mutters, then says to me, "She just said, 'You're dying,' and fuck, he looks mad."

Maybe he is. Maybe he isn't. He stands there looking at her without an expression and her spit rolling around his tongue, while she tilts her head, staring back at him.

She lifts her hand to touch his face, but he grabs her wrist, holding her harder than he has to. She flinches as if it hurts, but she doesn't lose that expression of compassion.

Carmine lets her go. She drops her arm and looks down.

I breathe, finally. Luna's going to get herself killed one of these days. I have to find a way to talk to her... another day. Today I have to get out of this, find Massimo, get him out, then... I don't know. Have a life? Maybe.

Carmine slides behind us again and moves to the next girl. One closer to me. I can fucking smell him the way I smelled him last night. He smells of nothing. He's a void of scent. A hole where a man should be. It's weird and uncomfortable.

I want Massimo to come and save me from Carmine, but I also want him to be far, far away from Carmine. I decide to pray for Massimo's salvation instead of my own.

CHAPTER 37

MASSIMO

The window Paolo got up on dropped six feet to a walkway with cannons pointing through "the teeth stones at the top." I took that to mean battlements.

Very jumpable, unless you're Aris, standing on the edge, holding up the works. He was one of the first to go up there, but though the six feet isn't enough to kill him, it's enough to stall him. The men have shucked their jackets and are now crawling on top of one another to get out.

"Just go, you cabbage!"

"Push him!"

"It's two stinking meters, for the love of Maradona!"

These guys are going to throw him over and get both his legs broken, so he better jump for Delfina's sake.

Aris looks down at me. I can't make him go, because I'm on the floor, nor can I yell, because I still feel only half-conscious. So I nod and mouth, "The boat," and give him a thumbs-up.

Corrado, who's staying for the "brass door" part of the

plan, cups his hands around his mouth and calls, "Go get your fucking sister!"

Aris nods, takes a breath, and jumps. Good for him.

I can barely think straight right now. I'm sure this plan has a hundred holes and a workaround. Thank God all the guys took to the execution so fast.

"Okay," I say to Corrado. "Now there's going to be chaos on that wall." I snap up the jackets.

Paolo turns out to be the helpful type and follows my lead.

"They'll hear the shouting going on in here first," Corrado says.

"Unless they're all at the line." I throw the last of the jackets on the pile.

Paolo's already knotting the shredded sleeves together. If he wanted to get cut in, they should've done it already. The man's a team player.

"Or eating dinner." Corrado makes a sleeve knot and tugs it. "It's just a party for most of these people. The line's barely a blip."

"The line is everything." There's a commotion on the other side of the door that rises as the men of the Quarter leap out the window. We're down to half and we haven't tied enough sleeves together. "Hurry."

Corrado and Paolo speed up the knotting, but it's me I'm talking to. The show of efficiency and decisiveness I'm putting on is just that. A show. I can barely stand on my own two feet. Even if I get out of here, I'm afraid I won't be able to run fast enough to save her.

The voices on the other side of the door are closer, while the voices at the window thin to nothing, leaving the last human stepstool under the window. He's six-five, at least. Paolo makes the last knot and tugs it.

"Go." I jut my chin toward the window as I tie the end of the string of jackets around a pillar.

"I'm staying," Paolo says, straddling the opposite pillar and pulling the other end.

"Me too," says the last stepstool, a thick guy with black hair on the tops of his hands, who kept his bowtie on and his shirt buttoned. "Carlos." He nods to all of us. "I will stay in front."

That's a suicide position. Corrado and I wanted someone there but quickly decided we couldn't ask anyone to take it.

"Okay, Carlos. Paolo, pull that tight."

He leverages all hundred-sixty pounds to pull the jackets taut, about a foot over the floor, then lets them drop. Thumbs-up. Corrado and I take either side of the door.

"What are you going to do when we get out of here?" I ask him.

"Find Angela. Drink and fuck."

"Yeah. Good plan." I blink hard, but my vision's still clouded. At least the room stopped tilting.

"You going back home to be king?"

"I need a vacation first."

There's a scrape, a snap, and a click.

The door opens.

CHAPTER 38

DELFINA

"Hello, Delfina Gargiulo," Carmine Montefiore says in a voice so smooth it almost slips outside the range of hearing. "You look well."

You're sick.

He doesn't look sick to me. He looks healthy, strong, polished. He's capable of atrocities I can't even imagine.

"I feel well. Thank you."

You're dying.

I am not aroused. He doesn't lay a hand on me. He doesn't sniff me, or whatever he was doing. He just stands there in my space. Is he trying to prove a point to everyone else?

"You did this with me already," I say. "In the alley."

"I should have seen before then. I'm a little disappointed in myself, frankly."

"Seen what?" I start to turn toward him.

"Face forward."

"You should have seen what?"

"That you're lovely, but you're not mine."

A laugh of relief catches in my throat, yet this isn't over for me or any of us. I still have Ario's leer to deal with and the one person who saw me truly, to the bottom of myself—not as a little girl or a convenience, but a full woman—is not here.

"Where's Massimo?"

"He's not your concern."

"He is, and you know it!" The last word echoes off the stones.

Ario smirks. I take the tenor down a notch. These men have all the power here.

"Don't hurt him. Please," I say.

"Ah. Sorry."

Sorry is not an apology. It's a taunt. A shrug. Sorry is a performance of regret for an audience of one. Sorry isn't an admission of responsibility or a description of the wrongs done. It's an empty hole he's opened up to tempt me. I am expected to pour my fears down it for his entertainment, and I determine that I will do no such thing.

"It's been lovely talking to you." He says it from a few inches farther away. Interview over. He's moving on.

"I want you to choose me."

"Do you?" I've stopped him for a moment. "Why?"

"So I can kill you myself."

"For that man?" He tsks. "It shouldn't matter to you. If he lives, he's one of mine. Wherever I go, he goes, and you…" Carmine steps away, and in the moment before he moves to Serafina, he collapses my world. "You're staying here."

Whatever resolve I built up leaves me through my eyes as salty tears. My lungs also fail me, hitching and snagging to take simple breaths. He didn't humiliate me by turning me into a pile of arousal with a touch. He did worse, and he enjoyed it.

He ignores Serafina and comes to the end of the line, pausing before he heads back to the center. Through the fog of my tears, I can only discern Carmine as a blob speaking to the two serious blobs in black suits. One is a little wider in the jaw and the other has a nose shaped like a lost streetfight, but they're otherwise indistinguishable. I wipe my face with my fingers flattened, sniff, then murmur softly, through hitching breaths, knowing he can hear.

"I hope Luna's right." I watch Carmine walk back to the center to address us. "I hope you're dying, and I hope it hurts."

He responds just as softly as I spoke. I shouldn't be able to hear it, but I do, clear as day. "It does."

Carmine claps his hands together, and the murmuring and whispering I hadn't noticed is immediately silenced. "You will remain silent and still. My cousins may do you the honor of choosing you."

The two serious men come to my side of the line.

Did he choose me? Isn't that what I wanted?

No. It's not what I want, but I was never, ever going to get what I wanted anyway.

The men split apart to either side of me. One takes Serafina's arm and pulls her away, and the other takes someone to my left.

We were all calculating the odds wrong. He chose two, and though neither one is me, I am angry that no one was given full information. I am also grateful, relieved, and sorry for Serafina. I am worried about Massimo, who may be dead or…

When the chosen girl on my left passes, my list of conflicts comes to a screeching halt.

"Luna?!" I cry. This can't be. She was just visiting.

"Delfina…"

That's all I understand. The room has broken into relieved sighs and chatter. I rush to Luna with my arms out. She pulls away from the man taking her out, bending her knees and yanking her arms. She gets one free, then curls up to draw him close, and with a move as fast as an angry toddler... she bites him.

"*Cazzo!*" he shouts.

"No!" Carmine's reaction is as sharp and heavy as an axe. "Let her say goodbye."

He lets go, pulling the sleeve up his bitten arm. I have only a moment to see there was no skin broken before Luna rushes to me and we hold each other. I can't understand a word she's saying, and I need to, so I try to memorize the sounds before we part. I'll repeat them to Massimo if he's alive, and if he isn't, I'll learn to speak English and ten other languages. This will never happen again.

Carmine leaves with his two new brides while the cousins step up to the line, and chaos ensues. Viaro slaps a candidate's ass. She recoils. The rest start for the door and are held back. There is no more line. No one has a place anymore, except Ario, who comes right for me.

CHAPTER 39

MASSIMO

Carmine's men rushed in exactly as we needed them to. Paolo pulled the jackets at the right moment, tripping anyone who ran in. Carlos started stomping heads, but I don't know how he finished, because Corrado and I had already gone out the door into a chaos more intense than I'd even hoped for. The guys who jumped out the window found a way back in. One swings a chair at the nearest Montefiore.

The vertigo comes back in the hallway just outside the ballroom. I lean against the wall, blinking hard against the relentless and unpredictable blur I've had since my head hit the side of a building.

"Hey!" I grab an old guy rushing past with his woman. "Where's the line?"

"What?"

"The line!"

"What are you talking about? Get off me!"

Fuck this guy.

"Corrado!" I shout, but he's gone inside the melee. It's just me, and this place is huge.

Against traffic, touching a solid wall, I enter a ballroom set up for a civilized dinner and destroyed. The last stragglers are running out. Tables and chairs are overturned. Cloth napkins bloom on the marble floor.

One guy in the middle of the room spins a baton.

"Hey!" I say. "Where's the line?"

"There's no line." His voice has the clarity and pitch of a pre-adolescent. Who let a kid his age into Armistice Night?

"There is. Did you see women in white dresses?"

"Sure did." He stops spinning and faces me—a pile of gray and white blobs.

"That's the line. Where is it?"

"There's no more line. He's chosen two and gone."

"Two." That doubles the chance she was taken. I shake my head a little. My vision clears.

The kid's tuxedo is pristine and the baton he's spinning is my father's cane. He can't be a day older than fourteen.

"The cousins are choosing now, but that's not a line. It's more of a—"

"Where?!"

"—whorehouse."

Shaking my head has cleared my eyes but rattled my brain. The world is on some kind of axis and when the boy moves toward me, he redistributes the weight of it all, tipping it. I fall back into a serving cart and lose what little balance I have, until I'm on the floor, looking up at a cracking fresco ceiling.

The boy stands over me and pokes my chest with my own cane. "You were never going to be the king of anything, were you?"

I grab the cane.

I may not ever be a king, but that won't keep me from my queen.

CHAPTER 40

DELFINA

Ario's not shopping around for a bride. He knows who he wants.

He comes right for me, blocking out everything. I put up my hands, ready to push him away. I'm going to scratch his eyes right out. Rip his skin off with my teeth. He can try to take my bloody, broken body away. I'm ready to die, but I'm not ready for him to freeze, wide-eyed, and look down at his chest.

He lurches forward. I back up until I hit the wall.

"Don't make this unpleasant," he says.

I kick him in the balls. He doesn't even try to block me. The contact is perfect, but he just laughs as if he knew this was going to happen and took steps to protect his little jewels.

"I'm not coming quietly."

"Nice. I like it fun too."

That's what he meant by making it unpleasant. My resistance is exciting. Obedience is boring. I lose either way.

He may enjoy the fight, but his pleasure isn't my problem.

I'm not getting carted away to be married to a beast. Not today.

I shift to the side. Ario moves with me.

"Cosimo is dead," he says. "The Quarter's going to be mine. You'll be chained beside me. My beautiful bride. Can you see it?"

"In my nightmares." I shift to the side again. There are too many sidesteps between me and the door, but I take another and he does not follow.

"Try to run," he says. "Go on."

It's too easy and too hard. I make a sudden move to run then jerk back. He tries to follow and goes off balance. Then I make a break for it. Two whole steps, then he catches me in a disgusting embrace. God, he has that same empty scent everywhere except his bloody, open wound breath right in my face. I push him away, but he's holding me too tight.

Ario's weight presses me down, bending my knees. I'm falling under him with a sharp pain to my chest, like a short blade just piercing the skin. I land on my back, lungs expelling air through gritted teeth. I am smashed between the floor and his bulk.

I open my eyes. Over Ario's shoulder, I can see a brass cobra sticking out of his back, and Massimo standing over us. He's as pale as death.

I push Ario's lifeless body away, but he's too heavy.

"I have you." He pulls Ario by the shoulder.

I push harder, and with that, I am free.

I leap up and throw my arms around Massimo.

The room is almost silent now. We are alone. He kisses my face over and over. His skin is cold and clammy.

"Carmine didn't choose you?"

"No."

"Then he's a cabbage." I get one more kiss before the sound of people running makes him pull away. "Let's go."

"Come on." He takes my hand and pulls me out the door.

I never thought I'd leave that room in one piece, much less with Massimo.

All I ever needed was this moment, running to a new life with him, to feel as if there's something outside the Quarter for me. Everything has gone wrong, but all of those wrong things led me to Massimo's hand holding mine, leading me down an empty hallway and outside where it's cool, and breezy, and desolate, with only the sounds of the sea fighting its way to shore.

We are on a flat, wide deck as big as our courtyard. Man-made right angles jut into the sea. Tables are overturned. Candles in cups have fallen over, spilling hot wax. Red tablecloths are strewn like bloodstains on the concrete.

I breathe deeply. The air is salt and moisture, and the horizon line fades to black.

Massimo lets go of my hand and puts it at the back of my neck, drawing me close. "It's going to be okay."

At first, I think of course it is. We're here. We have arrived. But all I have to do is look into the corners of his heart to know it's not okay. We are here, but we have not arrived.

"What's wrong?"

"There's no boat," he says through his teeth.

"Wait. What?" I spin 360 degrees and find the only way out is the way we came. We are stuck.

"Aris, you shit for brains!" Massimo shakes his fist at the sea, but keeps looking into the distance, hoping for a surprise. "Fuck."

"We could swim."

"Sure." A laugh escapes him, then his face gets serious as his thoughts turn inward.

"What is it, Massimo?"

He wakes up enough to meet my gaze. "I don't know if I can get you back through. I don't have my cane. What am I going to use for a weapon? All I have is…" He waves his arms at the broken desolation of the pier. "Tablecloths and…" He's at a loss for anything else. "God, I fucked this up."

"No, you didn't."

"Don't tell me that!" he shouts. "We're trapped. Being stuck out here… that's the definition of a fuckup. Jesus…" He runs his fingers through his hair. "I'm sorry, Delfina. I am so sorry. I've lost everyone I ever loved and now, to lose you—"

"You haven't lost me." I take him by the arms and stare down his desolation. "I am here, always with you."

"Okay. Listen. I need you to hide, while I go to—"

"No, Massimo, you're not hearing me."

"Just go." He takes my arm and pulls me. "Behind that table for—"

"No!" My cry is lost in the sea. I jerk my arm back. He doesn't let go. "I am not leaving your side. Ever."

"If something happens to you, anything, I'm—"

"I have faith, Massimo."

"I haven't earned that."

"You have. And I have faith in me, even if you don't."

He lets me go. "I do." He takes my face in both hands and puts his forehead to mine. "I have more faith in you than I have in myself."

"Let's go then." I hold his hands and pull them down. "The only way out is through."

"Okay." He lets one hand go so we can walk back into the castle together, side by side, hand in hand.

But we aren't alone. Our way is blocked.

"Very sweet," Carmine says. "Don't you think so, Ario?"

The bearded man grunts and smiles, fully alive.

CHAPTER 41

MASSIMO

My first impulse is to put her behind me, but I resist it, because I have faith in her. She needs to see what we face, and since we both need both of our hands, I let go.

"We're done here, Carmine," I say.

"You owe me something. Did you think I'd let you walk away without delivering it?"

"Escort her out first, then I tell you where the crates are."

"No!" She growls and stands between the two men and me. "You escort us out together, right now, or you can get out of the way."

"For the love of God," Carmine says. "Control her."

I stand next to Delfina. "Are we getting an escort or are you getting out of the way?"

Ario laughs, wheezes, puts his hand on his chest.

"Massimo." Carmine sighs my name, sounding exasperated. "You refuse to understand what ruling a kingdom entails. What kind of message would that send?"

"I'll tell you what you want to know," I say. "Once we're out."

With a flick of his hand, he sends Ario toward Delfina. We both step away, but Ario's faster, and as he grabs her, I see, unbelievably, my knife is still sticking out of his back.

Jesus Christ. Did I miss every single organ?

"You expose your weakness," Carmine says, coming closer.

It kills me that I have to watch Carmine, and not Ario and Delfina wrestling. She can't win, but I have faith that for another minute, she can manage to not lose.

"And you're making sure I don't tell you shit."

"Why is everything so complicated?!" Carmine's lost patience.

"You don't need her. You didn't choose her."

"I chose *you*!" He's frustrated by how thick I am—like a teacher who can't get a student to learn long division. I didn't even know we were in class.

"Me?"

Ario has Delfina in the same position as he did this morning, in the alley. They are both listening to Carmine instead of struggling.

"With your gunshot leg and the attitude, yes, you. An American they all hate. We'd bring the Colonia back into my System and declare victory. You'd have more than you could ever dream of. Not just a return to your kingdom, but a place in a colony—my family—forever. You'd never be alone again. All I had to do was crack you just enough to let in the light."

Maybe his offer would have been appealing a week ago, but on this pier, with Delfina being held back by a guy I already stabbed in the back, it isn't enough, and it's too much.

"Talk about complicated," I say. "That's fucking complicated."

"It's not. It's very simple." He holds his hand out to Ario and waves his fingers.

Ario lets Delfina go. She runs in my direction, but she only gets one step before Carmine grabs her. She fights him.

"Let her go!" I am boiling rage.

I don't have a single strategic thought in my head, all I see is her struggle and how strong he is. When I go for them, Ario gets between us, pushing me back. I'm going to have to deal with him first.

I reach for the cobra head sticking out of Ario's back and yank it out. First I'll kill him, then—

Suddenly, Carmine growls like a thousand angry lions and pushes Delfina away, holding his arm. Delfina backs away slowly, not knowing what to do.

Ario's frozen. Easy prey. I could stab him again, but instead I grab Delfina and draw her to me.

"You fucking bit him," Ario says in a shocked whisper.

Carmine's eyes go wide with surprise as a thin line of blood comes from a tooth mark in his arm and drops down his wrist. Then he is angry—a seething boil of rage over a stupid bite that'll heal in a day. Maybe he's afraid of infection. Maybe he has a weird thing with bites. But I can tell he's going to explode in half a second and I don't need to know why or what that looks like.

"You need to stay with me," he says through his teeth, still crouched over a bent arm.

"No," I say. "I told you."

"Massimo," Delfina says softly.

Taking my attention off Carmine long enough to hear her, I hear something else. A motor. The boat. It's Aris with the fucking boat. I'm going to kiss his face then beat his ass.

"Not you!" He stands and points at Delfina. "You."

"I won't." She steps behind me as Carmine steps forward.

"Don't come any closer!" I hold out the knife as if it doesn't feel too small, too light, too easily knocked from my grip.

Carmine stretches his neck to one side, then the other as if he's stiff from a long sleep. Ario's backed away like a man who knows a land mine's going to explode.

Face turned up, eyes closed, Carmine holds out his hand. "Delfina. Come."

Her fingers grip my shoulders.

"Once we're on the boat," I say, "I'll tell you where your shit is. But you leave us alone after that."

He sighs and opens his eyes. He's managed to box away all the anger and frustration. He's back to the emotionless monster he's always been.

"I'm afraid you may not want me to." He seems to truly regret my impossible future desire to contact him.

"We'll be fine."

"Aris!" Delfina calls. "Over here!"

"I can't tie on!" Aris shouts back. "You have to jump."

I didn't notice the tide and I can't look back now. Is the boat lower than the edge of the platform? Higher?

"How far is he?" I pull her behind me when Carmine moves. This time, she lets me.

"Too far. We might have to swim."

"Shit," I mutter under my breath.

"Massimo, if you continue to stand in my way, I will kill you." Carmine's changed and I don't understand it. He's not threatening me as much as revealing, with regret, what he'll have to do.

From behind, I feel Delfina move before she whispers, "Follow me."

She runs past me, then past Carmine toward the middle of the pier. He holds his hand up to stop Ario from going after her.

Carmine shouts her name as she runs past him and he reaches for her, but I get between them, slashing with the knife just to keep him back. She leaps off the edge of the platform, and just as she did when we jumped from roof to roof, she flies, landing just short, but close enough to loop one arm over the hull.

Aris pulls her over. Her feet aren't even wet.

She trusts me to come after her. She trusts I'm not going to sacrifice everything to make sure she's safe. I can do that or die trying.

The hard part is going to be outrunning Carmine, but he doesn't seem to give a shit about what I do or where I run anymore. He's just eye-locked on the fifty-foot boat Aris stole.

"I was careless," he says to himself.

"In the tunnels," I say. "A room between east and west."

He said I'd tell him to save my own life. In one way, he was right.

"What?" he answers me while moving toward the edge of the platform.

"Your stuff." I tuck the knife in my back waistband and hope I don't puncture my ass. "Ask the kids about the East-West Room. They'll know it."

"Bring her back, Colonia."

"No."

As fast as my bum leg is able, I run and launch myself off the edge of the pier the way I have off a hundred rooftops—and land smack in the water.

When I told Cosimo I was never much of a swimmer, I was understating the fact that I can't swim at all. Running and jumping off the edge, I'd forgotten to be afraid until I was in midair. Now I'm slashing wildly at the water, sure I'm going to sink like a stone. The boat bobs above me. Delfina and Aris lean over the rail, shouting things I can't make sense of past the whooshing in my ears.

Something splashes in front of me. It floats. I grab for the Styrofoam ring. It sinks a few feet, but I have it. I'm not going to drown tonight.

Delfina's leaning over the rail, waving. I give her a thumbs-up.

"I'm okay!"

"Aris is going to—"

The ring jerks forward with the boat. I hang on to it for dear life as it pulls me along, behind the scripted name of the vessel—*Tom's Arm*.

Carmine Montefiore gets smaller and smaller in the distance.

CHAPTER 42

MASSIMO

"Massimo!" Delfina shouts as I slap onto the deck like a full sack of seaweed. The trip to the open water was harrowing, but I held on to the ring for dear life and crawled up the ladder when Aris stopped the motor.

Delfina drops to her knees in a white dress and a blanket over her shoulders.

"You're okay?" Her hands run over my shoulders and chest to make sure I'm all in one piece. "You're okay."

"I'm okay." I cup her face and pull it down for a salty kiss.

"There's blood," Aris says, flashing a light onto the pool around me where the water is curled with red.

"Oh, my God!" Delfina cries.

"It's fine." I reach behind me and pull the knife from my waistband, letting it clatter on the wood.

"You cut your own ass." Aris picks it up.

"I did." All I have in my field of vision is Delfina. My brave jumping queen.

"Your cane had a knife in it the whole time?"

"Yes," I say, kissing my woman again and again.

"We should look at your butt," Delfina says.

I want to agree, but I can't stop kissing her.

"That's my fucking sister, asshole." Aris pushes my head with his foot.

Delfina swats it away. "Leave him alone."

"I love her, you cabbage." I can't let her go. She is mine, and no one will take her. "I'm going to marry her."

"Are you?" she asks.

"You gotta ask our father." Aris is farther away, climbing up the stairs to the helm.

"Do I?" I ask her. "I will if you want me to."

"You have to ask me." She sits back on her heels. The boat moves again. "Or maybe you need to wait until I ask you."

"How long do I have to wait?" I get up on my elbows. "Because this week's been ten years long."

She stands and holds out her hand. I take her by the wrist and she hoists me up.

"Ow. Jeeze, my butt." The salt water stings, but I can't help but laugh at my pain.

"Let's get your pants off."

I check on Aris's reaction, but he's not paying attention. He doesn't complain that his sister is too pure to take care of my sliced-up ass. He's busy fucking with the knobs. He's stolen boats before, but I'm not sure he's actually ever driven them anywhere.

"Where's he taking us?" I ask as she pulls me down to the cabin.

"Home."

The cabin has a long seat on one side that turns into a narrow bed, and a counter with cabinets above and below on the other.

"Lie down." She shoos me and randomly opens cabinet doors.

I hesitate before sitting on the cushion. I'm not sure I'll be sitting on anything for a while.

"Pants off," she adds, reaching for the first aid kit.

My wet trousers stick to my legs as I peel them off. The black fabric hid the amount of blood coming out of me, but my skin shines with streaks of red.

She puts the kit on the counter and flips it open.

The engine roars and I feel us turn.

"Where's home?" I ask, lying on my stomach.

"With you." She removes gauze and disinfectant. Scissors. Tape. Everything she needs is laid on the counter.

I didn't know she was the kind to take that kind of care. I'd just pick shit out as I needed it, but she has to run the whole process over in her mind beforehand to arrange it all first.

She finds a cloth towel, soaks it under the faucet, and wrings it. Every move is beautiful and I want to learn everything about her. Does she squeeze toothpaste from the bottom? What makes her laugh? How long does her patience last?

"That's sweet," I say. "And true. But where is he taking us?"

She sits on the edge of the cushion with gauze and inspects my ass. Her touch sends a message to my dick that it's time to wake up.

"I have no idea." She lays the wet rag on my ass and wipes the blood away, then kisses the wounds as if they're scraped knees.

"Is it bad?"

"My cousins have done worse to themselves." She runs her hand over my bottom as if appreciating it the way no nurse should. I look over my shoulder. She has a lost, inside-looking expression.

"Delfina?"

She snaps out of it and picks up tweezers. "The bleeding stopped, but you have some grit in here. This might hurt."

"Okay. Go."

She digs in and she was right. It hurts. I suck in a breath.

"Where do you want to go?" I ask.

"Someplace quiet."

"I'm from New York. I don't have a lot of experience with that." The grit seems to be out, but I haven't felt a cream or bandage. I look over my shoulder. She seems to be inspecting the bloody towel. "Hey. We'll figure it out."

"Yeah." She clears her throat. "So, it's three cuts. I'm going to disinfect and bandage them up and you'll be fine."

She finishes the job efficiently, without another word, and when she's done, she stands over me and kisses my cheek.

"You're still in that dress," I say.

"There are some clothes in the cabinets."

"Take it off."

She smiles and peels off the dress, stretching upward. The sight of her elongated torso gets me so hard I have to turn to the side. Once the dress is off, I pull her down with me, spooning her back against my chest. We barely fit on the cushion together.

"What does this mean for us, Massimo?"

"What do you mean?"

"If my father picked you to marry me, I would have been happy."

"Pretend he did." Moving her hair away, my lips find skin still salty with sweat and sea air.

"I know I love you."

"And I love you. I fell in love with you the minute I saw you, and I've loved you more every time after."

"I would have wanted you anyway."

"You have me. You're already mine," I say into her ear, drawing my hand down from her jaw to every piece of her that I name. "Your throat is mine. Your tits are mine. Your belly is mine." I pull her knee up to open her legs and touch her between them. She gasps wetly. I didn't think I could get any harder. "This is mine."

I circle her clit, grinding against her until we're both panting and groaning. I can't take it anymore.

"Massimo," she whispers. "Yes."

She answers a question I didn't have to ask. I shift her leg to give me access and enter her from behind, letting my hands roam where she needs them. I am gentle. Slow. There's no need to rush.

Over her shoulder, she looks at me, and I lean forward to kiss her.

"You okay?" I ask.

"Yes. But…" She pauses for a deep breath. "You don't have to pull out if you don't want."

She's not offering me a moment of ecstasy. She's offering me the most valuable of any treasure. Her life. Her full commitment.

I can accept it because I'm ready to return it.

"Are you sure?"

"Yes."

"I'm going to make you so happy, Delfina. You're going to beg me to stop."

"Don't. Ever."

I make her come with my hand and she's so beautiful in her pleasure that I can't hold back another second.

She drops against me with a sigh and thanks me, as if I deserve her gratitude. I thank her back and fall asleep with her in my arms, where she belongs.

CHAPTER 43

DELFINA

The boat rocks and bobs. I wake up with Massimo pressed against my back and his even breaths in my ear. The motor is off and the silence is deafening.

Gently, I get out from under his arm, then find loose sweatpants and a huge T-shirt in a bin of clean clothes. I leave the bin out on the kitchen nook and go outside.

We've stopped. The only light comes from the moon, the stars, and a few dim ambient bulbs set around the perimeter of the deck. Aris has fallen asleep in the captain's chair.

I go to the very front and lean into the angle of the metal rails, pretending I'm floating over the water with nothing holding me back. Just me, the sky, and the black sea. I can still smell Massimo's blood soaked into the towel. Still taste it on my lips after I kissed his wounds.

The waves splash against the hull. The seagulls scream above. To the north, a tanker blots out the necklace of human lights on the horizon, dulling the sound of my breathing with its faraway roar.

"There you are." Massimo is on the deck, wearing white pleated trousers that are three sizes two big and a yellow shirt he hasn't bothered to button. He is exactly right for me.

"You're up."

He looks around, spots Aris sleeping, and turns back to me. "Do you want to be alone?"

"I did." I reach for him. "Until you showed up."

He stands next to me, gripping the rail. "I should get some swimming lessons."

"I don't think I want to live on a boat." I get behind him and wrap my arms around his waist, laying my cheek between his shoulders. I can hear his heart beating. Feel the warmth of the blood in his veins. "It's not as quiet as I thought it would be."

He holds the hands I've laid on him. "We'll find a place for us."

"As long as you stay with me. Even if I want to be alone, I want to know you're there."

"No matter what, Delfina." He curls his arm back, over my head and around my shoulders, to pull me into him. "I am with you."

EPILOGUE ONE

SIX WEEKS LATER

MASSIMO

The first time Carmine finds us, we are on Isola di Ventotene, where Aris navigated to that first night. He doesn't come with an army. He doesn't attack. He just sits next to me and watches the sun set over the sea. The concussion is healed by now, so I have the presence of mind to not react. Delfina's in the house making dinner and I don't want to scare her.

"How's the head?" he asks like a friend just catching up.

"Better."

"They say it can take a year to fully clear a concussion."

"Really. Wow. What the fuck do you want?"

He doesn't respond right away. A V of birds arrows across the horizon, right over the last shimmering curve of sun.

"I see congratulations are in order." He nods toward the bloody slits scabbing at the base of my fingers.

Delfina and I decided to wed the Colonia way by being cut into marriage. As captain of our little ship, Aris was the one to open our skin with my cobra knife. Delfina and I locked fingers and exchanged vows, then received scars that would

EPILOGUE ONE

only line up when we locked hands a certain way. Then he took the little boat we traded for the stolen one and motored off to find Corrado.

"We just decided to make it official."

"I'm happy for you." He leans back, laying his ankle on the opposite knee. "This is nice, this place."

This place is an abandoned, overgrown, breaking down, borderline hazardous cinderblock box without running water or electricity. We sold some of the things on *Tom's Arm*, then traded it for something smaller and less stolen. I was able to access one of my small US bank accounts to buy some necessities, including a composting toilet and camping burner. We keep a vegetable garden and a couple of chickens we found roaming in the tall grass.

"It's pretty quiet."

"Yes. It is."

We sit together, appreciating the quiet, except that I'm on high alert. I've fashioned a replacement for the lost bottom of the cane, but the knife doesn't go in all the way or come out easily. I know where all the rocks are, if I want to throw one at him, but I know how capable he is. Unless he's walking away, nothing will touch him.

"How is Delfina?"

"None of your fucking business," I reply casually.

"I could just ask her myself."

I turn toward him finally. The sunlight is dimming into a haze. It'll be dark soon and I won't be able to fight him and win.

"Why would you go do that?" I ask.

"Because you won't tell me."

I sigh, but don't answer. This is my borrowed patch of earth. My quiet. My view. My wife.

"I'm not here as an enemy," he says. "Not this time."

"Why are you here then?"

EPILOGUE ONE

"I need you to trust me when I say, you don't want to know. Because if I tell you, your life will change. You seem content here for now. There's no reason to disrupt the peace with you."

"So this isn't about my peace, it's about you?"

"Sure." He shrugs. "It's a distinction without a difference. But if you like… yes. It's about me and what I want, which has nothing to do with you. I just need to know… how is she?"

"In what way?" I'm stalling because at some point, I've decided to tell him and I need a minute to come to terms with my capitulation.

He taps his fingers on the worn wood of the beach chair, then starts counting off the ways.

EPILOGUE TWO

DELFINA

At first, when I see them talking out the kitchen window, I assume Massimo is with the man living in the next abandoned house over. He's not very social, but once in a while he'll stop by to talk about the weather.

But I hear the vestiges of his voice curling under the breaking waves as if they're on a different sound spectrum. From out the window and across the yard, Carmine Montefiore makes me aware of his presence. I know things about him that I can't grasp, like the first wisps of a dream, when the worldbuilding is done but the sleep cycle hasn't started yet, and I wake wondering what happened to that reality. Like I know him, but I never did.

There's no threat surrounding Carmine. Even if I just took my cues from Massimo, I wouldn't be frightened.

Carbon and sulfur. Heat at my chin. The meat is burning, damnit. And it's not cheap either. I turn off the gas.

With an unbearable craving, I rip a piece from the raw top and eat it. It's dissatisfying. Lately, I have needs in places I didn't know existed and no shape fits inside. Not even Massimo, who is a balm to every emotional and physical ache I bring to him, can soothe what I can only call my weirdness.

I focus on Massimo, our love, our life. He's the only thing that makes me happy.

Carmine is holding up two fingers. Massimo nods and talks. I can't hear him as clearly.

When Aunt Sylvia couldn't stand the smell of garlic, she knew.

When Mrs. Tonio plowed through an entire loaf of bread, sobbing that she couldn't understand why everything seems so incomplete, we all knew.

I've eaten this mostly raw sausage down to the crispy, burned bottom, and I know.

It has to be. There's no other explanation for why my senses feel so hotly attuned, why my naps are so long and my appetite has changed.

Massimo and Carmine are standing now. They shake hands, and Carmine goes around the house to the road, while my husband walks toward the door. I rush out to meet him.

"Was that—"

"Carmine. Yeah. I'll tell you inside." He takes my hand. "What's burning?"

"Did you ask about Luna and Serafina?"

"It didn't come up."

"What?"

I playfully slap him on the arm, because I'm not angry, but I also need to know if they're training to be doctors in Florence or if they're captive wives.

Running after Carmine, to the front, I trip on a pipe hidden in the tall grass. I have to be careful now, but I run anyway, past the line where the property ends and the dirt road begins.

He's not here. No smell of car exhaust in the pristine air.

No sight of him in the moonlight. No smell or absence of it digging a hole in my senses. Just big black birds launching out of a juniper tree.

"Hey." Massimo puts his hand on the back of my neck. "Next time, we'll ask."

"Next time?"

"If he wants to find us, he's going to, and I'm not spending our lives hiding."

He's right. We agreed on this. We're here because we want to be. Massimo needed a place to heal and I wanted quiet.

I lean into him.

He pulls me close and kisses my forehead. "You all right?"

"Yes, but..." I wrap both arms around his waist. "Also. I don't want to say definitely but..." I slow down. Is this how a wife is supposed to tell her husband? Is there some ritual Mama never had the chance to teach me?

"But?"

"I think I'm pregnant?"

"Oh, wow." He pulls me tighter, kissing my head, then my eyebrows. "Wow. Really?"

"I'm not sure. It's just a feeling."

"Wow." He kisses my cheeks, my chin, my nose.

"So, you're happy?" I ask between wows.

"Oh, my God, Delfina." He picks me up under my knees and shoulders and I cry out with delight, laughing. "I've never been so fucking happy."

"Me neither."

He carries me through the tall grass, among the deafening noise of crickets, birds, rustling leaves, and sea wind, kicks open the door, and brings me into our little house.

AND THEY LIVED HAPPILY EVER AFTER

EPILOGUE TWO

Is this your first dance with the Colonias?
If so, you're missing out on a huge chunk of the story.
Read the sexy, dark trilogy, starting with *Take Me Capo*.

I was stolen on my wedding day and forced to marry a man who wants to get vengeance on my father. Now I'm falling for him and we're going to run away together... if my family doesn't kill us first.

Now if you're all caught up, you're going to want to find out what happens in my new mafia vampire world! Sign up for my newsletter and you'll be notified when ***Blood Bride*** drops. Scroll on to the Acknowledgements for the full lowdown on where I'm going with Carmine Montefiore.
It's going to be batshit, and you're going to love it. Pinky swear.

ACKNOWLEDGMENTS

The letter to the fathers of the System summoning their daughters was ripped off of Charlemagne's Summons to His Army c.804-11. Thanks, buddy.

I need to thank Becca, who made sure the groundwork for this story was rock solid before I started it. The two books before this one were late, so I didn't have a minute to spare. Without that grounding, I'd be crying right now. Well, maybe I'm crying anyway.

Brandie jumped in with a quick pre-edit to make sure Cassie's slower edit went smoothly, and the talent and professionalism of both these ladies got this book out on time.

THE NEWS>>> This book connects to my next series —*Immortal Empire*. Thank you to all the publishing professionals, authors, and readers who have loaned me their excitement and enthusiasm for the idea of mafia vampires. You're all about to be paid back with interest.

About that...

I've called *Mafia Kingdom* a bridge book, because it spans the distance between two subgenres—the contemporary mafia romance trilogies, *The DiLustro Arrangement* and *Manhattan Mafia*, and the Mafia Vampire Romances[1] that start with *Blood Bride,* book one of *Immortal Empire*.

This book is meant to tie up a loose end in *Manhattan Mafia* and give you a taste of the vampires, without explicitly mentioning vampires and keeping the characters from the contemporary series in the dark. No one in any of the previous books knows the vampires exist, nor does anyone in this book... except the vampires themselves, and once you, the reader, know about them, I think it's pretty obvious who they are.

So, in that way, it's a bridge, but it's also not that.

Imagine a bicycle wheel.

Mafia Kingdom is the hub. Every spoke will connect to an event or character in this book[2]. From here, you can go to any of the other series, contemporary or vampire, and see something or meet someone you recognize. You can choose your next spoke based on your preferences as a reader.

The spokes are my trilogies and series. They start with *Mafia Bride, Take Me Capo,* in the contemporary mafia romance world, and the mafia vampires starting in 2024 with *Blood Bride*[3]. The wheel wrapping around is the characters, touching each series and holding it together.

Some spokes will not be for you. You will be able to read any series without the others. If you don't like erotic vampires, I still respect you... I just don't understand you, LOL. But if that's the case, you can stop right here knowing that Delfina and Massimo got their HEA. You can go back to *Mafia Bride,* where Violetta is kidnapped and forced to marry the sexy mafia king, Santino DiLustro, and we get a taste of Cosimo's obsession with relics. Or read *Take Me Capo,* where Massimo's sister is kidnapped by Dario Lucari on her wedding day as vengeance on her father, and cut into marriage with him using the knife Cosimo covets.

Massimo and Delfina will appear again as parts of the wheel. Maybe not in *Immortal Empire,* and maybe not until 2027, but they'll show up.

She bit a vampire, after all.

How do you think that's going to go?[4]

I'll see you then,

Christine

If you're interested in the mafia vampires, all I can say is, I want you to know when it releases more than you can imagine and I'm going to do everything in my power to put it in front of you.

Follow me on Facebook, in the Facebook group, on Twitter, Tiktok, Instagram, or get on my mailing list. Follow me on Amazon, Bookbub and/or Goodreads.

A vampire can't enter your house without an invitation, so if you send a physical mailing address via This Form, I'll send you a goddamn engraved invitation.

If you want Carmine to poke you, those are all the methods we got.

---

1. Yes, I said it—MAFIA VAMPIRES.
2. This is a plan, not a guarantee. I reserve the right to connect them so loosely they fall apart, because though I see every moment of every series in my head, shit changes. If you followed the Drazen World, you saw it happen right before your eyes. It was for the best.
3. I have no preorder link, which is killing me. KILLING ME.
4. Me neither!

PAIGE PRESS

Paige Press isn't just Laurelin Paige anymore...

Laurelin Paige has expanded her publishing company to bring readers even more hot romances.

Sign up for our newsletter to get the latest news about our releases and receive a free book from one of our amazing authors:

Laurelin Paige
Stella Gray
CD Reiss
Jenna Scott
Raven Jayne
JD Hawkins
Poppy Dunne
Lia Hunt
Sadie Black

ALSO BY CD REISS

THE DILUSTRO ARRANGEMENT

Some girls dream of marrying a prince. I was sold to a king.

Mafia Bride | Mafia King | Mafia Queen

MANHATTAN MAFIA

I was stolen on my wedding day and forced to marry a man who wants to get vengeance on my father. Now I'm falling for him and we're going to run away together... if my family doesn't kill us first.

Take Me Capo | Make Me Cry | Break Me Down

THE SUBMISSION SERIES

One Night With Him | One Year With Him | One Life With Him

THE GAMES DUET

Adam Steinbeck will give his wife a divorce on one condition. She join him in a remote cabin for 30 days, submitting to his sexual dominance.

Marriage Games | Separation Games

ABOUT THE AUTHOR

CD Reiss is a Brooklyn native and has the accent to prove it. She earned a master's degree in cinematic writing from USC. She ultimately failed to have one line of dialog put on film, but stayed in Los Angeles out of spite.

Since screenwriting was going nowhere, she switched to novels and has released over two dozen titles, including two *NY Times* Bestsellers and a handful of *USA Today* bestsellers. Her audiobooks have won APA Audie Awards and Earphones Awards.

She resides in Hollywood in a house that's just big enough for her two children, two cats, her long-suffering husband and her massive ego.

To find out when her next book is coming out, sign up for her mailing list here or at cdreiss-dot-com.

Made in the USA
Las Vegas, NV
29 August 2023

76772605R00176